FINISHED OFF

Abby parked far enough off to the side to make sure her cart wouldn't block any emergency vehicles. "Jamie, thanks for jumping in to help. Zoe Brevik and the EMTs are headed this way. Even after you point them in the right direction, they might want you to stick around long enough to share any information you might have."

He took the two bottles of water she offered him. "Okay, we'll hang around."

He looked pretty relieved not to have to return to the injured man. It made her wonder how badly hurt the guy was. She headed off at a slow trot down the trail, looking for Spence. When she didn't immediately spot him, she called his name. He stepped out of the trees a short distance from where she stood, looking grim.

She slowed down, really not wanting to get any closer. Deciding that would be cowardly, she kept moving forward. "Zoe and the EMTs should be here in just a couple of minutes. Is there anything I can do to help?"

The former soldier was normally pretty cheerful, but not today. Whatever he'd seen down in the gully had left him looking badly shaken as he shook his head. "I'm pretty sure there's nothing anyone can do for him now."

Her stomach lurched and her pulse did a stutter step. "You mean he's..."

She couldn't bring herself to finish that sentence, so Spence did it for her. "Sorry, Abby, but I'm pretty sure he's dead . . ."

Alexis Morgan

DEATH by the FINISH LINE

Kensington Publishing Corp.
www.kensingtonbooks.com

CHAPTER 1

Five months ago

At ten o'clock on a weekday morning, the coffee shop in Snowberry Creek was blissfully quiet. Abby McCree sipped her favorite dark roast coffee and studied the puzzled expression on her companion's face. Finding it a bit worrisome, she asked, "Hey, are you all right?"

Her mother stared down at her own coffee and sighed. "All this time you've told me how you somehow ended up in charge of one committee or another without knowing how it even happened. To be honest, I never really believed it. You're no pushover, so I thought it was just your way of making excuses for jumping in to take on yet another major time-sucking project."

At this point she finally dragged her gaze up to meet Abby's head-on. "But after meeting Connie Pohler this morning, I get what you've been trying to tell me. The mayor's assistant is a lovely woman, so warm and friendly. At the same time, she has an absolutely terrifying ability to convince someone that they want nothing more in life than to help organize a charity run."

By that point, Abby couldn't help but laugh. She'd seen that same dazed expression on her own face on several occasions after talking to Connie. When her mom looked a bit put out by her reaction, Abby grimaced and apologized. "Sorry, Mom, I probably shouldn't laugh, but I warned you not to make eye contact with Connie. The second you do that, she's got you under her spell."

Abby pointed to the two plates on the table. "That's why I brought you here to Something's Brewing. The only way to console ourselves is with a great cup of coffee and a big piece of Bridey's best gooey butter cake. Besides, you only agreed to help on the weekend of the event. I'm in charge of the whole dang thing."

Throwing her hands up in frustration, she sighed. "What do I know about organizing the Founder's Day Salmon Scoot? The closest I've ever come to serious running is watching Tripp set off on his daily crack-of-dawn jaunt."

It couldn't be any fun to get out of bed to pound the pavement every day, rain or shine. But her handsome tenant, Tripp Blackston, rarely blew off his morning runs. He claimed that after twenty years in the army, the daily runs had become a habit he couldn't break. She wished he would try harder, mainly because she felt guilty for not dragging herself out of bed to join him.

Her mother managed a rueful smile. "Well, at least Connie did say she had someone interested in co-chairing the race with you. Maybe that person knows more about this kind of thing. At least you won't have to do everything by yourself."

If only that were true. "That would be nice, but it all depends on who it is and how much time he or she is willing to put in on the project."

Honestly, she'd rather do it all herself than have to nag her yet-to-be-named partner to make sure everything got done on time. More than one person—including Chad, her ex-husband—had pointed out Abby's control-freak tendencies over the years. It wasn't as if she didn't know that about herself, but those same people had benefited from her compulsion to make sure things got done right and on time. Unfortunately, it was also the reason she was near the top of Connie Pohler's list of favorite people to call on whenever a new project crossed her desk.

For now, Abby took solace in rich coffee and a decadent dessert while her mother did the same. She refused to feel guilty about consuming so many carbs. Earlier, she'd promised her furry roommate a long walk after she got back home, so she could work off at least a portion of the calories before the day was out.

A low rumble coming from out on the street drew their attention to the front window of the shop. A few seconds later, a double line of motorcycles rolled past, all being ridden by tough-looking men in black leather vests. Their presence in town didn't come as a surprise. The local motorcycle repair shop had a reputation for quality work, and people came from all over the area to get their bikes fixed.

What was a surprise, though, was seeing one of the bikes peel off from the pack to park right outside of Something's Brewing. It wasn't as if she thought bikers didn't drink coffee, but she'd spent a lot of time in Bridey's shop and had never seen any come in. She recognized this one, though, as soon as he dismounted and took off his helmet. It was Gil Pratt, co-owner with his brother of the repair shop.

She'd crossed paths with him several times since her move to Snowberry Creek. Gil might be a little rough around the edges, but he'd always been nothing but polite to her. Still, he seemed like the kind of guy who liked his coffee black, extra strong, and preferably brewed in a coffeepot that hadn't been thoroughly cleaned in years. But after setting his helmet down on the seat of his bike, he headed straight toward the door of the coffee shop. Once inside, he stopped to look around. As soon as he spotted Abby, he smiled and headed over to the counter to place his order.

"Do you know that man?"

Her mother sounded a bit horrified by that prospect. That came as no surprise. There was a lot about Abby's decision to make her new home in Snowberry Creek that her mother disapproved of, starting with the fact she'd become embroiled in four—count them, four!—homicide investigations since moving there. While her mother didn't blame Abby for divorcing her now ex-husband for cheating on her, she did question her decision not to immediately dive right back into the corporate world in Seattle. But thanks to a sizable inheritance from her late aunt, Abby had no need to rush things. For now, she was content to take her time setting down some deep roots in her new home.

"Yes, Mom, I know him. Gil is a member of the same veterans group as Tripp, and we've run into each other at a couple of functions. He and his younger brother own a very successful business here in town."

Well, that might be a slight exaggeration, but she didn't want her mother to base her opinion of the man solely on his ponytail, scuffed boots, and leather vest. Meanwhile, Gil picked up a tray holding three cups of coffee and headed straight for them.

She did her best to hide her surprise at his approach, offering him a quick smile when he stopped at their table. He gave each of them a quick nod as he set the coffees down. "Hi, ladies. I asked Bridey to make you another of whatever you were drinking."

Before they could respond, he hustled over to the counter to pick up a muffin that the barista had heated up for him before returning to their table. Clearly, this was no chance encounter. Abby's weird-o-meter was starting to register some pretty strange vibes, but she didn't want to jump to any conclusions. Falling back on the good manners both her mother and her late aunt had drilled into her, she pointed at the empty chair next to her. "Won't you join us, Gil?"

"Thanks, I don't mind if I do."

After he got settled, she said, "I don't think the two of you have met. Gil, this is my mother, Phoebe McCree. Mom, this is Gil Pratt."

He smiled at her mother. His eyes twinkled, suggesting he had a good idea of her mom's reaction to having a biker join them. "Nice to meet you, ma'am. I can sure tell where Abby gets her good looks. She has your dark hair and pretty hazel eyes. I do hope you know your daughter here has been a real godsend to our veterans group and others here in Snowberry Creek. She also helped me out of a bit of a rough spot a few months back."

One look at her mom made it clear she'd likely be grilling Abby on that particular subject later when they were alone. Great. All she'd done was to make sure the police knew Gil hadn't thrown the first punch when a bar brawl had broken out when she and Tripp had been at a local hangout playing pool with their friends. To her surprise, Gil had shown up on her front porch the next day with a bouquet of flowers to thank her for her efforts and for keeping him out of jail. Of course, she'd also secretly been checking him out as a possible suspect in a murder case, but what was a little suspicion among friends?

Somehow she doubted her mother would find that amusing, so she changed the subject. "Do you come in here very often?"

He gave a rusty laugh as he glanced around the room. "No offense to Bridey, but it isn't exactly my kind of place. Gary and I do stop in regularly to load up on some of her pastries, but we get everything to go."

After taking a careful sip of his coffee, he set the cup back down. "Actually, Connie Pohler thought the two of us should talk and that I could probably find you here."

By that point, Abby's brain was screaming "Mayday, mayday!" Even so, she thought she sounded pretty calm as she asked, "Well, you found me. What's up?"

Gil drew a deep breath and then slowly let it out as if bracing himself to deliver some bad news. "I'd like to partner with you to organize the run for the Founder's Day celebration, but only if you would be willing to work with me."

Without giving her a chance to respond, he added, "Look, I don't mean to put you in an awkward position, and I'll understand if you'd rather find someone else. Don't feel like you have to say yes."

She might have believed a negative answer wouldn't matter all that much to him, but it was hard to miss the tight hold he had on his coffee cup and the lines of tension bracketing his mouth. Even if she had qualms about accepting, she did feel compelled to give his offer some serious consideration.

"I have a couple of questions for you first, if that's okay."

He released the death grip on his coffee and eased back in his chair. "Ask away."

"Connie assured me a lot of the preliminary work is already done. Even if that's true, organizing something like this takes a lot of effort. Considering you own your own business, will you have the time?"

Gil nodded. "Good question. My hours are flexible. As long as we set up a regular schedule to meet, it won't be a problem. That's true even when we get closer to the actual race and need to meet more often. Gary knows I want to do this, and he's on board with paying a friend of ours to help him out at the shop a few hours a week if the work piles up a bit."

So this wasn't a spur-of-the-moment offer, and he'd given the matter some serious thought. Feeling more optimistic, she asked her next question. "Have you ever done anything like this before? It will involve keeping track of a whole bunch of information. At this point, I don't yet have a clear idea what all it will entail."

Gil leaned forward, elbows on the table and looking more relaxed. "I worked in supply back when I was in the navy. I tracked inventory, filled orders, and dealt with various suppliers to maintain stock. On a smaller scale, I do the same at our shop. I also keep all the books for our business, including doing our taxes. That's a pretty roundabout way of saying I've got a knack for tracking information."

Better and better. "How are you at riding herd on people? We'll need to recruit a bunch of volunteers to help, but unfortunately not all of them will be as reliable as they should be."

He shot her a wicked grin. "Try dealing with bikers day in and day out. Anything else?"

She found herself laughing at that, and even her mother was smiling by that point. "Yeah, I have one more question. Do you know anything about what this kind of event entails?"

Bless him, he was already nodding. "Actually, Gary runs in races several times a year, most longer than this one. I've helped him train and even volunteered to help out the day of the races a few times."

Wow, he'd just ticked all the boxes on her spur-of-the-moment questionnaire. She'd be foolish to turn down his offer to help. She stuck her hand out. "Well, Gil, if you're sure, then let's do this."

His callused hand gently engulfed hers and gave it a quick shake to seal the deal. She only hoped he didn't come to regret his decision.

CHAPTER 2

Present day

Life would be so much better without alarm clocks. Well, technically the irritating chirp that had dragged Abby out of a deep sleep originated from her cell phone, but the principle was the same. She grabbed the phone and debated whether she could risk turning on the snooze feature. Another fifteen minutes of shut-eye would feel pretty darn good.

Sadly, there was no way she could give in to that temptation. Today was the day she and her co-chair had been working toward for months, and she couldn't risk showing up late. Too many people were counting on her.

Throwing back the covers, she sat up on the edge of the bed. Zeke, her mastiff-mix roommate, lifted his enormous head to give her a grumpy look. "Sorry, boy. Go back to sleep if you want. I'm the only one who has to be up at this awful hour."

Taking Abby at her word, he dropped his head back down on his paws and was back to snoring before she reached the bathroom door. When she walked out twenty minutes later, showered and dressed, Zeke sighed and slowly dragged himself up to his feet to follow her downstairs. She let him out to make his morning rounds while she put together a quick breakfast for two people and one big dog.

When Zeke returned, he wasn't alone. Tripp, who rented the small mother-in-law house on the back of the property, followed the dog into her kitchen. She'd barely been able to dress herself at this hour, but Tripp was clean shaven, his dark hair neatly combed, and his dark eyes sparkled with good humor. He looked irritatingly chirpy, but then he was a morning person. Lucky for him, he had other redeeming characteristics to make up for that one serious shortcoming. After pouring each of them a cup of coffee, he set hers within easy reach on the counter and took his own over to the table.

"I bet you thought this day would never arrive."

She dished up the scrambled eggs and bacon before carrying their plates over to the table. "Yeah, it's been a long time coming."

Abby grabbed her coffee and took her usual seat beside Tripp. "All in all, planning this thing has gone pretty darn smoothly, thanks in large part to Gil. He's been a real trooper about picking up the slack whenever someone else needed help getting something done. Poor guy."

Tripp had been about to shovel a huge bite of eggs into his mouth, but he froze in position. "Why do you say that?"

"Because now Connie Pohler has him in her sights. I'm sure she's already plotting against him with an entire assortment of projects and committees she wants him to take on."

"Well, at least maybe that means she won't be coming after you anytime soon."

If only. She had no illusions about her chances of avoiding any further entanglements with town events, but that was a worry for another day. Right now, she needed to finish breakfast and then head off to the park where the race would begin in just over three hours. Tripp had loaned her his truck for the day so she could haul all the signs and other stuff that needed to be set up right before the race.

"Are you sure you want to ride to the park with me? You can drive my car if you'd like to wait until closer to starting time."

Tripp checked his watch. "No, that's okay. I got a text from Owen last night saying he and your mom will meet us there. I can hang out with him."

It had taken some time to get used to her mother having a man in her life, although Abby had grown to like Owen Quinn a lot. She liked his barbecue even more and ate at his restaurant far more frequently than she should. Even so, she still occasionally winced when reminded that whenever her mom came down from Seattle for a weekend, she now stayed at Owen's house rather than with her daughter. To be honest, though, it was probably better that way. Abby loved her mom and had no doubt her mother loved her in return. But if they spent too much time living under the same roof, things tended to get a bit rocky.

They made quick work of their meal and the cleanup afterward. "I'll grab my gear and meet you outside."

Tripp stopped long enough to toss Zeke a couple of treats before heading out the door. After gathering up the last few things she'd need to get through the day, Abby took one more look around the kitchen to make sure she hadn't forgotten anything. It was going to be a long day, but once it was over, life would slow down again. She couldn't wait. Tripp had just started another full load of classes at the university and had been training hard for the race. Between his schedule and her various committee meetings, they hadn't been able to spend as much time together as they usually did. She missed their movie and pizza nights, not to mention the long walks they often took together with Zeke.

It seemed as if their friendship had been teetering on the edge of becoming something more for a while now, but lately their busy lives had put a little distance between them. Now wasn't the time to worry about that. They had a race to get through.

Zeke sat by the door, clearly hoping his humans were going to include him in their outing. "Sorry to disappoint you, boy, but you'll have to hold down the fort by yourself today."

She accompanied her apology with a big hug along with a kiss on his wrinkly forehead. After tossing her buddy one more treat, she let herself out the back door, locking up as she left. Tripp was just stepping down off his porch.

She stashed her tote bag in the back of his truck and carried her small backpack around to the passenger side where Tripp stood waiting to open the door for her. He held her pack while she climbed up into the seat. "Are you and Gil both counting the minutes until this is over?"

There was no reason to lie about it. "You have no idea. Who knew how much went into organizing one of these things?"

He resumed the conversation after he joined her in the cab of the truck. "Sorry I haven't been around to help very much, but it seems like you have a pretty good crew of volunteers from what I could see."

"We do, and it was my lucky day when Connie pointed Gil in my direction. He's been amazing from day one. Always the first to volunteer to take on any job and never failed to get stuff done on time. I actually had to remind him that it was okay to delegate a little now and then."

Tripp glanced over at her. "I'm not the only one who was surprised to hear that he'd volunteered to co-chair this thing. From what I've heard, he's never gotten involved in anything like this before, especially on this scale."

"I was surprised, too. That just goes to show we shouldn't make assumptions about people. Heck, he's even managed to charm my mom. She even wants to have Gil and his brother over for dinner after all of this is over."

Tripp's laughter filled the cab of the truck. "I'm having trouble picturing that. Still, I'm really glad he stepped up and did such a great job."

"Me too, but he's spoiled me for working with anyone else. Maybe it's his military background. You know, like back when you dragooned me into setting up the fundraiser for your veterans group. One of your selling points was that people who'd served were used to working as a team and to taking orders."

She tried but failed to fight back a huge yawn. "Sorry. I'm not sure there's enough caffeine in the whole town to wake me up. I'm out of practice getting up at this hour."

Tripp immediately executed a U-turn and headed back in the direction of the main business district in town.

"Where are you taking me?"

"I'm going to make a quick stop at Something's Brewing. You're not the only one who'll appreciate a big cup of Bridey's best."

He didn't give her any say in the matter, but she wasn't about to argue. Unless there was a huge line, they would still make it to the staging area in plenty of time. She reached for her pack to fish out her wallet. Tripp shook his head. "Put that away. This one is on me."

If it was just her coffee he was buying, she wouldn't argue, but she suspected they should probably pick up a few extras. "I was going to ask you to get some for Mom, Owen, and Gil."

The stubborn man just shook his head. "I said I've got it."

He whipped into a parking spot a couple of doors down from the coffee shop and was off and running before Abby could respond. Tripp must have lucked out, because it was only a few minutes before he was back. She rolled down her window to take a cardboard tray holding six cups of coffee. When he joined her inside the cab, she asked, "Who is the sixth one for?"

He shrugged. "Whoever asks for it first. I thought Gary might be with Gil. If not, I'm betting Gage will be around early, and you know how much he loves coffee."

True enough. The chief of police was one of Bridey's best customers, at least when his teenage daughter wasn't around to catch him. He complained all the time about her nagging about his diet, but he always did it with a smile.

They were almost to the park. The 5K run wasn't the only event scheduled for the Founder's Day celebration that morning, so she wasn't surprised to see several different groups of people milling around in the parking lot. She pointed off to the left. "Gil's over there."

"I'll back in to make it easier to unload everything. After we're done, I'll drive the truck over to the event parking at the high school and catch the shuttle back."

"Is it even running this early?"

"If not, I can walk. It's not that far."

By that point, Gil had spotted them and was headed in their direction. When he reached the truck, she held up the coffees, which brought a huge smile to his face. He opened the door and took the tray. "Bless you, woman. I had some earlier, but it's already worn off."

"Don't thank me. Tripp's the one who made the emergency caffeine stop. There's an extra if Gary's around. Otherwise, give it to whoever needs it the most."

"Will do. I'll be right back."

He carried the tray over to a nearby picnic table and then returned to help unload the truck. "I have the water Owen Quinn donated for the race in my truck. A few friends from the veterans group should be here in a few minutes with a couple of hand trucks. I told them to divide most of the water up between the water stations and the medical tent and then bring the rest to the finish line. The people manning the water tables will let us know if they start running low after the race gets started."

That checked off a couple of items from Abby's to-do list. They had just finished carrying the last of their stuff over to the picnic table when Owen and her mother arrived. Abby handed them their coffee and caught her mom up on where things stood after Owen and Tripp left to drop their vehicles off at the off-site parking.

Abby handed her mother a clipboard. Her mom's job was to stand at the finish line and check off the names of everyone as they crossed the finish line. Someone else, a professional they'd hired, would handle recording the official race times. "Well, Mom, are you ready for this madness?"

"Yes, I think so. It will get pretty chaotic closer to race time, but you and Gil have things well in hand."

Crossing her fingers that was true, Abby grabbed her tablet and studied her to-do list. Gil had a small laptop that he used to track things, but he also kept printouts of everything on a clipboard. He said he'd had a few bad experiences in the past when something went wrong with his electronic files at the worst possible moment. This way they were covered no matter what happened.

The two of them went over the lists together to make sure nothing had been missed. When they were done, Abby took a big swig of her coffee and smiled at her partner. "Well, Gil, this is it. Pardon the play on words, but we're off and running."

He grinned as he picked up one stack of signs. "I'll start posting these. It shouldn't take long, and then I can help set up the tables at the finish line."

"I'll see you there."

It didn't surprise her when Connie Pohler was the next person to appear. "Good morning, Abby. I wanted to see if you needed any last minute help."

"Thanks for asking, Connie, but I think we've got it all taken care of for now. I'm sure some surprises will pop up over the course of the morning, but all the major stuff is covered. Gil and I both wanted to thank you for everything you did beforehand. It really helped that you already had all of the permits, insurance, and sponsors pretty much lined up before we even started."

"You're most welcome. I just appreciate how hard you and Gil have worked to make the race so successful this year, especially the way you promoted it. This is the first time that the registration filled up within five days of going live. That's huge. I'd really appreciate it if the two of you would update the notebook I gave you at the beginning, to show how you did things and any suggestions you might have for whoever takes over from you."

"We will."

She secretly suspected Connie had already penciled in the two of them on her list of victims for next year, although she'd probably call them "volunteers." Between now and then, Abby planned on polishing up her avoidance skills. Maybe she could get through one year without having her name heading up the crew on any of the town events. Yeah, fat chance.

Connie studied her tablet one more time. "Well, I've got a few other people to check in with, so I had better get moving. You've got my number if anything comes up."

Abby watched in awe as Connie charged off down the path, stopping briefly to confer with one of the ladies working on the silent auction being held in the large tent located at the far end of the parking lot. Her mother moved up to stand beside Abby. "Does that woman ever run out of energy?"

"Not that I've ever seen. We might all complain about her 'volunteering' us to take on one of her jobs, but Connie works harder than anyone I know to ensure our efforts are successful. I wasn't kidding about how much of the work had already been done or at least started before she brought us onboard."

"As much as she accomplishes here in Snowberry Creek, it's almost a shame that she isn't sharing her talents on a bigger stage."

Abby picked up the stack of the signs she needed to post. "I asked her about that once, but she said she grew up here and never had any interest in living anywhere else. Besides, her job for the city and the work she does for her church is enough to keep her busy."

Then she made a show of looking around to see if anyone else was close by. "I also suspect she has a thing for Pastor Jack, the minister who started the veterans group. It's not one-sided, either. I've heard rumors they've been spotted out on the town together a few times. I'm crossing my fingers that they figure how perfect they would be for each other. They're both nice people who deserve a bit of happy in their lives."

Her mom looked as if she wanted to say something but then thought better of it. Before the woman could change her mind, Abby handed her the remaining stack of signs. "We need to get these posted, Mom. Call me if you have any questions."

"Will do. Should I meet you at the finish line area when I'm done?"

"Sounds good."

Abby started off down the path to the right but had only gone a few steps when her mom called her name. "Yes, Mom?"

"I just wanted to make sure you know I'm proud of everything you've done to make this race a success."

Wow, that was a huge turnaround from how her mother had felt about Abby's growing connection to the town of Snowberry Creek and the people who lived there. Her eyes burned just a little from the sting of tears. She blinked like crazy to prevent them from falling. "Thanks, Mom. That means a lot."

"Well, it's nothing but the truth. Owen is impressed as well, and I suspect he isn't an easy sell. For sure, I had no idea how much work it took behind the scenes to pull something like this off without a hitch."

Abby winced, hoping like crazy her mother hadn't jinxed things with that last comment. It wasn't as if she was superstitious, but things had gone so smoothly that she secretly feared they were overdue for some kind of glitch to happen. Telling herself that she was being foolish, she hung up the first sign and kept right on going. After all, like her mother said, everything was on schedule and rolling along smoothly.

With luck and a lot of hard work, hopefully that would continue.

CHAPTER 3

Two hours later, Abby and Gil were in the process of dispersing their volunteers to monitor the race. As long as everyone did their job, they had plenty of people to keep an eye on things along the entire length of the course, which ran through the city park, looped through a nearby national forest and then back to the park. She had talked to people who had worked on similar events and compiled a list of the most likely issues to arise during the actual race. She'd gone over that with the team, gave them everything they needed to do their job, and then left it up to Gil to finish up their orientation by making sure they also knew how to respond if there was a problem.

He was about halfway through the list when one of his buddies from the veterans group came running over. He leaned in close to whisper, "Sorry to interrupt, Gil, but you might want to check out what's going on with your brother."

Abby didn't mean to eavesdrop, but she couldn't help but hear everything since she was standing right next to Gil. They both turned in the direction the man had indicated. It wasn't hard to figure out what had him worried. Gary was right up in another man's face and yelling at the top of his lungs. Most people gave the pair a wide berth, but others were looking on with a great deal of interest. The argument hadn't yet gotten physical, but she feared it was a distinct possibility from the amount of anger in their body language.

Both men were dressed for the race, and she couldn't tell who the other man was from where she stood. But from the curse words Gil muttered under his breath, he did. He shoved his clipboard into her hands. "Sorry, but I've got to deal with this, Abby. Can you finish going over the list for me? I was on number eight."

He took off running before she had a chance to respond. Rather than watch the drama play out, she drew everyone's attention back to her. "Okay, so raise your hands if you have the list of emergency contacts that Gil printed out for you."

After checking to make sure everyone had a hand in the air, she repeated the process for the remaining few items on the list. "Okay, people, thank you again for volunteering to help today. And I must say, you all look quite fashionable in your matching T-shirts. I know that particular shade of green might not actually occur in nature, but it does make you stand out in the crowd. Well, maybe not in a good way, but I guess that's the whole point."

That drew a few laughs, which was what she was hoping for. "I know it's a bit early yet, but feel free to head off for your assigned spot. Make sure you have water with you. I know the race isn't all that long time-wise, but it might get pretty warm if you're standing in the sun. When the race is over, you can go enjoy the rest of the day's festivities."

As soon as they began dispersing, she searched for Gil to see how things were going. By that point, the two brothers were off to the side having what looked like a heated discussion of their own. The other man was no longer close by, but she finally spotted him standing over near the picnic tables doing a few stretches to ready for the race. It was easy to pick him out of the crowd, thanks to the distinctive pattern on his running shorts. The main color was navy blue, but the sides had insets with starbursts of green, orange, and yellow. It took her a few seconds longer to put a name to his face. No wonder Gil was upset. That wasn't just some random guy or even one of the bikers who frequented their shop. No, it was James DiSalvo, upstanding citizen and proud member of Snowberry Creek's city council.

Mr. DiSalvo had apparently shaken off the effects of the argument, but it didn't look like Gil was having much luck calming down his brother. Finally, Gary stalked off and disappeared in the crowd of runners gathering for the race. Gil stared after him for another few seconds before walking back in her direction. He didn't say a word, but he was clearly upset.

Even though it was none of her business, she couldn't help but ask, "Is everything okay? Things are pretty caught up right now, so if you need to spend more time with your brother, I can handle the last few details on my own."

Gil smiled, but it clearly took a lot of effort. "No need, Abby. Gary's a hothead, but the idiot has got himself back under control."

Then he sighed. "He swears he didn't start the argument, that DiSalvo deliberately provoked him. It wouldn't be the first time."

There was obviously more to the story, but Gil didn't seem inclined to go into detail. "I'm sorry that happened. I know Gary was looking forward to the race, and I hope Mr. DiSalvo didn't spoil it for him."

Gil took back his clipboard and scanned the page as he spoke. "He'll be fine once he starts running. Gary finds it relaxing and says it puts him in the zone. Not exactly sure what that means, but he always comes home exhausted and happy. That's one reason I try to show my support even if I don't understand the appeal myself."

Abby laughed. "You and me, brother. Tripp runs every morning, rain or shine. Who wants to be out moving around like that before the sun comes up?"

Gil glanced around at the gathering crowd. "I might not like running, but I can understand why he likes to hit the road early. It's my favorite time to take my bike out. The roads are mostly empty, which makes it easier to relax and enjoy the ride. That's harder to do in traffic when you have to keep an eye on what all the other idiot drivers are doing. Cars and trucks don't always do a good job of sharing the road with motorcycles. I could tell you horror stories."

"I'm sure you could. That's one reason I've never been on one."

Gil's eyes flared wide in shock. "What? Never? Didn't you ever date a guy who owned a bike?"

"Nope, my mother forbade me getting anywhere near one."

"That's just sad, because there's nothing like it. Well, if you ever want to take a ride on the wild side, tell Tripp to give me a call. I've got a bike and helmets he can borrow, so the two of you can go cruising."

"What makes you think he knows how to ride a motorcycle?"

Gil rolled his eyes. "Seriously, Abby? I'm betting your boy has spent his fair share of time cruising on a bike. If not, I'll take you myself."

She mulled over the idea for a few seconds. Yeah, there would be a certain amount of risk involved, but the real question was if she trusted both Tripp and Gil to keep her safe. In the end, it turned out to be a no-brainer. "You know, I might just take you up on that offer. If Tripp doesn't ride, you and I can go for a cruise and maybe stop off at Gary's Drive-In for burgers on the way back. My treat."

The brief discussion seemed to have improved Gil's mood because he winked at her. "Anytime. Just say the word."

Sharing a smile with her partner, Abby looped her arm through his. "Well, we'll save that bit of excitement for another day. We'd better head over to the starting line. The mayor will be signaling the start of the race in less than ten minutes."

Chaos ensued, but she loved every minute of it. Abby joined in with all the hooting and hollering to encourage the crowd of runners poised to start the race. She caught Tripp's eye and gave him a thumbs-up. Her mother was equally vocal as she called out Owen's name and wished him luck.

Rosalyn McKay, the mayor of Snowberry Creek, held up a bullhorn and her watch. "Okay, ladies and gentlemen, one minute left to go."

A new wave of awareness went through the participants as they shifted in position, shaking their arms and hands to keep loose. Their excitement was contagious, and Abby's pulse raced as she counted down the seconds until the mayor would send the runners pelting down the course. This was it—the moment they'd been working toward for months. Soon it would all be over except for the cleanup. Hopefully everyone involved would walk away satisfied with their experience whether they were a volunteer, a runner, or a spectator.

Once again, Rosalyn's voice rang out over the crowd. "It's time! Get ready, get set, go!"

The amassed runners surged forward. For the first few seconds, they remained bunched up, but the group gradually began to spread out, giving everyone more room to maneuver. She was pleased to see Tripp was one of the lead runners and looking strong, but then she was a bit prejudiced. She waited until the majority of the competitors disappeared around the first bend in the route before walking away. Her mother caught up with her as they cut through the park toward the finish line.

"I meant to tell you that I finally saw the wall hanging your quilting guild pieced for the winner. It's beautiful. It's amazing how they captured all the motion of a race using nothing but fabric."

"It is. They all do beautiful work, but they surpassed themselves this time. I hope whoever wins it appreciates all the work they put into it."

The truth was the ladies hadn't told Abby that they'd taken on the project. They'd surprised her with it at one of their meetings, telling her it was their contribution to her request for donations to be used as prizes. "By the way, if you like it that much, they did another one with slightly different colors. They're selling chances on it over in the silent auction tent. The money will go toward funding the small quilts we give to the local law enforcement and fire departments to give kids whenever they respond to an emergency."

"I'll stop by and buy a whole bunch of tickets after the race."

Abby walked over to where Gil was manning their table at the finish line and sat down. It felt good to get off her feet for a few minutes. Her mom had a chair set up closer to the path where the first runners should start arriving all too soon.

Gil was making notes in the margins of the print copy of their spreadsheet. Finally, he set the pen down and leaned back in his chair. "Several people gave me some suggestions that might be worth considering next year. Nothing major, just a couple of things they'd seen done at other races that went over well."

"That's always helpful. We'll be sure to note them in our report to Connie. She keeps a file on every event in town with what worked and what didn't. Saves the next person who takes on a project from having to start from scratch. I'm sure they'll appreciate all the helpful tips we can give them."

He nudged her with his shoulder. "Is that your way of telling me that I'll have to drum up a new partner for next year's race?"

His question surprised her, but then maybe it shouldn't have. He'd been enthusiastic from the start. "Honestly, right now all I can think about is getting through the rest of today in one piece."

She turned to face him more directly. "I've said this before, but it's been great working with you. I really mean that, but I want a chance to recover from this year's race before I can decide if I want to commit to doing it again."

Her response seemed to really please him. "I understand. To be honest, I didn't expect to enjoy all the work as much as I have. I've gotten to know a lot of nice people along the way, present company included. It feels pretty good to get more involved in the community."

That was something she did understand. "I'm right there with you. When I inherited my aunt's house, I moved in thinking I'd likely put the place up for sale. But her friends on the quilting guild board made it clear they expected me to take Aunt Sybil's place as president of the group. It was their way of helping me forge connections with the people here. Now I can't imagine living anywhere else."

"It is a nice town, and most folks are pretty welcoming."

Interesting. His emphasis on the word "most" made it clear there were a few people in Snowberry Creek who hadn't been quite so welcoming. If so, that was a darn shame. Her own conscience made her cringe a bit. Gil had scared her badly the night she'd first spotted him walking across the dance floor at the local bar. The look in his gaze when they'd inadvertently made eye contact had left no doubt in her mind that he was capable of violence under the right circumstances. Looking back, though, she thought maybe he'd been aware of the men who were looking to start a fight with him.

When he'd stopped by her house the next day, her reaction to him was completely different. The two of them had sat out on her front porch and shared a plate of cookies. Even Zeke had taken an immediate liking to Gil, and she'd always found the dog was an excellent judge of character. Tripp insisted that Zeke's loyalty could be bought with two treats and a pat on the head, but that wasn't always true. While there weren't many people the big dog didn't like, the few exceptions had all turned out to be bad news.

But enough about that. She checked her watch. "The lead runners should be coming into sight soon. At least we've made it this far without problems."

No sooner had she said those words than Gil's phone buzzed. He listened to what the person on the other end of the line had to say and hung up. "That was the lady at the halfway point. She needs more water. I'll take care of it."

"Okay. I'll double-check that the snacks and drinks are ready at this end and then help Mom check off numbers as the runners come through. Call if you need me."

"Will do. Otherwise, I'll see you after the race."

A short time later, Abby was thrilled to see Tripp stagger across the finish line right behind the first two runners. One of her volunteers immediately shoved an open bottle of water in his hand along with a small bag of snacks. He carried them over to a grassy area and collapsed in a sweaty, tired heap. When a little more time had passed, her mother started shouting encouragement to Owen, pointing to where he'd just made the final turn toward the finish line.

After that, there was a huge rush that left Abby and her mom no time to think about anything except marking off names and numbers as fast as they could. That didn't keep her from smiling when Gary Pratt eventually trudged across the line to where Gil was waiting for him with a big hug and a bottle of water. He led his brother over to the same slope where Tripp and Owen were sitting on the grass. When Gary was settled, Gil returned to his duties.

Once the big rush was over, Abby left it up to her mother to finish checking off the last few runners. It appeared that the vast majority of the participants had made it to the finish line. Some were clearly happy with their times, others less so. The ones she got the biggest kick out of were the ones who celebrated the simple fact they'd made it to the end at all. One woman stopped to gasp that it was her third race, but the first one she'd actually completed. For her, that was a major victory.

After Abby reconciled her list with her mom's to see how many of the runners were unaccounted for, it appeared they had about twenty people to locate. She got out her list of the volunteers stationed along the length of the course so she and Gil could call them for an update. Within a few minutes, she'd determined the whereabouts of all but a few of the runners. No doubt they were all in one of the blind spots along the route. Eventually, she or Gil would do a sweep to make sure everyone either made it to the finish line or got whatever help they might need.

Gil hung up after checking with the last person on his list. "Well, so far, so good. We should be done right on time. The mayor texted to see when we'd be ready for her to present the medals to the winners. I told her another half an hour would probably be good."

A group of five women came into sight, who all wore matching T-shirts and visors. They looked a little worse for wear, but they linked arms and picked up the pace as they proudly stepped over the finish line together. After high-fiving each other, they grabbed their waters and snacks as other friends surrounded them with big grins. She laughed and applauded when the weary ladies managed a little victory dance.

Abby crossed their names off her list, which left a few people still unaccounted for. "I think it's time one of us makes a sweep of the route."

She pointed toward the golf cart Clarence Reed, a member of the veterans group, had dropped off for them to use for the duration of the race. "I've never driven one of those before, but Clarence gave me a quick lesson. But if you'd rather go, I'm perfectly happy to stay here."

"You'd better do the honors." Gil waited until a couple of people walking by were out of listening range and leaned in closer as if he was about to reveal state secrets. "This may come as a shock to you, but some folks find me a little bit scary."

He was teasing, but only sort of. More than once people had walked right past him to ask her their question, even though they both wore badges that identified them as being in charge. She feigned total shock. "Whatever could make them think that? Personally, I think you're a total charmer."

It was good to hear him laugh. "I think that's the first time anyone has ever said that about me. We should probably keep that our little secret, though. I wouldn't want Tripp thinking I've been flirting with his woman."

Abby wasn't sure Tripp thought of her as his, but she wouldn't really mind if he did. Now wasn't the time for figuring out the exact nature of their relationship, but at least they'd made plans to spend the rest of the day together.

"Okay, I'll head out." She picked up her tablet and pack. "I'll be back soon. If I run into any glitches along the way, I'll let you know."

She got off to a bit of a rocky start maneuvering the golf cart through the crush of people now gathered around the finish line, but several volunteers finally cleared a path for her. After that, it was clear sailing. As she passed the remaining few runners still making their way toward the finish line, she slowed long enough to make sure they were going to make it okay.

The people at the water tables were already starting to pack up. They were happy to report that there hadn't been any huge problems. From there, she stopped to check in with her friend Zoe Brevik, the nurse practitioner who had volunteered to head up the medical crew for the race.

"How did it go?"

Zoe looked calm as always. "We just discharged our last patient. I recommended the guy who hurt his ankle head over to the clinic to get it x-rayed. I'm pretty sure it was just a bad sprain, but I'd rather he get it checked out to make sure. Everything else was pretty minor."

That was a huge relief. "I should get going, but if you or any of your crew have suggestions for improvements for next year's race, let me know. I'd like to include the information in the final report Gil and I will do for Connie Pohler."

"Sure thing, but I can't think of anything right off the top of my head. I've got to say that you and Gil seemed like a pretty odd pairing to run this shindig, but I've heard nothing but praise on how things have turned out. Congratulations."

"Thanks. I'll share the good news with Gil. He's already mentioned the two of us working on the race again next year. Not sure I'll be up for that, but I'd only consider doing it if he was onboard to co-chair it with me again."

She got back in the cart. "Maybe Tripp and I will see you later."

Just past the next turn, the sound of someone calling for help had her slamming on her brakes. Thanks to all the surrounding trees that crowded close to the trail, it was hard to decide which direction the shouting was coming from. Finally, she started forward again. Driving slowly, she called Zoe. "Did you hear that? I think someone is calling for help."

"No, I didn't. If I'm needed, call me back."

"I will."

This was the crookedest stretch of the entire route, so she could see only a short distance ahead. As soon as she rounded the next curve, a teenage boy spotted her and started waving his hands. Abby sped up to reach him sooner.

"What kind of help do you need?"

The boy was breathing hard, but he managed to gasp, "Someone's hurt down at the bottom of a steep slope off the trail to the right. He didn't respond when my girlfriend and I tried calling out to him. Another man came running when he heard us shouting. He sent us to watch for help to arrive."

"Hop in and show me where." She drove one-handed

as she dialed Zoe. "It sounds like a man might be badly hurt. Do you want me to come back for you?"

"No, we're already on our way. Spence Lang called 9-1-1 and said the guy apparently fell down into a gully somewhere near the entrance to the national forest. Evidently a couple of hikers spotted him."

A teenage girl stepped out of the woods a short distance ahead. Her companion pointed toward her. "That's my girlfriend. The injured guy is about twenty yards off to the right. The trail is too narrow for your cart."

"Zoe, I'm going to leave"—she paused to glance at her young companion—"sorry, what's your name?"

"Jamie."

"I'm going to have Jamie and his girlfriend wait for you on the main trail. They'll point you in the right direction. From there, he said the trail narrows. You'll have to hike in."

She parked far enough off to the side to make sure her cart wouldn't block any emergency vehicles. "Jamie, thanks for jumping in to help. Zoe Brevik and the EMTs are headed this way. Even after you show them where to go, they still might want you to stick around long enough to share any information you might have."

He took the two bottles of water she offered him. "Okay, we'll hang around."

He looked pretty relieved not to have to return to the injured man. It made her wonder how badly hurt the guy was. She headed off at a slow trot down the trail, looking for Spence. When she didn't immediately spot him, she called his name. He stepped out of the trees a short distance from where she stood, looking grim.

She slowed down, really not wanting to get any closer.

Deciding that would be cowardly, she kept moving forward. "Zoe and the EMTs should be here in just a couple of minutes. Is there anything I can do to help?"

The former soldier was normally pretty cheerful, but not today. Whatever he'd seen down in the gully had left him looking badly shaken as he shook his head. "I'm pretty sure there's nothing anyone can do for him now."

Her stomach lurched and her pulse did a stutter step. "You mean he's . . ."

She couldn't bring herself to finish that sentence, so Spence did it for her. "Sorry, Abby, but I'm pretty sure he's dead."

CHAPTER 4

Spence's stark pronouncement left Abby with wobbly knees and a dizzy head. She wasn't sure how she looked, but it must not have been good. After one glance, Spence immediately lunged forward to grab her upper arms as if he expected her to collapse any second. She was pretty sure that was smart thinking on his part.

"Breathe, woman."

His barked order was enough to get her lungs working again. She drew in a long breath and let it out slowly, repeating the process several more times before he eased up a little on his steel-hard grip. When it was evident her legs would support her, he finally let his hands drop away and stepped back.

"Sorry, Abby. I didn't mean to send you into a tailspin."

She managed a harsh whisper. "Not your fault, Spence."

She finally risked a peek down the slope. All she could see were a pair of legs sprawled in an awkward angle. The shoes alone made it likely the man had been one of the runners in the race. If so, what was he doing so far off the course? She leaned forward to get a better look. He was also wearing running shorts, black or perhaps dark blue. There was also splash of color along the side of his thigh. Green and maybe orange, but it was hard to pick out many details thanks to the shadows cast by the surrounding trees and undergrowth.

"Did you recognize him?"

The fact that the former soldier didn't immediately respond was a bad sign. "Spence?"

He stared down the hillside and shook his head. "I'm not sure I should say anything before Gage gets here to deal with all of this, Abby."

She didn't press him for answers, not when her own mind was providing a possibility—one she really didn't want confirmed anytime soon. After winnowing down the list of runners still unaccounted for, there were very few possibilities left. But now wasn't the time for wild guesses. Instead, she turned in the direction of footsteps headed in their direction. Zoe and two of the EMTs were closing in fast, and it came as no surprise the chief of police and two of his deputies were right behind them.

Her phone ringing saved her from having to say anything. She stepped closer to the tree line on the far side of the trail to take the call. "Hi, Gil, I was just going to call you."

"What's going on, Abby? Gage Logan was talking to the mayor when he got a phone call. He shouted for his deputies to come with him, and the three of them took off running in your direction."

"Please don't share this information with anyone, but some hikers spotted an injured man on one of the side trails. The EMTs, Zoe, and Gage all just got here. That's all I know for sure right now. I'll fill you in on the details when Gage says I can."

Nothing but silence coming from the other end of the call. "Gil? Are you still there?"

"Yeah, I'm here." He let out a slow sigh. "The situation is bad, isn't it? Maybe real bad."

Gage would have her head if she starting blabbing before he'd even had a chance to investigate. She hated to withhold information from her partner, but she had no choice. "I didn't say that."

"You didn't have to, Abby. It's in your voice. Don't worry, I'll hold down the fort until you get back."

"Thanks, Gil. I owe you."

She hung up to find Gage standing right in front of her, a grim expression on his handsome face. "Who were you talking to?"

"Gil called. He saw you heading in my direction and wanted to know what was going on. I told him hikers spotted an injured man, but that was all I knew at this point. He agreed not to share even that much information until you gave us the okay."

"Good. Stick around until I see what we're dealing with. You know the drill."

Unfortunately, he was right about that. Even if the man's death was due to an accident like a fall, Gage would need to make a full report on his investigation. She remained where she was and did her best to stay out of the way.

Meanwhile, Gage carefully made his way down the steep slope to where his deputies and Zoe stood waiting.

It was impossible to hear what she was saying to Gage, but their expressions pretty much said it all. Spence had been right—they were dealing with a death. The only question now was how it had happened. It was hard not to cross her fingers and hope like crazy that it had been an obvious accident of some kind. That would make things so much easier on everyone involved if the cause of death was clear-cut, leaving no lingering questions of how or why it had happened.

But when Gage's deputies started marking off the area with the all-too-familiar yellow crime-scene tape, her knees went all wobbly again. Hoping no one would notice, she backed slowly toward the nearest tree and leaned against the sturdy support of its thick trunk. Unfortunately, Angela Grosskopf, one of the EMTs, frowned and headed in her direction.

"Abby, are you all right?"

This wasn't the first instance where their paths had crossed at a time like this, which meant there was no use in lying. "I'm a bit shaken, but I'll be fine. I just wasn't expecting to have something like this happen today."

Angela reached for Abby's hand and laid her fingertips across her wrist, checking her pulse. "Do you want to sit down for a while?"

Boy, Abby really hated drawing so much attention to herself. "No, that's okay."

When Angela gave her a doubtful look, she added, "Really, I'll be fine. My co-chair and I are in charge of the race today, so I need to stay here until I know for sure one way or another if this was related to the event."

She sort of hoped that comment would convince Angela to share whatever she'd learned about the situation, but that didn't happen. Instead, the EMT walked away, only to return a few seconds later with a bottle of water. "Drink that. If you start to feel dizzy or anything, give me a shout. This is a tough situation for anyone, and especially for you."

The sympathy in the other woman's eyes was almost Abby's undoing. Angela had been one of the first responders when Abby had discovered a body in the parking lot outside of a charity auction. At least this time she hadn't been the first on the scene. That had her asking, "Are Jamie and his girlfriend okay? This has to be especially rough on them."

"I understand Gage had one of his deputies take them home. He didn't want them to still be here when they finally move the body."

"Good thinking. This won't be easy for them, but hopefully they'll have their families around to support them."

Angela started to walk away, but she stopped to point down the trail. "Speaking of people, I think there's someone looking for you."

Sure enough, Tripp was standing on the other side of the line the police had cordoned off. They wouldn't let him come to her, so she headed in his direction. Angela kept pace with her until they reached the deputy that Gage had stationed there.

She stopped to speak to the man Gage had standing guard. "Deputy Chapin, Tripp and I are going to wait in my golf cart. Would you let Gage know where I'll be?"

"Sure thing, Abby."

He lifted the tape so she could duck under. Two steps later, she was wrapped in Tripp's arms. His voice was gruff with worry when he demanded, "What the heck happened?"

"Let's wait until we're at the cart. I really need to sit down."

He supported her with his arm around her shoulders as they made their way back to the main trail, stepping aside as two men wheeled a gurney toward where Gage and his people were waiting. She grimaced, wishing she could just head home where she could take refuge in bed with the blankets pulled up over her head.

As they approached the intersection between the two trails, Tripp pointed ahead. "There's already a crowd gathering down here. Gage probably wants to keep a lid on things for now. That said, there is no way to hide the emergency vehicles, first responders, and cops converging on the area. People are going to be asking questions."

"It's not like I have any answers, or at least not many. Two teenagers spotted a man down in the ravine. Fortunately, they never got near him. Spence heard them shouting for help, so he was the one who went down to assess the situation and then called 9-1-1. He didn't say if he recognized the man or what he thought had happened to him."

Sure enough, as soon as the two of them appeared, the people who had gathered around quickly surged toward them, asking rapid-fire questions.

Abby stepped away from Tripp and drew herself up to her full height. Holding up her hand for silence, she waited until it was quiet before speaking. "Please save your questions for Gage Logan or one of his deputies. That's all I'm allowed to say."

There was some mild grumbling, but Tripp planted himself between her and the other people long enough for her to take refuge in the golf cart. She leaned back and closed her eyes, wishing like crazy that she would wake up and find it had all been a nightmare. The cart rocked a bit when Tripp climbed in next to her.

"Your mom is helping Gil wrap up the last few things that needed to be done. When I headed this way, the mayor was getting ready to hand out the prizes and medals."

She popped her eyes open at that comment. "Shouldn't you have stuck around for the ceremony? You came in third overall. There was a medal for that, and a prize as well."

"Owen offered to let the mayor know why I left, so she wouldn't waste time looking for me." He slid his arm across the back of the seat, letting his fingers lightly rest on her shoulder. "You might want to text your mom and let her know you're okay. She looked pretty worried, but at least she let me come looking for you alone. I figured you didn't need her hovering over you right now."

"True enough."

It hadn't gone well when her mother had been with Abby the last time she'd stumbled across a murder victim . . . not that this case was anything like that . . . no, this was an accident. It had to be. She wasn't sure she could go through getting tangled up in another murder case. It had happened all too often since she'd moved to Snowberry Creek. Maybe there was something in the water or about the town itself that brought out the murderous tendencies in a few residents. That was hard to imagine, though, considering how many of the people she'd met were so great. Especially the one sitting next to her, the man who always stood ready to offer her his own brand of rough comfort.

The minutes ticked by slowly, her mind caught up in an endless loop of dread and denial. She really hoped that Gage Logan would complete his preliminary investigation of the scene and find nothing that indicated the death had been anything other than a tragic accident. Death by natural causes would be even better.

She tried to focus on what she and Gil had left to do, now that the race was officially over. But thinking about Gil brought his brother back to mind, and suddenly the argument between the city councilman and Gary Pratt started playing out in her head in stark clarity. She hadn't pressed Gil for any details, and he'd shown no inclination to talk about it when he'd returned to their table. Besides, it was really none of her business.

The surrounding crowd continued to grow, but at least no one seemed inclined to approach her and Tripp. That didn't keep them from gathering in small groups to ponder the situation, although she was only guessing at the topic of their conversations. Lost in her own thoughts, she had no idea how much time had passed, but the increased volume in the chatter had her looking around to see what had everyone stirred up.

The gurney, no longer empty, rolled past. The police provided escort and held people back as it was wheeled down the trail to where an ambulance waited. The sight made it all too clear that something tragic had happened that day. At least no one appeared to be making wild guesses as to who had died.

She shuddered and leaned in closer to Tripp. "I hope Gage lets me go soon. I feel really guilty leaving Gil to shoulder responsibility for everything that still needs to be done."

"He'll understand, Abs. He knows you'd never duck out on your duty. You would've covered for him if the situation were reversed."

And it was probably petty of her to wish he had been

the one to do the final sweep of the course. Telling herself that she didn't really mean that, even if she actually did, she began the tedious process of pulling herself back together. Once Gage did send her on her way, she needed to jump right back into the thick of things and help her partner wrap things up. She'd been looking forward to spending the rest of the afternoon and evening with Tripp, hitting the food trucks gathered in the parking lot at city hall for a late lunch, and then a second time for dinner. There was also a concert in the park to cap off the evening.

"I don't know how much energy I'm going to have left after we finish up here today."

Tripp gave her shoulders a gentle squeeze. "Not a problem. Just do whatever you need to. Meanwhile, I'll catch the shuttle to city hall and pick up some lunch and a few things we can reheat for dinner. After that, I'll go back to the house for a badly needed shower and change of clothes. Just text me when you're done, and I'll come get you."

Bless the man, he knew just how to make her feel better. "Sounds good, especially since I hadn't planned to cook tonight."

"Any preference for what you want me to get?"

"Pretty much anything sounds good right now. Sandwiches, barbecue, Chinese, Italian." Then she mustered up a teasing smile. "I don't have to remind you that some dessert would be greatly appreciated."

That was an understatement, especially considering the man's love of all things gooey and sugary. He took the teasing well. "It will be a toss-up between the elephant ears and the peach cobbler I've heard people talking about."

"Get one of each, and we'll split them. That way you won't actually have to choose."

His eyes lit up. "Or I could buy two of each. That way neither of us has to make do with half measures. Don't forget, I just ran a race. I need to up my carb quota for the day."

That might work for him, but she hadn't run in the race. Supervising one probably didn't count as exercise as much as she wished it did. On the other hand, surely stress had burned a few extra calories. "Fine, but if I can't finish mine tonight, don't think you get the leftovers. There's always tomorrow."

For the second time, the crowd grew restless. This time, Tripp looked around for the cause. "Gage is headed this way, and he doesn't look happy."

He never did when he was on the job, which made her feel a bit guilty for forgetting about the dead man long enough to tease Tripp about desserts. Regardless, she suspected the chief of police would both forgive and understand her need to step back from the image of the dead man's body sprawled in the woods.

She sat up straighter and waited for Gage to reach them. It didn't take long. When someone approached him, his curt response had everyone backing up a few steps to give him room.

"Thanks for waiting, Abby. I know you'd rather be anywhere else."

"So would you, Gage, but here we are. What do you need from me?"

"For now, just the basics. Like I said earlier, you know the drill."

Sad, but true. She drew a slow breath before launching

into a summary of the events as she knew them. "Clarence Reed loaned us his golf cart for the day. We waited until the vast majority of the runners had crossed the finish line or were otherwise accounted for before doing a final sweep of the course to look for stragglers. My co-chair preferred to man our table, so I offered to do the honors. I stopped at the water tables and then at the medical tent to check in with Zoe and her crew. After verifying that we had no major issues there, I continued on down the course."

When she paused for a breath, Gage spoke up. "I take it the co-chair you're referring to is Gil Pratt."

"Yes, he and I headed up the committee to organize the race."

"And how has that worked out for the two of you?"

Was he simply curious or was he asking for some hidden reason? Her answer would've been the same regardless. "It's been great. Gil's job in the navy was detail oriented just like my job was in the company my ex-husband and I owned, so our working styles are surprisingly compatible."

For the first time, Gage's mouth quirked up in a small smile. "Who would've seen that coming?"

He wasn't the only one who'd questioned their pairing. "Evidently Connie Pohler did. She's the one who suggested we partner on the project."

Gage just shook his head. "That woman's mind works in mysterious ways."

No arguments there. Abby picked up her narration where she'd left off, quickly explaining how she'd heard Jamie yelling for help, and that she'd left him on the main trail with his girlfriend while she'd hiked the short distance to find Spence. Other than her calls to Zoe and the one from Gil, she hadn't talked to anyone about what had happened, except Tripp.

"Okay, got it. You can go now. I'm guessing people who want to know what happened may come at you from all directions. Just refer any questions you get back to me and my department. There's no hiding the fact that someone died, but I'm not giving out any information until we've had a chance to notify the next of kin."

She'd figured as much and had no inclination to ask the man's identity. That way if anyone asked, she could honestly say she didn't know anything beyond what was already public information. Besides, if her suspicions were correct, she really didn't want to know any more than that. It was bad enough she'd already brushed up against Gage's preliminary investigation. She had no desire to get sucked in any deeper. It was past time to get going. She started the engine on the golf cart. "I'm sorry this happened, Gage."

"Me too, Abby."

Then he patted the roof of the golf cart and stepped back. She took her time pulling away and steering past the people still cluttering up the path. When they broke clear, she punched the gas pedal and picked up speed. Just before they reached a curve that would take them out of sight, she glanced at the rearview mirror. Gage was still watching them, maybe to make sure she was able to make a clean getaway. She lifted her hand in farewell. He did the same and then disappeared back into the trees.

She glanced at her silent companion. "I hate this, Tripp. I don't know why I keep getting caught up in stuff like this, but I really hate it."

He met her gaze, his expression a strange combination of sympathy and anger. "Me too, but there's nothing we can do now but ride it out. Finish up what you have to, and then we'll head home and shut the world out for a while."

She silently added she'd also be crossing her fingers the world wouldn't come knocking on her door anytime soon.

CHAPTER 5

Abby dropped Tripp off near the parking lot before circling back to the finish line to check in with Gil. As much as she wanted to go straight home, staying busy would at least help her focus on something other than the scene in the woods.

The first person she ran into was Clarence Reed, the owner of the golf cart. She forced a smile as she slowed to a stop. "Hi, Clarence, I'm sorry if I've kept you waiting. I didn't expect to be gone anywhere near this long."

He shook his head. "Not a problem, Abby. I heard you ran into a situation. That had to take priority."

"Thanks for being so understanding."

She turned off the engine and handed him the keys. Before accepting them, he asked, "Are you sure you won't need it again? I can swing back by later to pick it up."

"Thanks, but we should finish up here soon, and then my crew will be free to enjoy the rest of the festivities."

Hopefully the rumors about the death wouldn't cast a pall over the other events that were part of the Founder's Day celebration. Everyone had been looking forward to the concert later in the evening. She and Tripp had planned to attend, but she really couldn't keep up a brave front for that much longer.

After thanking Clarence one last time, she headed toward their table, which was currently unoccupied. Darn it, she'd really hoped to get back in time to help Gil. When she sat down, she spotted a note he'd left for her. He'd been called away to help with a problem that shouldn't take longer than half an hour. Based on the time he'd jotted at the bottom of the paper, he should be back anytime now.

While she waited for his return, she read through the notes on his clipboard, updating her own to-do list in the process. Boy, the man had been busy. Almost everything was done. She felt a little bit guilty about that, but it was a relief to know she wouldn't have to stick around much longer.

"There you are!"

After marking off the last item on her list, Abby looked up to greet her mother. "Sorry, I didn't mean to go missing in action. I hope things weren't too chaotic after I left."

"I'm not worried about me, Abagail. It's you I'm concerned about. I heard you ran into another . . . unfortunate incident."

Well, that was one way to describe what had happened, but she didn't quibble. "I'm fine. I had to stick around in case Gage needed me. Once he had everything under control, he let me go. I'm waiting for Gil to see what still needs doing, and then Tripp's going to come back to pick me up. We've decided to stay in tonight."

Her mother was already shaking her head. "But we were supposed to attend the concert together."

"I know, Mom, and I'm sorry to disappoint you. But honestly, I'm exhausted. You and Owen should go, though. I know you've been looking forward to the music."

One thing she and her mom had in common besides their hair color was a healthy dose of stubborn determination. For once, she really wished that wasn't true. Even now, she could see her mom trying to come up with an argument that would convince Abby to change her mind. It didn't take her long. "How much energy does it take to sit on a blanket and listen to a band?"

"I don't know, but it's more than I have at the moment."

Fortunately, Owen walked up in time to hear the last bit of their conversation. He gave Abby a sympathetic look before turning his attention to her mother. "Phoebe, Abby has been running at full tilt for days while she and Gil got this race organized. They did a fabulous job of it, but she's bound to be exhausted. Even if you did manage to convince her to drag herself to the concert, she wouldn't enjoy it, especially with what she's just been dealing with."

The man meant well, but she really wanted to avoid that particular topic of conversation. It was one more thing she didn't have the energy for right now. Her mom stared at Abby with a slight frown on her face. Finally, she leaned into Owen, smiling slightly when he automatically pulled her in closer to his side. "I'm sorry you don't feel up to going, Abby, but it's understandable. Do you want us to bring you some dinner later?"

"Thanks, but Tripp is already taking care of that. He's hitting the food trucks at city hall on his way home. I'm supposed to text him when I'm finished here. Right now, I'm just waiting for Gil to get back so he can fill me in on what still needs to be done."

Owen looked off to the left. "Talk about perfect timing. There's the man now, so we'll make ourselves scarce. I need to check on my food truck, and I've got a hankering for some ice cream. Text us if you need help with anything. Otherwise, we'll see you at the diner in the morning. Is eight o'clock still okay?"

"Sounds good."

Although it really didn't. The breakfast date had slipped her mind, so she was grateful for the reminder. Sleeping late would've been nice, but her mom needed to get an early start on the two-hour drive back to Seattle tomorrow in order to get caught up on her laundry and other things before going back to work on Monday. There would be plenty of time later in the day for Abby and Zeke to enjoy a long nap.

She waved at the couple as they headed toward the parking lot to catch the shuttle down to city hall. Then she turned her attention to her partner as he dropped down into the chair next to her. Gil looked a bit frazzled, which surprised her. "Is everything okay?"

"Yeah, I just had to meet up with my brother. He managed to wrench his knee in a fall along the race route. It's stiffened up enough that riding his bike wasn't a good idea. I caught the shuttle down to the high school and brought my truck back for him to use. We traded keys so I can bring his bike home when we're done here."

Funny that Zoe hadn't mentioned Gary's name as one of the patients they'd treated today. "Is he okay?"

"He'll be fine after he ices his knee and knocks back a couple of cold ones." Gil looked a bit disgusted. "It's not the first time he's had to hobble the last part of a race. I've tried telling him he's going to mess up that knee bad enough to the point they'll have to replace it. And if that happens, who does he think will play nursemaid while he sits on the couch and watches television all day? Not me, that's for sure. I'll be alone at the shop doing everything that needs to be done. Someone's got to keep the money coming in and the bills paid."

It was hard not to laugh at Gil's grumbling about Gary, knowing full well it was worry and not anger driving his complaints. Anyone who spent five minutes in their company knew the two brothers were extremely close. "So what are you taking home for the invalid's dinner tonight?"

Gil's cheeks, flushed a bit red, said she'd hit a bull's-eye with that question. Finally, he chuckled. "I bought some of Owen's barbecue with all the fixings for Gary to take home in the truck. I could've carried it in the saddle-bags on his bike, but he would pitch a fit if anything leaked on the leather. I should've done it just for spite."

She gave in to the need to laugh, but at least Gil joined in. "I promise I won't tell anyone that you're an old softie at heart. Besides, I can't point fingers when it comes to needing to be fussed over a bit. Tripp was buying both lunch and dinner for the two of us on his way back to the house. We plan to take it easy and stay home tonight."

Gil winced. "Does your mom know that? She sounded pretty excited when she told me that the four of you had plans to go to the concert together."

"Yeah, I told her. She was disappointed but understood why I wasn't up to staying out that late."

"Is it because of the race or having to deal with whatever you ran into out there on the trail?"

So he hadn't heard any details. Not surprising, though, since he'd been busy dealing with his brother. "Mostly the latter. I checked in at our water stops and stopped to talk to Zoe at the first aid tent. A few people needed fluids, and there were some other minor injuries. The worst was an ankle injury, but she was sure that was a sprain. She didn't mention Gary, though."

"He probably didn't bother to have them check his knee. It's happened before, and there wasn't much they could do except tell him to ice it and take it easy for a few days."

That made sense. "Anyway, I'd just left there when I heard a couple of teenagers yelling for help. They'd been hiking one of the side trails and spotted a man who'd fallen down at the bottom of a ravine. Spence Lang got there before I did and called it in. Zoe and the EMTs got there next, followed by Gage Logan and his deputies."

"Was he badly hurt? The guy, I mean."

There was no reason not to tell him the truth, considering how many people had seen the body being taken away. "Unfortunately, he was dead. I don't know who it was. Gage won't be releasing any details pending notification of the next of kin."

Her explanation of the events was met with shocked silence. Then Gil gave her a rough pat on her shoulder. "I figured it was bad, but I was envisioning someone with a broken leg or something. I'm so sorry, Abby. I wish I'd done the loop so you didn't have to deal with that. I know it's not the first time you've stumbled across a tough situation, but that doesn't make it any easier."

He picked up his clipboard and flipped through a few pages. "There's really nothing left to do that can't wait until we meet to debrief with our committee members on Tuesday. A couple guys are coming to pick up the tables and chairs. I can wait around for them to make sure there aren't any problems. That bunch of middle school kids did a great job of picking up the discarded water cups the runners tossed all over the place. They also carried the recycling out to the bin in the parking lot. I signed off on their paperwork so they'll get credit for their community service work."

Boy, he had accomplished a lot. "So, how did the award ceremony go? I'm really sorry I missed it."

"The mayor rocked it, and the newspaper reporter was on hand to take a bunch of pictures. Everyone loved the Salmon Scoot logo on the medals we had made for the winners. Connie also let the people who won prizes know they could pick them up at city hall on Monday if they didn't have a way to take them home today. I'm guessing that's where Tripp's stuff was taken."

"I'll let him know."

They went over a few more odds and ends, which didn't take long. Abby boxed up all of their paraphernalia. "I'll take this stuff home with me. That way you don't have to carry it all on Gary's bike. We wouldn't want to risk the cap coming off one of the highlighters and staining his saddlebags."

"Yeah, I'd never hear the end of it. I swear that guy babies that bike like it's his child. I'm actually surprised he trusts me to ride it the two miles back to our house."

She couldn't help but tease Gil a bit. "So I shouldn't give him a call to see if it's okay for you to give me riding lessons on it before you bring it home?"

Gil's grin turned wicked. "You know, it might just be worth it. Well, except for all the whining he'd do."

"Tell him I said hi and thank him for hobbling in our race today."

"I'll do that."

While Gil gathered up all their paperwork for her, she called Tripp to come get her. "I'll be going. I hope you don't have to hang around too long. I'd hate to find out that Gary had time to finish off the barbecue before you get home."

"He wouldn't dare. He knows he'd end up with a few more bruises and two bad knees. We Pratts don't take kindly to being messed with, even amongst ourselves."

Gil wasn't looking at her at the moment, so Abby wasn't sure if he was kidding or not. She chose to think that he was. "I'm going to go now. Enjoy the rest of your weekend, and I'll see you on Tuesday at my house."

He gave her a hopeful look. "Any chance you'll have some of those lemon bars you served at our last meeting?"

"For you, I'll make a double batch so you can take a bunch home with you. I'll leave it up to you to decide if you'll share them with Gary."

"That depends on whether he parks his backside in the office at the shop on Monday to catch up on the paperwork he let slide while I've been working on the race."

"I'll cross my fingers for you both."

As she walked away, Gil mumbled something under his breath about needing all the luck they could get. What was he referring to? But since he hadn't actually directed the comment to her, she wrote it off to just more grumbling about his brother and his bum knee. When she glanced back, he was laughing with the guys who'd just arrived to pick up the tables. Rather than interrupt, she continued on down the path to the parking lot.

After all, Tripp was on his way, and she shouldn't keep him waiting.

CHAPTER 6

The next morning, Tripp held Abby's hand as they strolled along Main Street. "That went well, although I'm not sure my heart would survive that much cholesterol on a regular basis."

Abby couldn't disagree. "Frannie's omelets are absolutely huge, so were those lemon scones. Health-wise, we would've both been better off if we'd ordered one breakfast and split it."

Looking horrified, Tripp shook his head. "No way. You know what happens to people who insult Frannie's cooking. Even if we think splitting an order isn't rude, she would. The last person to tick her off was banned from the diner for a month. I can't go that long without a piece of her pie."

"It's far better to sacrifice our health than Frannie's desserts." She smiled up at the blue skies overhead. "I'm glad we decided to walk down to meet Mom and Owen. The exercise will do us both good, and the weather is perfect."

"Not to mention you can relax since the race is over. Of course, it's only a matter of time before someone else wants you to run something else for them. An auction, a dinner dance, the world."

"Bite your tongue, Tripp Blackston. After the wrap-up meeting on Tuesday, my calendar is clear for the next month except for the quilting guild meetings. I plan to enjoy every minute of free time I can."

"If I were a betting man, I'd place all my money on you getting suckered into something else within four weeks. Five, tops."

"Did you not hear what I just said?"

He held up two fingers. "I have two words for you—soft touch. Better yet, just one—sucker!"

She was still sputtering in outrage when a familiar car slowed down and stopped next to them. The passenger window rolled down, and Gage Logan leaned over the console to look up at them. They would normally be happy to see him. But right now, his usual smile was missing, and he was sporting his official police chief expression.

"Hi, Gage, what's up?"

"Sorry to intrude on your morning, Abby, but I was about to stop by your house. I need to talk to you about yesterday."

Abby immediately regretted having eaten such a huge meal. Suddenly all those eggs solidified into a huge lump of tension in her stomach. "I told you everything I knew at the scene."

"This is about something else."

It was hard not to demand details, but standing out on Main Street wasn't the place for this discussion. She looked at Tripp to see how he was reacting to the intrusion. The grim set to his jaw said it all. There was nothing he hated more than her getting drawn into a police investigation. Maybe it would be better to buy a little time to calm down. "We'll meet you at the house in fifteen minutes."

Gage looked as if he might offer them a ride to speed up the process. Instead, he finally jerked his head in a quick nod. "I'll be there. And again, I'm sorry, you two."

With that, he rolled up the window and then drove off.

"What's that all about?"

She shrugged as she started trudging down the sidewalk. "No idea. You were there when I told him everything yesterday. If someone didn't like something about the race and how it was run, I would think they'd either bring their complaints directly to me or even the mayor's office. There would be no reason to involve the police."

"Let's just forget about it for the moment. No use in getting all tied up in knots over what might turn out to be nothing."

They both knew Gage wouldn't bother her if it wasn't important. Rather than stew over it, she shoved the worry to the back of her mind and enjoyed the rest of their walk as best she could.

As it turned out, Gage ended up calling to say he'd been delayed and would be over a little later. Abby spent the time working in the backyard and talking to Zeke as he alternated between soaking up some sunshine and then stretching out in the shade when he wanted to cool off.

She was always amused by the way he moved from spot to spot, lying first on one side and then the other, his version of circuit training.

Tripp was out front edging the sidewalk, probably as an excuse to keep an eye out for Gage. He'd already made it clear he wanted to be in on the discussion, whatever the subject might be. She wasn't sure how Gage would feel about that, but she would appreciate the moral support. When the weed trimmer shut off suddenly, she stripped off her gardening gloves and tossed them in the five-gallon bucket where she'd been putting the clippings from the bushes she'd been trimming.

"Time to go in, Zeke."

The big dog dragged himself up to his feet and gave himself a good shake before trotting up onto the porch. She followed him inside and headed to the front door to greet the two men standing on her porch.

"Hi again, Gage. Come on in."

Tripp immediately muscled past him to enter first. At least Gage didn't insist he had to speak to Abby alone. They both knew that wasn't going to happen, not without a major argument, anyway.

"Kitchen or living room?"

"Either's fine, Abby. This shouldn't take long."

She opted for the kitchen. Giving a statement to the police was thirsty work, at least it always was for her. While the two men got settled at the table, she poured three glasses of iced tea and filled a plate with some cookies and sliced nut bread. She was still full from breakfast, but Tripp and Gage were both big men with a definite appreciation for sweets of all kinds. They also knew about her compulsion to offer any and all guests refreshments regardless of the circumstances. If she failed to set out a plate of goodies, they'd wonder what was wrong.

Once she sat down, Gage reached for the spiral notebook he used when he was taking a statement, a clear indication that something serious was going down. He clicked his pen a couple of times as if hesitating over where to start. Finally, he gave Tripp a pointed look. "None of what we discuss here is up for public discussion. I trust you to keep your mouth shut."

If that was true, then why did that sound more like a threat? Tripp hadn't liked Gage's comment, either. He leaned forward, elbows on the table to glare at his friend. "Fine. The lips are zipped, but don't use that tone with Abby or this discussion will be over before it gets started."

Gage slammed his pen down on the table. "Would you rather I take her down to my office? Maybe you'd prefer I use the room where we interview criminals."

Enough was enough. She waved her hand up and down between the two men to break their staring contest. "Tripp, you know Gage is only here because he has to be. Give the man a chance to tell me what's going on before you get mad."

When Tripp leaned back, she turned to the other guilty party. "Having said that, I don't need the threats, Gage. If you have questions, ask them."

He had the good grace to look chagrined. "You're right, Abby, and I'm sorry. That apology extends to you, too, Tripp. It's been a rough twenty-four hours."

Abby took a long look at him and decided to be honest about what she saw. "Have you been up since yesterday? Because frankly, you look pretty awful."

Tripp just had to pile on. "Yeah, I've seen roadkill that looked healthier."

"All right, you two, that's enough. I did manage to sneak in a couple of hours of sleep."

He'd been smiling, but now his expression reverted to cop mode. "I'm sorry to say that the incident in the woods yesterday has turned into a murder investigation. That's bad enough, but the fact that the victim is a member of the city council adds to the pressure to make an arrest, and sooner rather than later."

Tripp asked, "Who?" at the same time Abby blurted out, "James DiSalvo was murdered?"

Both men turned to stare at her as she slapped her hand over her mouth as if that would somehow cancel out what she'd just said.

"We haven't released the name yet, Abby. What makes you think it was him?"

Why couldn't she have kept her mouth shut? But there was no avoiding the discussion now. "I never went near the dead man's body, but I did catch a glimpse of his running shorts. I could see they were dark with a splotches of bright green and orange on the side. When I saw Mr. DiSalvo before the race, he had on dark blue shorts with a pattern of green, orange, and yellow on the side panels."

Gage looked incredulous. "There were one hundred and fifty runners in the race yesterday, but you somehow remember what one man was wearing."

"Yeah, well, his shorts were pretty distinctive."

She didn't think it necessary to explain she'd only paid attention to him in the first place because of his heated discussion with Gary Pratt. The two men had separated and gone their separate ways. Whatever had happened to the councilman had taken place long afterward. At least she hoped so.

Gage had a way of looking at a person that had them wanting to confess anything and everything, and she was no exception. "I'm guessing there's some reason you took note of his attire that has nothing to do with the style of his shorts."

She should have known it wasn't going to be that simple. "I saw him talking to someone before the race."

He immediately prompted her into telling him more. "And that would be?"

She really hated to rat out the Pratt brothers, but Gage had left her no choice. She closed her eyes and sent a silent apology winging its way to her co-chair. *Sorry, Gil, but I can't lie to Gage.*

Swallowing hard, she dove right in. "Earlier in the day, before the race even started, I happened to see Mr. DiSalvo talking to Gary Pratt."

"Just talking?"

If he already knew what had happened, why hadn't he just said so? "I was too far away to know what the topic of discussion was, but I admit that neither of them looked happy."

Gage flipped back to an earlier page in his notebook. She was beginning to hate that stupid thing. When he found what he was looking for, he started reading. *"I heard some yelling, but couldn't make heads or tails out of what they were saying. By the time I got close, the two men were standing toe-to-toe glaring at each other. About then, Gary Pratt's older brother charged up to insert himself into the conversation, after which both men took a step back. Finally, James DiSalvo muttered something under his breath right before he walked off that left both Pratts glaring at him. For a second, I thought Gary would go charging after him, but Gil planted himself right in front of his brother. After that, Gary stalked off in the opposite direction than Mr. DiSalvo had gone. Gil then returned to where Abby McCree was waiting for him."*

Gage looked up from his notes. "Does that sound about right?"

"I have no idea who started the argument or what it was about. Someone told Gil there was a problem, and he went to deal with it. A few minutes later, he came back to the table, and we got back to work on the race. We never talked about what had happened."

That earned her another long look, but he finally shoved his notebook back into his pocket. "Were you and Gil together the rest of the time?"

She closed her eyes as she quickly replayed the morning's events. "We weren't connected at the hip, but we were always in the same general area. I'm certain we were never apart long enough for him to get all the way down to where the body was found and back again. For the record, Gil Pratt worked his backside off on the race, both in the days leading up to the event and all morning yesterday to make sure it was a success. I've never had a better or more hardworking co-chair. If he asks me to take on another committee with him again in the future, I'd do it in a heartbeat. I consider him a friend, and he's a good man. If anyone says differently, they'll get an earful from me. And that includes you, Gage Logan."

If she sounded a bit angry and a whole lot protective of Gil, too bad. It was nothing but the truth. Tripp looked like he was fighting the urge to laugh, and even the police chief had a suspicious twinkle in his eyes. She glared at both of them. "What's so funny?"

Gage was the one who answered. "I'm just glad I'm usually on your good side, Abby. You're pretty scary when you get all worked up defending someone you care about. Just so you know, Gil is not on my radar for this."

"That's good."

It was hard not to notice that he didn't say the same about Gary. She didn't know him as well as she did Gil, but he'd always been polite to her. She really, really hoped that Gage had other leads, ones that didn't point straight at Gary. Admittedly, neither of the two brothers had pristine police records, but a few bar brawls were nothing in comparison to possible murder charges. The prosecutor on the case might very well look at those fights as evidence of Gary being prone to violent behavior. It would kill Gil to see his little brother locked up on murder charges.

"Do you have any other questions for me?"

"Not right now."

"I know not to press for details in your investigation, but when will the cause of death become public knowledge?"

"I'll be releasing what details I can to the press later this afternoon. I'd appreciate it if you keep this to yourselves for now, but he died from blunt force trauma. The rest of the investigation is a work in progress. That's all I can say right now."

There were so many questions flying around in Abby's head, but she kept them to herself. Gage couldn't answer them anyway, and Tripp would worry that she might be drawn deeper into the case.

Up until that point, neither of the two men had shown much interest in the refreshments she'd set out. But now that she'd given her statement and Gage had told them as much as he could, everyone seemed to take that as a signal that it was time to relax. She topped off their drinks and added a few more cookies to the plate.

Gage took a long sip of his iced tea and turned the conversation to more pleasant subjects. "So, Tripp, I hear you came in third overall. Was that your best ever time?"

"Yep, it was. I hear that I not only earned a fancy medal, but I also won a prize. I left before the award ceremony to find out what kind of mess Abby had gotten herself into this time, but I can pick my stuff up at the mayor's office this week."

"Any idea what kind of prize you're getting?"

"Nope, I didn't ask. I thought I'd let it be a surprise."

Actually, Abby knew exactly what he'd won, and she was pretty sure he'd like it. Three of her friends in the quilting guild had donated a really nice quilt, the kind that was meant to be enjoyed, not just admired. It was sturdy enough to hold up to years of everyday use. That didn't mean she couldn't tease him a little. Jean, one of the three ladies, had a habit of showing up on Tripp's doorstep with one of her special tuna casseroles. Some were better than others, but he always ate every bite after thanking her for her generosity.

Abby gave in to the temptation to tease him just a little. "I can give you a hint, Tripp. You know, just so you're forewarned."

Now he looked truly worried. "Don't tell me."

She hid a small smile behind her glass of tea. "Jean donated this particular prize. She'll be thrilled to learn that you're the one who will benefit from all her hard work."

Gage was openly grinning now while poor Tripp looked a little sick. "I said not to tell me."

She hit him with her best innocent look. "Oops, my bad."

CHAPTER 7

Gage left half an hour later while Tripp returned to the front yard to finish edging the sidewalk. For her part, Abby headed upstairs to Aunt Sybil's sewing room. In the months since she'd inherited the house, she'd gradually come to think of the big Victorian as her own, with the exception of the one room that was quintessentially her late aunt's special place. It had taken her quite a while to get up the courage to finish the two quilts Sybil had started before her death, but she loved having that small connection with her aunt.

Upon entering the room, she studied the shelves piled high in fabric, hoping to find inspiration for a baby quilt among the various colors and prints. When Abby had stopped in at Something's Brewing the prior week, her friend Bridey had shared the great news that she and her husband had just learned they were expecting their first child. That gave her plenty of time to make them a quilt.

Since they weren't sure if they wanted to know in advance if they were having a boy or a girl, going with a mix of bright colors seemed like the best option. She'd found a simple pattern that used hexagons in primary colors connected together with small triangles in a neutral shade. Thanks to the time she'd spent with the ladies of the guild, her quilting skills had improved. That didn't mean she was ready to dive into something too complex.

She pulled different fat quarters off the shelves, needing ten different colors plus the neutral one used to connect the large hexagons that made up the design. After spreading them out on the cutting table, it didn't take her long to narrow the pile down to five solid colors and five animal prints done in the same shades. Satisfied with her choices, she put the rejected fabrics back up on the shelf out of the way. After getting out the rotary cutter and various rulers, she prepared to dive right in.

Unfortunately, her phone buzzed, which put a hold on her plan. She checked the caller ID to see if she wanted to answer. Huh, why was Tripp calling her? Only one way to find out.

"Hi, what's up?"

"There's someone here to see you, and I wasn't sure if I should let him on the property. You usually don't like talking to him."

She peeked out the window that overlooked the front yard. That's all it took to destroy her good mood. Tripp was right about how she felt about the man standing beside him. What did Riley Molitor want now? This wasn't the first time the surprisingly tenacious reporter for *The*

Clarion, Snowberry Creek's local newspaper, had showed up on her doorstep unwanted and uninvited.

There was a hint of menace in Tripp's voice when he spoke again. "Should I let him in or play kickball with him?"

She could hear Riley's protest in the background, not that she blamed him. Tripp had threatened to toss him out in the road to see how high he would bounce on at least one previous occasion. He'd also hinted he had a few hand grenades tucked away, left over from his time in the army, if that's what it took to convince Riley to leave her alone. He was kidding about that, of course. At least she hoped he was.

"Did he say what he wants?"

"I didn't ask, but I can."

She couldn't make out much of the ensuing muffled conversation between the two men, but it wasn't long before Tripp came back on the line. "He swears he just wants to talk to you about the Salmon Scoot race for an article he's doing for the paper. I think we can trust him on that, mainly because he knows I won't be happy if I find out he lied to me. Is it okay if I let him in?"

As one of the co-chairs for the event, she was pretty much obligated to cooperate. The race had become an annual event to raise money for the music and athletic departments at the local high school. Even if she decided not to organize the race next year, she wanted to do whatever she could to ensure its continuing success.

"I'll be down to let him in."

"Want me to join the party?"

That made her laugh. "No, I can handle Riley, especially if I have Zeke there to supervise."

"Okay, I'll tell him to wait on the porch."

She hustled down the stairs to her bedroom on the second floor. Considering Riley hadn't called in advance to see if she was available, he could wait a few minutes while she checked her appearance in case he wanted a picture for some reason. After all, it wasn't the first time he'd showed up uninvited.

Basically, it was Riley's own fault if he felt less than welcome. He'd first appeared with no warning the day after she and Tripp had uncovered a dead body. She'd still been in her pajamas and hadn't yet had her first cup of coffee when he came knocking. When he'd demanded to know how her late aunt's archenemy came to be buried in her backyard, Abby had slammed the door in his face and taken cover. Not her finest hour.

After running a comb through her hair, she put on a touch of lipstick. Deciding that would have to do, she trotted downstairs and opened the front door. Riley looked relieved to see her, probably because Zeke was sitting next to him. The mastiff mix weighed in at a solid ninety-five pounds and could look pretty intimidating at times. As soon as Zeke spotted her, he gave a happy bark as his tail started wagging.

"Hi, Riley, come on in."

"Thanks for seeing me, Abby."

Zeke waited politely for the guest to enter first. If anything, that left the reporter looking even more nervous.

"Why don't we head back to the kitchen? I could use a cold drink about now."

"Sounds good."

She let Riley lead the way down the hallway, keeping herself between him and Zeke. Riley picked a seat at the table while she opened the refrigerator. "I have iced tea, pop, water, and a couple of beers. What sounds good?"

"I'd like a cola if you have one."

He got settled and booted up his laptop while Abby fixed their drinks and debated whether or not to break out other refreshments. Deciding that would only delay things, she handed him a glass of ice and a can of pop. She also set a couple of Zeke's favorite treats within easy reach.

"You might as well make friends with Zeke while you're here. He loves those peanut butter doggy cookies."

The dog was on his best behavior as he carefully accepted the cookies from the nervous reporter. As soon as he finished eating them, he slurped his tongue on Riley's arm to express his gratitude for the treat. It was hard not to laugh at the expression on the man's face, something between relief and disgust. Maybe he wasn't fond of dog slobber, but there was no accounting for taste.

As she opened her own drink, she asked, "So, what did you need to talk to me about?"

"I'm doing a follow-up article for this week's paper on the Founder's Day celebration. Since you organized one of the major events, I wanted to ask you a few questions about the race." He looked up from the keyboard. "By the way, everyone has been talking about what a great job you did."

"That's good to hear. If you'd called ahead, I'm sure my co-chair would've liked to have been here, too. Gil Pratt played a huge role in making the race a success."

Riley looked doubtful. "Seriously?"

"Yes, seriously. Thanks to his time in the navy and his experience running his own business, Gil has a lot of experience in organizing and keeping track of information. He also recruited a lot of the volunteers we needed through his connection with the veterans group here in town. I couldn't have done the job without him. Well, him and Connie Pohler, who provided us with many of the tools we needed to succeed."

Riley immediately cut loose with a rapid-fire series of questions that she did her best to answer. He also asked if he could use a picture of the logo they'd had designed for the race and offered to print the names of the winners in the paper. She agreed to e-mail him a JPEG of the logo and the list as soon as possible.

"I was going to ask if I could take a picture of you wearing one of the T-shirts that you handed out to the vol-unteers at the race; now I'm thinking I should include Gil in the shot. Any chance you two will be together before my deadline on Tuesday evening?"

"Actually, we're meeting here on Tuesday to wrap up everything. The whole committee will be here at ten o'clock. I'll let Gil know that he should come at nine thirty and that you'd like him to wear his shirt for the pic-ture."

Riley grinned a little. "I'm not sure I've ever seen him without his leather vest. Should make for an interesting shot."

He wasn't wrong about that. "Who knows, he may sur-prise us both."

"Okay, I'll be back on Tuesday. If anything comes up between then and now, you can reach me at the paper."

He shut down his laptop and then finished off his drink. "Thanks for seeing me today, Abby. And do me a favor—tell Tripp I behaved myself."

That made her laugh. "I will."

She followed him down the hall to the front door. As he stepped out onto the porch, he paused as if he had something else to say but wasn't sure if he should. Finally, he gave a quick nod, his decision made.

"Abby, I swear this isn't for any article I'm writing, but I just wanted to say that I'm sorry about what happened at the end of the race. That had to be hard to deal with after everything else you've been through since moving here."

"It was hard for everyone involved, but thank you."

Once again, her innate sense of curiosity stirred to life. It was so tempting to ask what Riley had learned from the briefing Gage had planned to give reporters about the case. With some effort, she resisted the urge and turned the conversation back to the race instead. "I do appreciate the extra coverage of the race, Riley. It was a lot of work, but all for a good cause."

"Anytime, Abby. Enjoy the rest of your day."

"I'll try. See you on Tuesday."

She watched until he drove away. Zeke kept her company until she stepped back from the window. His protective duty done, he flopped down in his favorite sunbeam in the middle of the living room floor for his afternoon nap. She left him contentedly snoring away as she went back to playing with fabrics.

There would be plenty of time later to e-mail Gil about the photo op. She wasn't sure if he would be any happier about having his picture in the paper than she was, but too bad. They'd been an effective team, and she wanted everyone in town to know it.

As she headed back upstairs, it occurred to her that Gage and Tripp had been right about one thing. She was protective of the people she cared about. They could tease her all they wanted to, but as far as she was concerned, her friends deserved nothing less.

* * *

Tuesday morning, Gil frowned as he studied their image in the mirror on her entryway wall. "Abby, I would've been fine with just you being in the picture for the paper. I'm sure Riley won't object to leaving me out of the photo."

"No way. We're in this together. You should get equal credit for the work we did. Besides, it will be good advertising for the bike shop. Think of all the new business it could bring in."

"If you say so, but I'm not sure how many of our customers actually read *The Clarion*."

He might be right about that. "Okay, fine. The real reason I want you in the picture is that I don't want to be the only one forced to wear this screaming green T-shirt. It's not exactly my best color."

Gil batted his eyelashes at her. "And you think it's mine? It does nothing for my complexion. I wear basic black because it brings out my eyes. Everyone says so."

The doorbell saved her from having to respond to that bit of outrageousness. "Looks like Riley is right on time."

She invited the reporter inside, but he suggested they take the picture in the yard. As they joined him out on the porch, she performed introductions. "I don't know if you two have been officially introduced. Riley Molitor, this is my good friend Gil Pratt."

She didn't know which man looked more surprised by her assertion about her relationship with the biker. Their doubtful expressions were pretty similar, but she didn't care. She didn't pick her friends based on their job description or what kind of vehicle they owned.

"Where do you want us?"

Riley pointed toward a trellis along the side of the yard

that was covered with a large pink climbing rose bush that was in full bloom. He quickly snapped half a dozen pictures with her and Gil standing in slightly different positions. The three of them studied the different poses, finally settling on the one that Abby and Gil both liked best.

Riley stuck his phone back into his shirt pocket. "I'll be turning the article and the photo in to my editor this afternoon. I can't promise he'll have room for both the shot of the medal you designed and the picture of the two of you, but I'm hopeful. He's pretty good about fitting things in, especially since your committee bought a big ad for this edition."

Another car pulled up front. Recognizing Clarence Reed, Abby smiled and waved at him. "Looks like our committee members are starting to arrive. Is there anything else you need, Riley?"

"Nope, I'm good. Thanks, you two."

She waited for Clarence to join them before heading back inside the house. "I've set us up in the dining room. Help yourselves to coffee, water, or tea while I get the rest of the refreshments from the kitchen. I'd appreciate it if you guys kept an eye out for the rest of the group and let them in. I'll be right back."

It took another fifteen minutes for everyone to get settled in and the meeting organized. Abby passed around copies of the agenda she and Gil had worked up. "Okay, if all of you have everything you need, let's get started."

She loved working with this particular group of people. All of them had understood from the very first meeting that everything flowed more smoothly if they stuck to the agenda as much as possible. That didn't mean she was completely inflexible if an unexpected issue arose in the course of the meeting. She made sure every member knew they were free to bring up any and all concerns they had. As this was their last meeting, she'd allotted an extra big chunk of time to let every person talk about what had gone smoothly and where they saw room for improvement.

They were almost done going around the table when Gil's phone rang. He apologized for not muting it beforehand and declined the call. No sooner had he set the phone back down on the table than the screen lit up again. He rolled his eyes and sighed as he studied the text message on the screen.

"Sorry, everyone. I'd better call this guy back. He's been helping out at the shop lately while I've been working on the race. Gary wouldn't have him call me when he knows I'm in the middle of a meeting if it wasn't important."

If it was that urgent, why hadn't Gary called Gil himself? "No problem. We're almost finished here."

He stepped out into the hall and closed the pocket doors while she did her best to get everyone back on topic. It didn't take long for the last two people to share their personal takes on how the race had gone. She took copious notes so she could give Connie Pohler a detailed report for the notebook. If she and Gil didn't take on the race next year, their successors would appreciate all of their insights and suggestions.

She was about to launch into thanking everyone for their help when she realized that she was having to speak over the sound of Gil talking out in the hall. Doing her best to ignore the increase in volume on his end of the phone call, she covered the last few points. "And finally, Gil and I both want to thank each of you for everything you contributed to make the race a huge success for both the participants and the town as a whole. When Connie has the final figures for how much we earned for the music and athletic departments at the high school, I'll send out a group e-mail. All indications are that we exceeded all expectations."

That resulted in a spontaneous round of applause that didn't quite drown out Gil's voice coming from the other side of the door. Whatever had happened had to be pretty serious if his obvious agitation was any indicator. Doing her best to hide her concern, she pasted a smile on her face and hoped it looked more genuine than it felt. "I think we've covered everything. Please help yourselves to more refreshments."

Clarence raised his hand to catch her attention. "Have you and Gil decided to head up the race again next year?"

"We've talked about it, but we both decided we needed some downtime before we make up our minds. Once we know for sure, we'll let everyone know, in case you want to join in the fun again. Of course, if one of you wants to step up and take charge"—she paused to give Clarence a pointed look—"I'd be glad to relinquish any claim to the position."

The man in question immediately shook his head emphatically. "No thanks, Abby. I wouldn't mind helping out again, but I wouldn't want to try to fill your shoes after the whiz-bang job you two did this year."

She feigned disappointment. "So if I'd screwed up, you would've stepped up to make sure next year's race was done right?"

Clarence laughed. "Pretty much."

After that, she started passing the platters of sliced fruit, cookies, and muffins around the table. "Please take a few things home with you. I don't need all those tempting calories sitting around in my kitchen."

She'd already packed up some of everything for Gil to take back to the shop to share with Gary as well as their temporary helper. It was her own way of thanking not just Gil for all of his work, but the other two men as well for freeing up his time to get it all done.

As the goodies made the rounds she got up, intending to pour herself another cup of coffee, when Gil yanked the pocket doors open hard enough to rattle the pictures on the wall. Everyone in the room fell silent as he walked into the room, his eyes looking wild. She set her cup down and headed straight for him. "Gil, what's happened?"

"That was Casey, the guy who's been filling in for me."

Seeing how pale Gil looked, she asked, "Is Gary all right?"

It took him several seconds to answer. "I honestly don't know."

Aware that they had an audience, Abby debated what to do next. She was pretty sure Gil was so upset by whatever Casey had told him that he'd forgotten they weren't alone. Maybe it was time to shoo everyone else out.

"Sorry, but I need to help Gil. Can you all see yourselves out? Just leave the dishes. I'll take care of them later."

Without waiting for them to answer, she took Gil's arm and propelled him down the hall toward the kitchen to give them some privacy. She got him seated at the table and then poured him a glass of ice water. Meanwhile, she could hear Clarence making sure everyone had what they needed. The front door opened and closed several times before the house finally got quiet. She sat down next to

Gil and waited for him to tell her what was wrong. When he didn't immediately speak, she tried to prompt him. "What did Casey tell you, Gil? Did Gary get hurt somehow?"

He blinked and slowly shook his head. "No, that's not what happened, leastwise not that I know of. Seems Gage Logan and his people showed up at the shop waving around a search warrant, which Gary didn't take kindly to. Apparently, he tried to block them from coming into the shop, which went over about as well as you think it would. Gage slapped him in cuffs and had his deputies haul him off to jail to cool his heels. From what Casey said, Gage said there may be other charges involved, depending on what their search turns up."

"Did he say what kind of charges?"

Gil had been looking a little better, but her question sent him into another tailspin. His eyes were bleak when he looked up at her. "There's only one case that Gage is focused on right now."

He didn't have to say which one. They both knew solving James DiSalvo's murder would be Gage's top priority. She trusted him to do the job right. When he made an arrest, it would be based on hard evidence. But considering Gary Pratt's very public argument with the man before the race, he had to be leading Gage's list of suspects.

CHAPTER 8

The silence dragged on for several seconds while Gil paused to take a long drink of water. When he set it aside, he let out a long sigh as his shoulders slumped as if exhausted. "Casey said they were going through the shop like a swarm of locusts. They bagged up a bunch of stuff, but I won't know what all they took until I go through things later today. And if Casey heard Gage right, they plan to tear through our house next if they don't find whatever they're looking for, or maybe just for grins. It's hard to tell. I could be wrong about what case has Gage's tail in a twist, but I can't imagine what else it could be."

A flash of anger had him sitting up straighter, his hands clenched into fists. "Abby, I swear Gary didn't do anything wrong the day of the race, and we're not involved in anything illegal, even if I can't say the same for a few of our regular customers. But even if one of them got on Gage's bad side, you'd think he would've told Gary at least that much. That still wouldn't explain why they're rifling through all of our toolboxes and parts. I can only imagine what kind of mess they're making of the place."

She knew he was more worried about his brother than the shop. "Do you want me to drive you down to the jail?"

Gil frowned. "No, it will take a while to process him in, and Casey wasn't sure if they took him to the jail here in town or the county lockup. I'll learn more if I go over to the shop and talk to Gage."

She was already up and moving. "I'll get my keys."

Gil reached out to stop her. "No need, Abby. I've got my bike parked out front."

That wasn't happening. Not as shaky as he looked right now.

"I'm sorry, but you shouldn't be driving right now. I'll bring you back to pick up your bike after we figure out what's going on."

That Gil didn't argue spoke volumes about how upset he was. Before he could change his mind, she quickly locked the front door, picked up her purse, and led Gil out the back to where her car was parked. It came as no surprise when Tripp stepped out on his porch. He would've guessed something was going on the second he spotted her hanging on to Gil's arm as they crossed the yard.

She unlocked the car so Gil could get in while she filled Tripp in on what had happened. "I don't know how long I'll be gone. Could you let Zeke out if this takes a long time?"

"Sure, but do you need backup?"

"No, I don't want Gage thinking we're ganging up on him. He already won't be happy to see me showing up, but Gil really shouldn't be driving right now. What his friend told him about what was going on with both his brother and the shop has left him pretty upset."

Tripp looked past her to where Gil sat staring out the front window of her car. "Call if you need anything."

"I will."

The drive to Gil's shop was less than fifteen minutes. She'd never been there but knew it was located at the far end of a dead-end street near the bar where Tripp and some of his friends played pool on a regular basis. Thank goodness she didn't have to depend on Gil for directions. He hadn't said a single word since leaving her house. Instead, he stared out the side window, his mind filled with all kinds of unhappy thoughts.

Even if she wasn't sure which building housed the bike shop, the deputies swarming around the place would've made it obvious. She parked as far from the police cruisers as possible and left the engine running. "Gil, how do you want to play this? I can go get Gage and ask him to come talk to you out here."

His immediate response was to unfasten his seat belt and open his door. "Wait here, Abby. No need for you to get mixed up in this. In fact, just drop me off. Someone will give me a ride back to pick up my bike later."

No way was she going to leave him on his own. Yes, he was an adult, one who could take care of himself. But Gil would be no help at all to his brother if he did something stupid that could land him in the cell right next to Gary's. After shutting off the engine, she was out of the car and hustling after Gil, barely catching up with him before he reached the closest pair of deputies.

The expression on all three men's faces pretty much ensured this wasn't going to be a pleasant encounter. Rather than let any of them launch the opening salvo, she did her best to take charge of the conversation.

"Deputy Chapin, I'm so glad to see you."

Normally the young deputy might have felt the same way. This time he only gave her a cursory glance before focusing his full attention on her companion. "Mr. Pratt, I'm sorry but we can't allow you any closer to your shop."

His tone hinted he wasn't really sorry at all. If she'd ever doubted the young deputy could play hardball if the occasion warranted it, the cold chill in his voice would've dispelled that error in her thinking. "We are executing a legally obtained search warrant. Once we're finished, Chief Logan will advise you about what happens next."

She braced herself and waited to see what Gil would do. To her surprise, he looked around the area before responding, his voice quiet and calm as he spoke. "Look, Deputy, I'll have plenty of questions for Gage about this search. I also would like to know where my brother was sent. Right now, though, I'm more concerned about Casey. A big brouhaha like this was bound to throw him for a loop. Can you tell me where he is?"

For the first time, there was a hint of sympathy in Deputy Chapin's voice. "We transported your brother to the Snowberry Creek jail, not county."

"Thank you for that much."

From the way Gil's tension level dropped appreciably, that was good news, or at least not as bad as he'd feared. Meanwhile, Deputy Chapin was talking again. "Mr. Kasper did get pretty shaky, so Chief Logan had a deputy escort him to the bar up the street and get him something to eat. Gage figured you'd show up sooner or later, and he told your employee that we'd send you his way."

The deputy looked back over his shoulder. "I'm not sure how much longer this will take, Mr. Pratt, but I'll let the chief know you've arrived."

Gil nodded but made no move to leave. Finally, after studying the scene in front of them for a few seconds longer, he abruptly stalked off in the direction of the bar without saying another word. Abby figured he needed a minute, so she waited long enough to offer the deputies an explanation neither of them had asked for. "In case Chief Logan wonders why I'm here, Gil was at my house when he got the call from Casey. Gil and I co-chaired the Salmon Scoot race this past weekend, and we had a meeting with our volunteers to wrap things up. Hearing his brother had been taken into custody upset him considerably, which should be no surprise to anyone. I didn't think he should be driving his motorcycle right now."

Deputy Chapin nodded. "We'll tell the chief, Abby. Should I assume you'll be at the bar, too?"

"For now, anyway. I want to make sure Gil and his friend are both okay before I leave."

She risked a small smile. "I have no intentions of getting in the middle of whatever Gage is up to in there."

When she got back to her car, she glanced back toward

the two deputies and waved. She'd never met the other one, but Deputy Chapin grinned and shook his head. Then they both headed back toward the garage, no doubt to update Gage on the situation. Maybe she should stop in the bar only long enough to tell Gil she was leaving. She could even simply send him a text to call her if he needed a ride back to her house to pick up his bike. Either of those choices would be the smart thing to do.

Evidently she wasn't feeling all that brilliant right now. But rather than go charging into the bar with no plan in place, she pulled out her phone to text Tripp.

I'm out front of your favorite bar. Gil is inside waiting for Gage to come tell him what's going on. I thought I'd keep him company and have lunch while I'm at it. Do you want to join us? My treat.

She could imagine his reaction to that bit of news. They both knew this fine establishment could get pretty rough, especially on the weekends. But that wasn't usually the case during the day, when it did a pretty brisk business serving lunch to the locals. That didn't mean he'd be happy that she was skating along the edge of whatever trouble Gary had gotten himself into. She was about to give up and go on in when her phone chimed.

NOT HAPPY, but on my way. Order me a double cheeseburger, fries, and onion rings. Darn straight it's your treat.

It was amazing how that man could pack so much growly crabbiness into the written word. **See you soon.**

When she stepped into the dim interior of the bar, she spotted Gil sitting in a booth toward the back. The other man must have been his friend Casey, but there was no sign of the deputy who had escorted him to the bar from the shop.

She cut straight across the room to where they were sitting. Gil didn't look in her direction until she reached the table. "Abby, you don't have to hang around. I'll be fine."

Maybe that was true, although she had her doubts. His friend, however, looked pretty rattled at the moment. "Actually, when I let Tripp know where I was, he told me to order him some lunch. We both love the burgers here."

Since neither man issued an invitation for her to join them, she looked around for an empty booth or table for her and Tripp. "I'll be right over there if you need me for anything."

She might as well have been talking to herself for all the attention they paid to her. Any other time it might have hurt her feelings, but it appeared that Casey was holding himself together by the skin of his teeth. It was understandable that right now all of Gil's attention remained focused on calming his sometime–employee.

When the bartender himself brought her a menu, she asked if Gil had requested anything to eat. Finding out that he hadn't, she ordered for herself and Tripp and then asked the bartender to add whatever Gil usually ate to her tab.

While she waited, she used the app on her phone to start an e-book she'd checked out of the library a few days back. When a tall shadow appeared on her table, she looked up, expecting to see Tripp, only to find Gage. The police chief slid into the opposite seat without saying a word. He crossed his arms over his chest and stared at her long enough to have her thinking about making a break for the exit.

Finally, she blurted out, "I didn't press Deputy Chapin for answers, and I don't plan to ask what's going on. I was worried about Gil, so I gave him a ride. That's all. You will note I'm not sitting with him right now, so you're free to go talk to him without worrying about me listening in. And if you're wondering, I'm waiting for Tripp. We're having lunch together. He's on his way."

"Actually, I'm already here."

Abby jumped. She'd been so focused on Gage that she'd missed seeing Tripp arrive. How had he gotten there so quickly? She moved over to make room for him on her side of the booth. "Our burgers should be here any minute."

Good manners made her ask, "Gage, have you eaten? You're welcome to join us if you're hungry."

He was still sporting his tough-cop expression. "This isn't a social occasion, Abby. I'm here on business."

Really? Did he think she didn't know that? Besides, if he was so focused on the job at hand, why was he sitting with her instead of Gil? "Of course you are, sir. Please tell me how I can be of help with your professional endeavors today, Chief Logan."

Okay, she probably should have toned down the snark, but she really wasn't in the mood to play guessing games. Tripp gave her a nudge. "He was actually waiting for me. Gage asked me to come check on Casey. He's a member of the veterans group, and I'm one of his contacts when he needs help. I was already on my way here when you invited me to lunch."

"You could've told me that much when we were texting." Then she pointed her finger at Gage. "And you could've told me when you sat down."

Neither man apologized for their mistakes, which didn't improve her mood one bit. Fortunately, the one man who was doing his job well right now was the bartender. He appeared beside their table with two plates heaped high with big burgers, fries, and onion rings. "Sorry, I'm down a waiter today, so things are a bit squirrelly. I just realized I forgot to get your drink orders. What can I get you?"

She didn't give Tripp or Gage a chance to answer for themselves. "I'll have iced tea. These two can have tap water, no ice, and they'll be grateful to get that much."

The bartender fought back a laugh. "Got it."

He walked away before either of her companions could protest. After delivering Gil's lunch, he headed back to the bar, presumably to get her tea and two plain waters. When he delivered them a couple of minutes later, Gage's mouth twitched just enough to hint that he found her snippy behavior amusing, at least a little. Without cracking a smile, he picked up his glass and nearly drained it before setting it back down on the table.

For his part, Tripp dug right into his lunch as if he'd gone days rather than just hours since his last meal. Abby turned her plate so that the fries and onion rings were closer to Gage. "Help yourself to a few. There's more than I can eat by myself."

Actually that wasn't true, but it was definitely more than she *should* eat all on her own. At least Gage accepted the peace offering. He glanced over to where Gil and his friend were still talking. "Casey's looking a whole lot calmer than when I called you, Tripp. Sorry if I dragged you over here for no reason."

"Not a problem, Gage. I'm getting a free lunch for my efforts, so it's all good. Well, not completely. If only they served a cold beer in this fine establishment instead of lukewarm water, it would be perfect."

Abby elbowed him in the ribs. "Very funny, Tripp."

Gage stole a few more fries. "Well, I'd better go talk to Gil. My people were finishing up at his shop. I'll send Casey over to check in with you, Tripp."

Did that mean the police would be heading over to Gil's house next? She really hoped not. Having his place of business invaded was bad enough, but having strangers pawing through his personal possessions would take the sense of violation to a whole new level. Sadly, she knew that from personal experience. It hadn't been all that long ago that the police had descended on her house to search it from top to bottom. She hadn't been the one suspected of murder, but that didn't make the experience any less distressing.

As soon as he walked away, Tripp asked, "How are you holding up?"

"I'm fine. I'm more concerned about Gil. He's worried sick about his brother. In case you didn't hear, Gary has been arrested. We don't know for what."

Well, not for sure anyway. "At least it looks like calming Casey down has helped Gil regain control. He told me I didn't need to stick around, but I couldn't leave until I knew he would be okay."

Tripp glanced over to where Gage stood talking to the other two men. "No surprise there, Abs. He's become a friend. There was no way you'd let him face this . . . whatever this is, on his own."

"Pot, kettle, Tripp."

He didn't dispute her observation. After all, he was sitting there in the bar in case a fellow veteran needed him, and they both knew he would've come running to be with Abby anyway. Casey said something to Gil and then headed toward them. When he slid into the other side of the booth, he nodded at Abby but spoke to Tripp. "Hi, Sarge. Gage said he'd called you. Thanks for coming."

"No problem. Gage felt bad you got caught in the middle of what had to be a tough situation. He thought you might need a ride home."

"I'd appreciate it if it's not too far out of your way. Well, unless Gil wants my help straightening the place up once the cops are done poking around. I told him I'd stick around until he got done talking to Gage. Hope that's okay."

"There's no rush. By the way, Casey Kasper, this is Abby McCree. She's friends with not just me, but Gage and Gil, too."

The veteran looked to be in his forties and could've used a few more pounds on his lanky frame. He wore a fatigue shirt over a T-shirt and jeans, all a bit worn, but neat and clean. "Nice to meet you, ma'am. Gil spoke real kindly about you. He said to thank you for the burger. Also that he would offer to pay for it himself, but he figured you wouldn't let him."

Casey's eyes held a suspicious twinkle when he added, "Something about being plum stubborn about some things."

Abby shrugged. "I guess he knows me pretty well."

After that, Casey shot a worried glance toward where Gil and Gage sat talking. The conversation looked understandably tense, but at least they weren't yelling at each other. "Things got bad as soon as the cops showed up.

Gary went ballistic, cussing and yelling at everyone, but no surprise there. Gil is more level-headed, leastwise most of the time. Don't know what the cops were looking for or if they found it. Once they hauled Gary off to cool his heels at the jail, Gage sent me up here to wait. He even bought me lunch, which was decent of him."

He turned back to Tripp. "I told Gil that I don't think Gage set out to arrest Gary today, but the man didn't leave him any choice. Maybe if he had just calmed down and behaved himself, he'd be sitting over there with Gil instead of behind bars."

Surely that meant Gary hadn't been arrested for anything connected to the DiSalvo murder case, at least not yet. She really hoped that didn't change. She ate the last bite of her burger and pushed her plate aside. It didn't take Tripp much longer to finish off his. "Looks like Gage is about to leave."

They all three watched as the police chief walked out of the bar, leaving Gil staring at his back. After a few seconds, Gil headed their way. "Casey, I'm going to lock up the shop for the day. I need to head home to keep an eye on things while Gage and his people do their thing. He still hasn't said what they're looking for or if they've found it. I haven't had a chance to read the warrant. Evidently Gary tossed it in the trash back at the shop."

Shaking his head at the stupidity of that, he patted Casey on the shoulder. "You'll still get a full day's pay."

"You don't have to do that, Gil. Just pay me for the three hours I actually worked."

"It's not open for discussion, man. You showed up. It's not your fault everything went off the rails."

Turning his attention to Abby next, he said, "Thanks

for being there for me earlier. I might not have acted grateful at the time, but it meant a lot."

There was one more thing she could do if he'd let her. She separated her car key from the others on her ring and held it out to him. "My car is parked out front. I can catch a ride home with Tripp, and you can bring my car back and pick up your bike when things calm down a bit."

He seemed torn but finally let her drop the key into his hand. "Thanks. That will simplify things."

"What did Gage say about Gary?"

"My idiot brother shot his mouth off and tried to interfere with their search. Bottom line was that he left Gage no choice but to get him out from underfoot for a while. I'm hoping they'll kick him loose later this evening, at least for now."

What did he mean by "for now?" He didn't give her a chance to ask, and this wasn't the time or place anyway. "I'll get your car back to you as soon as I can. Casey, do I need to drop you off first?"

"Nope, Tripp already offered."

"Okay, I'd better get moving."

They all remained seated until Gil had disappeared out the door. As they waited, it crossed Abby's mind that Tripp might want some time alone with Casey to make sure he really was all right. It was unlikely the man would feel comfortable talking in front of someone he'd only just met.

"If you two will excuse me, I'm going to go settle the tab, and I need to stop off in the restroom on the way back."

Tripp got up to let her out. She'd only taken a couple of steps before he sat back down, leaned forward, and started talking low and fast to the other man. Leaving them to sort things out, she stopped at the bar and got out her credit card. It took the bartender a couple of minutes to finish up an order before he could process her payment. When he apologized for the delay, she assured him it wasn't a problem.

In the restroom, she took time to redo her ponytail. After that, she checked her e-mail and read a funny article from the newsfeed on her phone. Hoping she'd given Tripp and Casey enough alone time, she left the restroom and saw her two companions were waiting over by the exit. She hurried to join them and looped her arm through Tripp's. "Well, gentlemen, shall we hit the road? I don't know about you two, but I could use a big dose of peace and quiet after all this excitement."

Casey opened the passenger door for her and waited until she climbed into the narrow back seat before getting in the front seat. She'd move up front with Tripp after they dropped Casey off. For now, having her in the back would also make it easier for the two men to talk if they needed to.

Once they were under way, Casey glanced back over his shoulder and then at Tripp. "Would you mind just dropping me off at the grocery store instead of taking me home? It's not that much farther."

"No problem."

With that decided, Abby leaned back and thought about everything that needed to be done when she got home, starting with cleaning up the mess left from the abrupt end to their meeting. After that, she'd get back to work on the baby quilt. Doing something creative would go a long way toward banishing her worry about Gil and his brother or at least might hold it at bay for a while.

For Gil's sake, she really hoped he was right about Gary not being responsible for James DiSalvo's murder. She didn't know much about the victim except for the few times she'd heard him speak at the town council meetings. He'd had strong opinions on many subjects, but he was far from the only one. Still, maybe someone else had run into problems with the man on the day of the race. Regardless, she trusted that Gage and his men would pursue any and all avenues of investigation. All she could do was cross her fingers and hope that those avenues wouldn't end right on Gary's doorstep.

CHAPTER 9

Wednesday started off much more peacefully than the previous day had. As a result, Abby made good progress on the baby quilt. After all the pieces were cut, she'd sewed the triangles on the long sides of the hexagons to form squares. When that was done, she laid them out on the worktable and moved them around until she was satisfied with how it all looked. She carried the first row of squares over to the sewing machine. With luck, she'd have most of the quilt top sewn together by the end of the day.

She was just finishing up the first row when her phone buzzed to signal she had a new text message. It was from Tripp. **Are you home? I knocked but no answer.**

Sorry I didn't hear you. I'm upstairs in the sewing room. Come on up.

He had a key and could've just let himself in, but he

rarely did that without asking first. Part of the agreement he'd made with her late aunt when he'd first rented the mother-in-law house was that he would work off part of his rent doing yardwork and small chores in the house itself. Him being able to come and go as necessary when he was working on a project only made sense.

Meanwhile, she quickly pressed the seams on the strip she'd finished sewing and laid it back on the worktable. After that, she stacked the next set of squares to sew. The steps creaked in warning that Tripp was almost there. It came as no surprise when Zeke came trotting in first. He sat down just inside the door and waited impatiently for his buddy to catch up. The dog knew Tripp wouldn't have neglected to pick up a few of Zeke's favorite cookies as he passed by the treat jar in the kitchen.

Sure enough, as soon as he walked into the room Tripp tossed Zeke one of the peanut butter pawprint cookies she'd baked last night. They both had a tendency to spoil the dog, but she refused to feel guilty about it. He'd been abandoned and most likely abused by his previous owner, so it had taken him a while to trust people again. Fortunately, he'd come a long way since that time.

Tripp wandered over to the worktable to study the single strip of squares with a puzzled expression on his face. "What are you working on?"

"A baby quilt."

"It's kind of small, isn't it?"

Okay, he wasn't that dense. He was just jerking her chain, but she played along. "Well, I thought I'd add on to it as the baby gets bigger."

He finally grinned at her. "On the subject of quilts, I finally had a chance to stop by city hall to pick up my prize this morning. You could've told me what it was."

"Why would I have done that? It was a lot more fun to let you think you might have won a year's supply of tuna casseroles from Jean. We both know how much she loves making them for you."

He handed her one of the two bottles of water he'd brought with him and then sat in the upholstered chair in the corner. Zeke immediately joined him, laying his head on Tripp's leg and giving him a hopeful look. After slipping him another cookie, Tripp asked, "Do the ladies in the quilting guild know about your mean streak?"

Despite his teasing, she could tell he was upset about something. She opened her drink to buy herself some time while debating if she should ask him what was wrong. Deciding it would be better if she let him tell her when he was ready, she took a sip of water and then set the bottle aside. Tripp stroked Zeke's big head and stared out the window as she began stitching the next row of squares together.

She'd finished two more strips and pressed the seams before he finally spoke again. "Have you talked to anyone this morning? Besides me and Zeke, I mean."

Okay, this was getting more and more worrisome. "No, I haven't."

"And you didn't watch the local news?"

"Nope, and I didn't read the paper."

He looked pretty disappointed by her answers. Clearly something was up. "Why? What did I miss?"

"I really didn't want to be the one to tell you, but Gage didn't release Gil's brother last night. Instead, he arrested Gary Pratt for murder. From what I heard, his arraignment will be sometime tomorrow."

His words flipped a switch in her head, abruptly turning off her good mood and leaving her feeling sick. Gil had returned her car yesterday afternoon, but he hadn't stopped to chat. Tripp had been working out in the yard at the time, so he'd left her key with him. If he'd known about the change in his brother's situation, surely he would've said something. When she'd asked Tripp how Gil was doing, he'd said he looked tired but otherwise okay.

Hoping Tripp's source of information wasn't top tier, she asked, "Where did you hear that?"

Tripp leaned forward, resting his elbows on his knees. "I ran into your buddy Deputy Chapin at the grocery store. He thought you'd want to know."

"I guess that means they've found something that clearly implicated Gary."

"I guess so, but Chapin didn't share anything about that. Probably couldn't. Either way, I'm sorry, Abby. I know you were hoping this wouldn't happen."

"Poor Gil. This has to be so hard for him. Well, and Gary, too, of course."

She shut off the sewing machine and the iron, no longer interested in working on the quilt. "Let's go to the kitchen."

Tripp followed her down the stairs. "What are you going to make this time?"

The man knew her too well. It was probably silly, but baking was her go-to cure for life's bumps and bruises. "I don't know. Maybe a casserole for Gil? And a pie of some kind to go with it?"

"I'm sure he'd appreciate whatever you come up with."

A quick survey of the refrigerator showed she had the makings for a beef and noodle dish that Tripp liked a lot. Hopefully Gil would as well. It would be easy to double the recipe, which would take care of her own dinner. Tripp's, too, for that matter. On the other hand, she didn't have enough of any kind of fruit to make a pie. Maybe a coffee cake would be a better idea. She could always send along a container of cookies from her freezer.

When she started gathering all of the ingredients for the casserole, the package of ground beef slipped from her hands. Only a quick move on Tripp's part kept Zeke from helping himself to a special treat while almost knocking Abby over in the process. After making him sit, Tripp released his hold on Zeke's collar and then pointed to the far corner of the kitchen and snapped an order. "Dog, go lay down."

Zeke's head drooped as he slunk off to curl up in his bed with a sad sigh. It was hard not to smile at his attempt to garner her sympathy as he followed every move she made with his big, so-sad eyes. She might have felt sorry for him, but she knew full well that the dog wouldn't remain banished for long. All would be forgiven by the time Tripp finished making a fresh pot of coffee.

She'd let the two males sort out their differences while she browned the hamburger. Right now, she needed to focus on what she was doing. The news about Gary had rattled her badly, and her shaky hands were evidence of that. As soon as she started to dice the vegetables, she managed to send the onion bouncing onto the floor to roll under the table. Worse yet, she'd nicked her finger in the process.

Muttering a bad word under her breath, she yanked open the drawer where she kept bandages for just such an emergency. Naturally, she scattered them all over the counter when she tried to fish one out of the box.

"Here, let me help." After setting the onion on the

counter, Tripp ripped a paper towel off the roll and held it out. "Wash the blood off and hold this on it for a few seconds."

After gathering up all the other bandages and stuffing them back in the box, he returned them to the drawer. He peeled the paper off the one he'd kept back and gently wrapped it around her small wound.

"Sorry I'm making such a mess of things. I'm not sure why I'm so upset."

"We both know this isn't the first murder case you've come across since moving to Snowberry Creek. Having experience doesn't mean it gets any easier to deal with, especially when a friend is involved."

"Gil didn't do anything wrong."

"I know that, but you're worried about how all this is affecting him. Even if Gary is proven innocent, this has got to be tearing Gil up inside."

Her eyes were dry, but they burned as if tears were imminent. At least she could blame it on the onion. "I know he looks all tough and everything, but he's not like that. Not really."

Tripp huffed a small laugh as he tugged her in close for a badly needed hug. "Yeah, he is, Abby. One reason their shop is so successful is that they can stand toe-to-toe with the rough crew that bring their bikes in for servicing. He might have a soft spot when it comes to you, but Gil is as tough as they come. So is Gary. They'll get through this."

She leaned into Tripp's strength for a few seconds more. "I hope so. We both know how hard it is to see someone you know living under the shadow of suspicion. Being innocent doesn't make it any easier."

"No, it doesn't."

She finally stepped back. "I'm okay . . . or at least better. I need to get back to work or risk burning the meat."

Tripp took over chopping the vegetables while she put on a large pot of water to boil. Once the noodles were cooked, she'd combine everything and then divide it into two different baking pans before putting it in the oven. That way Gil would just have to heat his up whenever he was hungry.

While she let the meat simmer with the vegetables and the marinara sauce, she started working on the coffee cakes. "Should I make blueberry or apple?"

"Blueberry is always my favorite, but whatever is easier is fine with me."

Tripp signaled Zeke that his time-out was over, reassuring the dog he was still loved with a thorough scratching followed by a small piece of bison jerky. "I'm going to take this guy out for a long run if that's okay. While we're out, I'll check in with Gil to see when I can drop by with the casserole and dessert."

"You don't have to do that, Tripp. I can run them by his house."

He was already shaking his head. "You don't need to go anywhere near that place right now in case some of his biker buddies are there."

Right after Abby had first crossed paths with Gil, Gage had told her that while Gil probably presented no direct threat to her, he couldn't say the same about some of his associates. Gil himself had agreed with that assessment. If she took both men at their word, letting Tripp handle the delivery was just plain common sense.

"I would appreciate it if you've got the time. They should both be ready to go in about an hour or so. If he says to stop by later than that, I can always put the casserole in the fridge. I can heat ours up whenever you want to eat this evening. Just let me know."

"Will do." He clipped on Zeke's leash. "We'll be back in a while. I think we both need to take the edge off right now."

By the time Zeke scratched at the back door, the coffee cakes were cooling on the counter. He immediately disappeared down the hall to pick out the perfect spot to lie down on the living room floor. Tripp came in a minute later and grinned as soon as he spotted Zeke. "I think I wore the poor guy out, but I think he has the right idea. A nap sounds pretty good about now."

Abby pointed toward the couch. "You're welcome to crash here if you want. I was about to make myself a cup of tea and kick back with a book for a while."

Tripp eyed the couch for a few seconds. The one in his own living room was a love seat and far too short for a man who stood several inches over six feet. Then Zeke stirred and let out a snore that she swore rattled the windows. That was a record breaker even by the dog's usual standards.

Evidently sacking out on her comfy couch was fast losing its appeal. When the first loud rumble was followed by another one, Tripp started backing out of the room. "Thanks for the offer, but I should take a shower before I sack out. Besides, I think I'll have an easier time sleeping over at my place."

He'd disappeared down the hall toward the kitchen when she realized he hadn't mentioned what he'd learned about delivering the food. She hurried after him, catching him just as he opened the back door. "Were you able to make contact with Gil?"

"Oh, yeah, I did. Sorry, I meant to tell you he said you

shouldn't have bothered . . . yada, yada, yada. I told him he should know you better than that by now. I promised to drop them by around five thirty. If something comes up where he won't be home, he'll call me."

"Thanks, Tripp. The casserole's in the fridge, so he'll need to heat it in the oven for about twenty minutes. So, how did he sound?"

"He's hanging in there okay. He met with a public defender this afternoon and said the guy was going to see what he could do about getting Gary out on bail. He didn't sound too hopeful considering the nature of the crime involved, but he thought it was worth a try. It's not like Gary is a flight risk, and he has strong ties to the community."

"I hope the attorney is successful."

Tripp didn't look so sure. "I have to wonder how the people in town would feel about Gary walking around free right now. I've heard mumblings that the Pratts and that DiSalvo guy have had a bad history. Not sure what the problem was, but they've evidently had some pretty public run-ins with the man. I know you want to believe Gary is innocent, but not everyone thinks that way."

Her first instinct was to leap to Gary's defense, but she couldn't help but remember the argument she'd observed herself. She hadn't heard the verbal exchange, but there had been a whole lot of anger in Gary's body language. DiSalvo's, too, for that matter. It would be easier to gauge the seriousness of their disagreement if she had some idea what it had been about. Gil hadn't chosen to share the topic of the discussion, and she'd had no reason to ask at the time.

"Surely Gage has other leads that he's still working on."

Tripp didn't look convinced. "I wouldn't get your hopes up. I don't think they would've actually pressed charges without some pretty convincing evidence. All we can do is wait and see how things go. I'll be back to pick up the stuff for Gil a little after five, unless I hear otherwise from him."

She closed the door behind him. It was time to make some tea and try to get lost in the book she was reading. There wasn't anything she could do to help Gil beyond what she'd already done. At least he knew she cared enough to worry about him, even if it felt like she hadn't really done anything at all.

CHAPTER 10

When Abby's doorbell rang early Thursday afternoon, the last person she expected to see standing on her porch was her mother. Why wasn't she at work? She hadn't mentioned taking time off work for any reason. Had something gone wrong either at her job or with her relationship with Owen?

And wasn't she being a pessimist? Taking a calming breath, she opened the door. "Mom, this is a surprise."

Whether or not it would be a pleasant one was to be determined. Her mom stepped inside and immediately swept Abby up in a quick hug. Then she stepped back and held Abby at arm's length. "Are you all right? When Owen told me about Gil's brother being arrested for murder, I just had to come check on you. I knew you'd be absolutely devastated."

Maybe that was overstating the case, but there was no

denying the news had hit her hard. "I'm okay, Mom, but I'll admit that it did knock me for a bit of a loop. I just really hate this for Gil."

"Have you talked to him?"

"Not directly. I baked him a casserole and a coffee cake yesterday, but Tripp delivered them in case a bunch of Gil's biker friends were there. I'm sure most are okay like Gil and Gary, but others not so much."

Looking pretty somber, her mother released her hold on Abby. "You know how much I like Gil, so don't take this wrong. But do you think there's any chance Gary is guilty?"

Abby wished she had a clear-cut answer to that. "Gil insists his brother didn't do it. I want to believe him."

Which wasn't exactly saying that she did, not 100 percent, anyway. No matter how hard she tried to convince herself Gary was innocent, a small niggle of doubt continued to linger. But rather than share her misgivings on the subject, she headed into the kitchen right behind her mother, who then all but shoved Abby into a chair at the table. "I'll make coffee. Do you want something to nibble on while it brews?"

Abby couldn't help but snicker. "I guess I'm not the only one Aunt Sybil indoctrinated with the need to offer refreshments in trying times."

That had her mom smiling. "Probably so. At least I don't feel obligated to break out the fine china and linen napkins on every occasion. Sybil was the only person I've ever known who could pull off the whole high tea thing at the drop of a hat."

"Me too."

After pouring the coffee and setting out the refreshments, her mom finally joined her at the table. Abby nibbled on a piece of cheese for a few seconds, still wondering about her mom's decision to make the two-hour drive from where she lived just to check on her daughter. "Mom, if you were worried, you could've just called."

"I know, but I wanted to see for myself that you were okay. If I'd called, I wouldn't be able to tell if you were just putting on a brave front."

"Are you going back tonight?"

"No, I plan to stay until Sunday. I have vacation time accrued, so I took both this afternoon and tomorrow off. Owen wants us to meet him for dinner at his restaurant. He said to invite Tripp, too."

Anytime Abby didn't have to cook was cause for celebration. "I'll text him."

She had no sooner hit "enter" than the doorbell rang again. "Well, I'm certainly popular today. Normally, I can go days at a time without anyone stopping by."

"Maybe it's Tripp."

That was doubtful. "He almost always comes to the back door since it's closer to his place. You can wait here while I go see who it is."

She might as well have saved her breath, because her mom followed right after her. Even Zeke abandoned his sunbeam in the living room to join their little parade. A quick peek out the narrow window in the entryway had her hurrying to open the door. "Gil, I'm so glad to see you."

He glanced past her toward her mother. "Hi again, Mrs. McCree. I'm sorry, Abby. I didn't stop to think you might have company. I wanted to bring back your empty pans and thank you myself for feeding me."

The poor guy looked as if he hadn't slept well or even much at all since she'd last seen him at the bar. His worry about Gary was etched in the deep lines on his face, and a good, stiff breeze would probably knock him over. After taking the pans, she stepped back to invite him in. "We've got fresh coffee and snacks. You'd be welcome to join us. I could also make you a sandwich if you haven't had lunch."

Still he hesitated, but her mother made the decision for him. "I'll get started on the sandwich and see what else I can find to go with it."

She was off and running before Gil could protest. Abby shrugged. "What can I say? The woman's decided you need to be fed. We both know it never pays to argue with a determined mother."

His expression lightened up just a little. "If she's anything like my mom was, she'd probably chase me down to force feed me the sandwich if I tried to escape."

"True enough. She can be tenacious."

Her mother already had the sandwich makings scattered on the counter by the time the two of them reached the kitchen. She offered Gil a bright smile. "Mayo or mustard? Wheat or rye? Ham or bologna? Cheddar or dill Havarti?"

It took Gil a few seconds to sort through the rapid-fire questions. "Mustard, rye, ham, and Havarti, I guess. Not sure what that is, but I'm willing to give it a try."

Abby pointed him toward the seat at the head of the table as she poured him a cup of coffee. "Good choice. It's one of my favorite cheeses. It's creamy and goes well with ham."

He seemed content to sip his coffee while her mother finished whipping up a quick meal for him. She finally produced a sandwich piled high with deli ham and a small fruit salad she'd somehow put together in record time. Gil stared at the plate and slowly smiled. "Thank you, ma'am. Other than that casserole Abby made for me, I'm afraid I haven't had the energy to fuss much with food."

"That's understandable, Gil. We know things are pretty tough for you and your brother right now. And I know it's the mom in me making me say this, but you've got to make sure you eat right and get proper rest. You won't be any help to Gary if you let yourself get run-down or sick. He needs you to be strong right now."

"It's nice of you worry about us, and I'll try to do better. I'm all he's got right now. Even his attorney seems to only be going through the motions. They're transferring Gary to the county jail either today or tomorrow. I'll likely have a harder time getting in to see him there."

His words made Abby's heart hurt. "Do you know what evidence the investigation has turned up that convinced them to press charges?"

Gil's shoulders slumped. "Yeah, but it doesn't make sense, not that Gage or anyone will listen to me about that."

Her mother interrupted the conversation. "Abby, why don't we let Gil eat before we ask any more questions?"

She was right. "Sorry, Gil. Please eat."

He dug right in, finishing off every bite in quick order. When he was done, he carried his dishes over to the sink. "Thank you, ladies. That really helped."

"Was it enough? I could fix you another sandwich in no time."

"Thanks, Mrs. McCree, but one was plenty. It really hit the spot. I feel better already."

Abby waited to see if he'd sit back down or head for

the door. To encourage him to stay longer, she pushed the plate of cookies closer to where he'd been sitting. There were a couple of lemon bars, his favorite of all the cookies she'd served him in the past. Recognizing the bribe for what it was, he returned to his chair.

"There's more where those came from."

"Abby, you're going to spoil me rotten, not that I mind. I'd never admit this to Bridey, but your baking rivals everything she serves up at Something's Brewing."

"That's some compliment, Gil."

He finished off his cookie and was eyeing a second one when he picked up the conversation about his brother's case where they'd left off. "For you to understand what was really going on between Gary and DiSalvo, I should give you some background, starting with how much Snowberry Creek has grown in population over the past thirty years. Most of us who grew up here still think of it as it used to be. You know, not much more than a wide spot in the road where folks could buy groceries and gas or eat a meal at Frannie's diner. Things have really changed, though. Gotten fancier, for lack of a better description."

Abby had witnessed some of those changes firsthand herself. "I used to come stay with Aunt Sybil and her husband when I was little. Going to the Creek Café for dinner was a big deal. This neighborhood is pretty much unchanged, but a lot of the current housing developments didn't exist back then. My uncle always worried all the new arrivals would change the feel of the town."

Gil nodded. "Sounds like he and James DiSalvo might have had some of the same thoughts on the subject. DiSalvo was a developer, so he was all for growth. That didn't mean he wanted just anybody to move to town. That's pretty much why he eventually set out to get himself elected to the city council. He wanted to have a bigger say in how things got done."

Abby frowned. "From what I was told, your family has been here a long time."

Gil leaned forward to rest his elbows on the table. "Yeah, my dad's side of the family moved to this area two generations back. But having deep roots in town didn't mean anything to DiSalvo if you didn't fit the image he had of what kind of folks deserved to live here."

Abby's mother got up to top off everyone's coffee. As she poured Gil's, she said, "I'm guessing bikers didn't fit into his world vision."

"You've got that right. Anyway, when my dad's health took a downturn, he had to retire. Since Gary and I were both in the navy at the time, that meant the original motorcycle repair shop closed down. When we moved back to take care of Mom, we pooled our money and reopened the business. Same name, different location. DiSalvo fought us getting the licenses we needed to set up shop, but he wasn't on the city council at that point. He was just a jerk who liked to throw his weight around."

"He clearly didn't succeed in stopping you."

"No, he didn't, but he never quit trying to find a way to run us out of business. That brings me to why he and Gary had words at the race. He went out of his way to tell Gary that he thought he'd gotten the votes he'd need to shut us down along with other unsavory businesses in the area. I'm guessing he meant the bar would have to go, too. There's no way to know if any of that was true because DiSalvo didn't share any details other than we and all the other undesirables should surrender to the inevitable and start packing up shop."

No wonder Gary got mad. "So, in short, your brother was there to enjoy the race, and DiSalvo went out of his way to spoil it for him."

"Pretty much. Gary should've ignored the man, but it's not the first time those two have ripped into each other in public."

Gil looked pretty disgusted by the whole situation. "Anyway, I'm sure folks who witnessed the idiots going at it told the cops what they'd seen and heard. Considering who the victim was, I figured Gage would take a close look at my brother. I just wish Gary had handled the whole search warrant thing better. Nothing like trying to prevent the cops from doing their job to convince them he had something to hide."

"I take it they found something."

"Apparently. They went through every tool Gary owned and took a few from both the shop and the house, all wrenches of different kinds but mostly the torque wrenches. As far as I can tell, they pretty much left my stuff alone. We each have our own work areas at the shop and mark the tools with our initials to help keep everything straight. It makes for a more peaceful work environment." He paused to smile a little. "We never outgrew the need to make sure we kept our grubby mitts off each other's toys. The one thing we have in common is a compulsive need to keep everything in its proper place."

He drifted off into a brief silence. "At the time, I had no idea what made them think DiSalvo was killed with one of our tools, but then the attorney told me they found a torque wrench stuck up on a low branch in a tree near where the guy was killed. They're pretty sure it was the murder weapon. At least it was the right size and right shape."

That alone shouldn't have been enough to point the finger at Gary. "But lots of people must own torque wrenches."

Gil only looked more depressed. "That might be true, Abby, but those wrenches don't have Gary's initials etched on the handles, his fingerprints all over them, and DiSalvo's blood gumming up the works."

That imagery left her a bit queasy. No wonder Gil was so dejected. What could she say to that? The thought of Gil going back home alone to sit and worry about his brother made her so sad. Come to think of it, there was one thing she could do about that last part at least.

"Gil, we're all going out for barbecue at Owen Quinn's restaurant, and you're coming with us."

She didn't know who was more surprised by that announcement, her mother or Gil. He looked as if he had no idea what to say. He divided his attention between her and her mother. "I am? You sure you two should be seen with me right now?"

At least her mom came through for her. "The McCree women stick by their friends, Gil. If other people have a problem with it, they'll get an earful from me."

For the first time since Gil arrived, Abby felt like smiling. "And me. The only question is whether you want to meet us there at six or do you want us to pick you up?"

Still looking as if he was having trouble keeping up with the conversation, he pushed back from the table. "I need to take care of a few things at home, so I should get going. Thanks for lunch. And if you're sure you want me, I'll meet you there."

"We're sure. Come on, I'll see you out."

As they started out of the room, her mom called after them, "I'll text Owen to add another chair to our table."

Gil remained quiet until they were out on the front porch. He looked back inside, maybe to make sure her mother wasn't right behind them. "To be honest, returning your pans wasn't the real reason I came by today. I wanted to ask a favor, one I've got no business asking. In fact, I'm pretty sure Tripp would come after me with both fists if he finds out I even thought about it."

"Just spit it out, Gil. If it's something I don't feel comfortable doing, I'll tell you."

"Fair enough. I don't want to get you in trouble with Gage or the prosecutor's people. I mean that, but here's the thing. You have connections here in Snowberry Creek that I don't. I was hoping that by getting involved in the race, I might be able to create some goodwill among the people at city hall toward our business. It was working, too. Even the mayor went out of her way to thank me for all the work I put in on the race. I thought it would help counter any negative stuff that DiSalvo might have in his arsenal."

He shoved his hands in his back pockets and rocked back on his heels. "Obviously that was all for nothing because all people are talking about now is the murder. Anyway, I was wondering if you'd let me know if you happen to hear anything that might help my brother's case, especially if anyone else might have had it in for DiSalvo. I don't want you doing anything risky, mind you. Just share any gossip you hear along the way."

Getting involved in murder investigations had not gone well for her in the past. In fact, things had turned deadly before it was all over. Tripp would go ballistic if he caught wind of her poking around even the edges of the case, and Gage would likely make good on his previous threats to toss her into a cell for her own good. She opened her mouth to tell Gil she was sorry, but it was a risk she couldn't afford to take. Not again.

Unfortunately, what came out was, "Sure thing, Gil. I'll see what I can find out."

CHAPTER 11

As usual, Owen Quinn had reserved the large table in the back corner of his restaurant for Abby, her mother, and Tripp. It was separated from the main dining room by a partial wall and was located close to the kitchen door, which allowed him to keep an eye on things when he joined them for dinner. Abby wasn't sure if Gil would know where to look for them, so she waited near the door. As soon as she heard the deep rumble of a motorcycle, she stepped outside to wave at him. He parked in a nearby spot and hustled over to where she waited under the awning. "Hi, Abby. Were you worried I wouldn't show?"

"No, you would've let me know. I wanted to make sure you could find us inside. The place is packed, and our table is on the other side of that wall over there. I hope you brought your appetite. Owen wants us to test out a couple of new spice rubs he's come up with. I think he said one was based on Texas barbecue and the other one is from St. Louis."

Gil grinned and rubbed his hands together greedily. "Don't tell him, but it might take a whole lot of ribs before I'll be able to make up my mind."

Cute. "Tripp said pretty much the same thing, but don't worry. Owen said he doubled the usual number of racks he cooked today for that exact reason."

"Smart man."

"By the way, he never lets us pay when we eat here. There's no convincing him otherwise, so don't even try. All he asks is that we're generous with tips for his staff."

As they stepped inside, Abby pointed toward the far corner. "Mom and Tripp are over there. Now, we just have to plow our way through the crowd to get to them."

Gil gamely took the lead and cut a trail through the hodgepodge of tables and booths that got them to their goal in good time. Abby couldn't help but notice the ripple of interest that spread through the other patrons as they caught sight of her companion. She was sure Gil could hear the whispers, too, but he never gave any indication that it bothered him at all. It was tempting to tell everybody to go back to stuffing their fat faces and leave the man alone. Figuring that would only make things worse, she did her best to ignore them.

It was with some relief when they reached their table. The wall provided a handy barrier between them and the nosy folks on the other side. She returned to her seat next to Tripp while Gil took the chair on her other side. Her mother offered him a welcoming smile. "Glad you could come. I hope Abby told you that Owen has already ordered for all of us. Well, meat-wise, anyway. I'm sure you can have whichever sides you want."

"Whatever he ordered will be fine with me. I love everything on his menu."

Their waitress appeared and took their orders for drinks. As she made the rounds, Abby leaned closer to Gil. "How are you and Gary doing? Were you able to see him today?"

Gil reached for one of the breadsticks the waitress had put on their table and began breaking it into tiny pieces on his plate. "I didn't see him, but I had a long phone call with his public defender. He's pushing Gary to seek a plea bargain to avoid a trial. I don't know what he's thinking. Admitting to a crime he didn't commit would mean spending decades behind bars. I argued against it, but the attorney seems to think the prosecution has a pretty airtight case between Gary's past run-ins with DiSalvo and the fact that the murder weapon was one of Gary's tools."

"Do you think Gary will listen to him?"

"I hope not, but he's got to be worried. It's not like we have a ton of money squirreled away to pay some high-priced attorney. We do own the house outright, though. I've got an appointment at the bank on Monday to see about taking out an equity loan. Depending on how that goes, I'll be looking for an attorney who's been out of law school for longer than six months."

Tripp had been listening to their conversation. "If DiSalvo was that much of a jerk to you and your brother, there has to be other people he treated the same way. I can't believe he would've zeroed in on the two of you like that but was all sweetness and light to everyone else."

Gil nodded. "He's also hassled the bar owner a few times over the years. Liam already let Gage know, not that he particularly wanted to draw the law's attention in his direction. He just figured someone should be aware the councilman had a habit of throwing his weight around."

Owen had just joined them. "DiSalvo lit into me about my food truck. I admit it isn't exactly a thing of beauty, but he actually claimed it was bringing down the property values all along Main Street."

He laughed. "Not sure how that's possible considering it's usually parked out back where no one can see it as they drive by. Besides, the owner of the coin-op laundry next door said he didn't mind it, and the muffler shop on the other side couldn't care less."

Abby asked, "What did you tell him?"

"That I had all the proper permits and licenses to do business here in Snowberry Creek, and that any attempt on his part to interfere with my ability to earn my living would result in a lawsuit. I also made sure he knew my attorney ate people like him for breakfast and had been feeling a bit peckish lately."

Owen Quinn was not only handsome, but also quite charming. Those characteristics along with his most excellent barbecue accounted for why his restaurant was so popular. But every so often, his inner shark peeked out. It was a reminder that the man had spent years in the military before being recruited to work for another government agency. He'd never shared the details about what that had entailed other than he'd walked some pretty dark roads before a mission went south and he'd retired. She bet a bully like James DiSalvo had backpedaled big-time once he caught a glimpse of the real Owen.

Gil was studying the other man with interest. Maybe he'd read between the lines and recognized the sharp edges that the man normally kept hidden. Owen must have picked up on it because he met Gil's gaze and lifted his chin in acknowledgment.

Before the conversation could continue, their waitress was back with their drinks. After passing them around, she ducked back into the kitchen to return almost immediately with a huge tray. It contained platters of ribs along with large bowls of baked beans, slaw, green beans, and corn muffins.

"That's just for starters. Let me know if you need anything else." Then she eyed both Gil and Tripp. "Okay, knowing you two, I should have said let me know *when* you need anything else. In fact, I'll save myself some time and go tell the cook to start piling up another platter of ribs now."

Tripp looked smug. "You know us too well, Judy."

Owen shook his head, feigning great sadness. "Maybe I should have tripled the number of ribs I smoked today instead of just doubling it."

Gil joined in. "Don't worry, Owen. If you run short on ribs, we'll be happy with pulled pork or those burnt ends you make from brisket. We're not picky."

It was nice to see Gil looking a little less grim. Abby leaned over closer to him. "Don't forget to leave room for dessert. I heard an interesting rumor from a reliable source, someone who claims to have gotten the facts straight from Owen himself."

Abby dropped her voice to a stage whisper. "I suspect the woman in question unleashed her feminine wiles on the poor man. But regardless of how she came by the info, I'm glad she shared it with me. Owen has somehow convinced Frannie to bake a few pies for his restaurant. Isn't that right, Mom?"

Her mother's face flushed a bit rosy, but she didn't deny it. "Peach, coconut cream, and Dutch apple."

Owen took her hand in his and gave it a squeeze. "Actually, it was Phoebe's idea. Frannie would only sell me a few of each flavor, so get your orders in early. Once we sell out, that's it until next week."

He had a pen and paper ready to take orders. Abby went with the coconut cream, always her favorite. Gil and her mom opted for the peach. Tripp bit his lower lip and frowned. "They're all great. I suppose it would be selfish of me to order a slice of each kind."

Owen gave him a hard stare. "Darn straight, soldier boy. You know firsthand how dangerous people get when food is being rationed and find out someone is hoarding it."

"Fine, be that way. I'll have the Dutch apple." Tripp pretended to look suitably chastened. "But for the record, I didn't say they had to be big pieces."

That sent a ripple of laughter around the table as everyone loaded up their plates with the main course and dug right in.

"I'm not sure I can walk after eating all of that."

Her mother was exaggerating, but Abby knew just how she felt. "I don't regret a single bite of what I ate, but tomorrow I'll have to live on lettuce and water to make up for it."

Tripp studied the huge pile of rib bones on his plate. "Yeah, I might've overdone it this time."

Abby rolled her eyes. "Ya think? I'll have to get out

my wheelbarrow and haul you from the truck to your front porch."

Seriously, he and Gil had turned dinner into a contest to see which of them could make the largest dent in Owen's stockpile of ribs, adding in big servings of burnt ends and a little pulled pork just for grins. If that wasn't impressive enough, they'd still managed to find room for pie.

Owen wiped his hands on a napkin and tossed it on the table. "Before you two collapse into a barbecue-induced stupor, what did you think of the new flavors?"

Both men gave him incredulous looks. Tripp pointed at his plate and then at Gil's. "The evidence speaks for it-self. They were both terrific. In fact, if you bottle those rubs to sell, put me down for half a dozen of each. They'll make good presents for some of my buddies."

Gil pulled out the wallet he kept attached to his jeans with a heavy chain. After tossing a couple of bills down on the center of the table, he said, "I liked the Texas-style best, Owen, but they were both great. Thanks for feeding me."

After Tripp contributed to the tip pile, Abby did the same.

"I agree with Gil, but it was a close race. It goes without saying that we'd volunteer to be your guinea pigs anytime you decide to try something new. I've enjoyed the company, too, but it's time for me to get home while I can still walk."

Gil and Tripp both stood up when she did, and her mom came around the table to give her a hug. "I'll call you before I head back home. I'm going to hang out here with Owen until the place closes."

Abby gave her a quick squeeze. "Okay, Mom. Tonight was fun."

"It was." Her mom surprised Tripp with a hug next. "Keep an eye on her for me."

He grinned as he slipped his arm around Abby's shoulders and tugged her in close. "I'll try, but you know that's a full-time job."

"Hey, you two. I'm not that bad."

When no one leapt to her defense, she took the high road. "Fine, be that way. Thanks again for dinner, Owen. Mom, I'll talk to you soon."

She headed for the door of the restaurant with Tripp following a short distance behind. Gil fell into step beside her. "They're right, Abby. Forget what I said about asking around about DiSalvo. I don't want to see my brother go to prison for something he didn't do, but neither of us would want you to put yourself in a situation that could get pretty risky."

He was right about the potential for danger even if she did her best to be careful. The little voice in the back of her head telling her to walk away from the problem sounded an awful lot like Tripp's. After all, more than once he'd been the one to throw himself into danger to save her life.

She waited until they were outside to speak again. "Fine, Gil. I'll stay out of it for now. I won't go out of my way to ask questions. But if I do hear anything during the normal course of things, I'll be sure to let you know."

Tripp finally joined them with a couple of brown bags in his hand. He held them out to Gil. "Owen sends his regards. Evidently he didn't think you got enough of the burnt ends you like so much. Judging by the weight of the bag, I think he sent along enough sides to make a full meal of it."

Gil didn't look like he knew how to react to Owen's generosity. "That was nice of him, but I should split this with you, Tripp."

"That's all right. Well, unless he included two pieces of Frannie's pie." Then he shook his head. "No, don't tell me if he did. I'd have to fight Abby for it, and I'm not up to it tonight. You never want to get between her and a piece of coconut cream pie."

She punched him on the arm. "Hey, again I'm not that bad."

"I call them like I see them."

At least their mock argument had Gil smiling again. "Well, I'd better get these loaded into my saddlebags before things get ugly around here."

Abby gave him a quick hug. "Get some rest, Gil."

"I will."

As he walked to where he'd left his bike, three older women were headed toward the restaurant. As he passed by them, one woman gave him a scathing look. "Well, apparently they'll serve anyone here, even thugs. He should be in jail just like his brother."

She'd pitched her voice loud enough to carry across the parking lot. Other than a slight hitch in his step, Gil ignored the old witch and her snooty companions, refusing to let them know if the insult scored a hit. Abby, on the other hand, had no compunction about defending her friends. She rang Owen's number. "Owen, there are three women about to come in. They just went out of their way to insult Gil. Said you'd serve anybody, even thugs."

"They'll learn differently." His voice turned icy. "I'll take care of it."

Tripp didn't say a word, just took her hand as they walked toward his truck. As they passed by the women, she gave them a sweet smile and said, "The barbecue was especially good tonight, and the dessert special was some of Frannie's best pies."

She didn't wait for them to reply, instead hurrying to where Tripp's truck was parked. As he opened the door for her, he murmured, "There goes that mean streak of yours again."

He glanced back to where Owen was blocking the door and refusing to let the women inside. By the time Tripp got in on the driver's side, the three women were stalking back toward their car. As he turned the key in the ignition, he grinned at her. "But that was nicely done, Abby."

"Nice" wasn't the right word for it. "Satisfying" came closer. She might have spoiled their plans for the evening, but that didn't erase the damage those women had caused. She just hoped Gil could find a way to forget their cutting remark and remember the fun they'd had at dinner. Maybe tomorrow she'd drop by his shop with a batch of lemon bars.

For now, she was going to go home and shut out the rest of the world for a few hours.

CHAPTER 12

Abby awoke on Monday feeling out of sorts. She couldn't quit thinking about Gil and his brother. Tough guy that he was, Gary still had to be scared out of his wits. What if he caved and took a plea deal even though he was innocent? It would ruin his life, not to mention his brother's. Knowing Gary would spend his life behind bars would hang heavily over Gil every day that he walked free.

This was the day Gil was supposed to talk to the bank about a loan against the equity in their house. Even if he was approved, would the bank give him enough to finance a topflight defense? So many questions and no good answers.

Rather than prowl the house, she bent down to pat Zeke on the head. "I'm going to go run a few errands. We'll walk when I get back."

The big dog blinked up at her sleepily before stretching back out on the carpet and closing his eyes. His easy acceptance had her smiling for the first time all morning. If only the rest of the world was as easy to please as he was.

Outside, she headed over to where Tripp had the hood up on his truck as he stared at something in the engine compartment. When he heard her approach, he straightened up and turned to face her. Wiping his hands on a rag he pulled from his back pocket, he leaned against the truck fender.

"Heading into town?"

"Yeah, I have a few errands to run. Need anything at the store while I'm there?"

"Nope, I'm good. I'll be leaving for class after I get done here."

She peeked at the tangled mess of wires and metal parts under the hood. It all looked fine to her, everything bright and shiny, not that she knew anything about engines. If someone told her they ran on magic, she would be inclined to believe them. "Is there something wrong or are you just tinkering?"

"Just routine maintenance."

"That's good. See you later."

Before she'd taken two steps, Tripp had planted his size thirteens right in front of her, blocking her path. "What's wrong, Abby?"

"Nothing." Actually, that wasn't true. She sighed. "I can't keep from thinking about Gil and his brother. There's nothing I can do to help, but I really wish there was."

Tripp edged closer, studying her face for several seconds. Finally, he brushed a lock of her hair back behind her ear. "You helped Gil the other night. For the length of our dinner, he was able to set aside his worries for a little while. He knows you care. I know from personal experience how much that helps."

"It doesn't feel like enough."

"I know you want to fix things for everyone, but sometimes that's not possible."

His voice sounded rougher. She'd closed her eyes, but she knew when she opened them that Tripp would have that same look on his face that he always got when he was flashing back to his time in the military. It was time to lighten the mood.

"I might stop by Bridey's place on my way back. If so, I could be persuaded to bring back something special."

Tripp immediately perked up. "And what form should this persuasion take?"

"I think I'll leave that up to you. Now, I need to be going."

She coupled that announcement with attempting an end run to get past Tripp to reach her car. Her ploy almost succeeded, but then the man unleashed some of the sneaky ninja skills he'd picked up in the Special Forces. He caught Abby's arm and used her own momentum to spin her back around right into his embrace. Before she could protest, he kissed her, hard and fast. Just as quickly, he released his hold on her and stepped back.

The maneuver left her slightly stunned, not that she minded in the least. This wasn't the first hit-and-run kiss he'd given her, and it packed quite a punch. Her mood considerably better than it had been only seconds before, she found herself grinning up at him.

"So, do you want a piece of Bridey's gooey butter cake or something else?"

"Surprise me."

"Will do."

She was still smiling an hour later when she reached her last stop. It was unlikely Bridey would have time to chat, since the high school was due to let out soon. Soon teenagers would come pouring into the coffee shop, making it one of the busiest times of the day for her friend. Besides, she had groceries in the car and shouldn't stay long anyway. She'd enjoy a quick drink at the shop and then head back home.

She had to leave her car on a side street five blocks from Something's Brewing. The short walk wouldn't hurt her, and it wasn't worth the effort to keep driving around looking for a closer parking spot. When she turned the corner onto Main Street, the first person she saw was Gage Logan. Spotting the cup in his hand, she figured he'd most likely dropped by the coffee shop on his way back to his office at city hall.

He wouldn't appreciate her grilling him on the murder investigation. But if she was careful with her questions, she might be able coax him into sharing a little information with her. When she started in his direction, he smiled and waited for her. They were less than a block apart when an SUV screeched to a halt right near Gage.

The driver left the vehicle running as she double-parked and got out, heading right for him. Pointing at his drink, she snarled, "So that's where you hide out, Chief Logan. I'll be having a word with the mayor about this.

I'm sure your official duties don't include hanging out in coffee shops when you're supposed to be working."

Even from a distance, Abby could tell he didn't much appreciate being confronted on a public street, but the man was no coward. Gage calmly stood his ground and waited for the woman to come closer, probably hoping they could continue the conversation without all the shouting. Abby slowed down, worried that any abrupt movement on her part might draw the woman's attention in her direction. The last thing she wanted to do was get in the middle of the brouhaha.

In the end, Abby coasted to a stop a few feet short of where the woman was still haranguing Gage. Rather than stare at the couple, she made a pretense of checking her cell phone for messages and then answered an e-mail. She'd just sent it when the woman stepped closer to Gage, her voice once again rising in both volume and fury.

"I don't care about your rules and regulations, Mr. Police Chief. You can't keep me out of my father's house forever. I need to find his will and other legal papers. His business attorney is stonewalling me, too, telling me I should just be patient. That these things take time."

Poking him in the chest, she continued her rant. "And you're not helping matters at all. I'm his only family. If nothing else, someone has to make the funeral arrangements when they release the body. God knows what kind of extravaganza Dad has planned out for himself. I certainly can't afford to pay the expenses myself while I wait for you and that idiot prosecutor to do your jobs. You've got the guy who killed my father. What else could you possibly need to know before you okay the release of the house and everything else?"

Abby hadn't known anything about James DiSalvo's family situation, but obviously she was looking at his daughter. This whole thing had to be hard for her, but it wasn't Gage's fault. It was amazing that he was able to remain calm as he gently pushed her hand away from his chest.

"Mrs. Denman, we're moving as fast as we can. Murder cases can't be rushed, and the investigation has to be done right. You don't want your father's killer to walk free on a technicality."

"That's the least of my worries. Whether or not that guy is in prison won't bring my father back, and I have more pressing problems to worry about."

Her voice cracked as her shoulders wilted. "I just want this to be over."

"I know you do. I know the prosecutor is in court today on a different case, but I'll try to check in with him later this afternoon. If he has any news, I'll let you know."

Instead of calming Mrs. Denman, it was as if his attempt at placating her threw another match on her explosive temper. "Trying isn't good enough. I want an update by this evening, one with a specific day and time when I can get inside Dad's house. If I don't hear from you, my next call will be to the mayor, the county executive, or the governor if necessary. Someone has to have enough clout to get things done around here."

She spun around to head back to her car, which was still blocking traffic. That was when she spotted Abby. "What are you looking at? This is a private conversation."

That assessment of the current situation was laughable. If she'd wanted privacy, she shouldn't have confronted Gage on a public sidewalk right on Main Street. Abby didn't respond, instead continued to hold her phone up to her ear. She wasn't sure how well the ploy worked considering the nasty look Mrs. Denman shot her before stalking back to her car. When a passing car honked at her, she muttered something under her breath as she got in and peeled off down the street.

Abby slowly approached Gage. "Are you okay?"

He stared at Mrs. Denman's car as it disappeared down the street. "You know, sometimes I really hate my job."

After sipping his coffee, he grimaced and tossed it in a nearby trash can, crushing the cup as he did. Glancing at Abby, he said, "It's gone cold."

Really? Rather than call him on the lie, she looped her arm through his and tugged him back in the direction of the coffee shop.

"Come on, I'll buy you another one."

Gage looked back in the direction Mrs. Denman had gone. "I probably shouldn't."

"You can get it to go." But only if he insisted. "If you've got time to sit a spell, I'll up the ante to include dessert."

That sealed the deal because he picked up speed. "We'll have to make it fast. The high school will be letting out, and there's a good chance my daughter will head this way with her friends. You know how she gets when she finds out I've been hanging out at Bridey's more often than she likes. I try to convince her that I'm the adult in the room, but that has ceased to be an effective defense."

Abby laughed at his grumpy comment. Gage's daughter had been nagging her father about his diet since she was a little girl. He might complain once in a while, but it was clear he and his daughter were close. The fact that he was in a high stress and potentially dangerous job only added to her concerns. He was a single parent, and he tried not to worry her too much.

"If it will help, we can split something. That way you can tell her you only had half the calories."

He looked horrified by that prospect. "There's no reason to go that far. If I'm going to risk another of her long lectures and extra time on the treadmill, I'm going to deserve it."

When they stepped inside the shop, Bridey came to the counter to take their orders. "Need another latte already, Gage?"

"The other one got cold before I had a chance to drink it."

Bridey looked surprised, but she didn't say anything as she took care of their orders. When they were ready, Abby followed Gage over to a table in the back corner.

As she sipped her coffee, she pondered how best to start the conversation. Gage broke off a piece of his muffin and ate it. "Go ahead and ask whatever questions you want, Abby. No guarantees that I'll answer, though."

He knew her so well. "I take it that was James DiSalvo's daughter."

"Yeah, her name is Francine Denman. Can't say I know much about her. Despite her assertion that her taxes pay my salary, she doesn't live here in town. Her father never talked about her around me."

"Were you and Mr. DiSalvo friends?"

Gage snorted. "Not hardly. He considered me part of the hired help."

Then he winced. "Sorry, I shouldn't have said that. It was unprofessional if nothing else."

"Don't worry. I won't repeat it to anyone." She meant that. Gage often complained that she somehow managed to get him to tell her things he shouldn't, especially when it came to his job. The last thing she wanted to do was cause him any unnecessary problems.

"I really didn't mean to listen in out there on the sidewalk, but I didn't know what to do. I suppose I could've walked on by, but I didn't want to risk interrupting your conversation. I couldn't help but notice how angry she was, and I'm sorry she took it out on you."

Gage leaned back in his chair. "It comes with the territory. She's really pushing to get into her father's house, but the prosecuting attorney wants us to finish sifting through everything before we allow anyone inside. DiSalvo was a widower, so no one else lives there."

"I'd ask what he's hoping you'll find, but I figure you couldn't tell me even if you wanted to."

"Nope, I couldn't. I know you've become friends with Gil and don't like that we arrested Gary for the murder."

She sipped her coffee before responding. "You wouldn't have done that without some pretty convincing evidence."

"And you want to know what that is."

"I didn't say that." Not that he was wrong.

He smiled just enough to set her teeth on edge. "You didn't have to, Abby. I can hear the cogs spinning inside your head."

"No, you can't."

"Let's just say that the two of us have crossed swords on enough other cases for me to understand how your mind works. All I will say is that I hope you trust me enough to know that I would never act without good reason."

Which meant the evidence against Gary was pretty damning, and Gil was right to be worried about his brother. With that realization, all the flavor in her gooey butter cake disappeared. And if that wasn't a tragedy, she didn't know what was.

CHAPTER 13

Gage left a few minutes later, saying Mrs. Denman wasn't wrong about him not being paid to sit on his backside drinking coffee. He'd only gone a handful of steps when he reversed course long enough to say, "Thanks for the coffee and muffin, but especially for the pleasant company. My mood has improved considerably, something my staff will appreciate when I get back to the office."

"Anytime. Nothing like Bridey's pastries to brighten the day."

"You're right." He glanced back toward the glass-fronted counters that held all the tempting items Bridey had on display. "In fact, maybe I'll have her box up a bunch for the office to spread the joy."

"You're a nice man, Gage Logan."

And a darn good chief of police, no matter what that Denman woman thought. He worked as hard or harder than anyone else in his department, and right now it showed. It was impossible to miss the dark circles under his eyes. His job wasn't nine-to-five at the best of times. When he had a big case, especially one that involved a high-profile victim like the local councilman, the number of working hours in his days stretched to double digits.

After he left the shop carrying a huge box, Bridey walked over to Abby's table with a carafe of coffee in her hand. She sat down after topping off Abby's cup. "Whew, it feels good to get off my feet for a couple of minutes."

"How are you feeling?"

Bridey smiled and rested her hand on her still flat tummy. "Pretty good most of the time. The biggest problem so far is Seth's unfortunate tendency to hover. While I appreciate that he's excited about our pregnancy, it's hard to get my early morning baking done with him underfoot. He keeps leaping up to get things for me, which only slows me down."

The smile on her face indicated Bridey was more amused than irritated by her husband's actions. "I'll bet there'll come a time that you'll really appreciate his efforts."

"True enough. When I get all roly-poly about month seven, I'll be glad for his longer reach."

"No doubt."

Bridey's smile faded. "I don't mean to be nosy, but Gage didn't look happy when you two came in. He was fine right before that. Did something bad happen?"

"He was accosted out on the street by Francine Denman, Mr. DiSalvo's daughter. She's upset about how long the investigation is taking. It didn't help that she spotted him coming out of your shop."

To put it mildly, the woman had been beyond furious.

"But Gage already made an arrest. What more does she want from him?"

How much should she share? Considering Mrs. Denman had ripped into Gage right out in public, it wasn't as if Abby would be sharing anything confidential.

"Evidently the prosecutor and the police still have Mr. DiSalvo's house cordoned off while they finish their investigation. I guess the problem is that means Mrs. Denman can't get access to the place while all of that's going on."

Bridey looked puzzled. "I know he was her father and all, but why does she feel it's so urgent to get in? It's not like they were close or anything."

Scenting blood in the water, Abby sat up straighter. "But the woman acted totally distraught about her father's death."

Bridey winced and glanced around the shop, probably to make sure they were still alone. "I probably shouldn't have said anything, but the two of them had a very public falling-out about ten years ago. As I recall, the problem stemmed from Mr. DiSalvo having pretty high standards when it came to the men he thought suitable for his only daughter. When she came home from college engaged to someone who didn't fit his criteria, he ordered her to break it off."

Abby knew how she would've reacted if either of her parents had tried to dictate her dating life. "I take it that didn't go over well."

"Nope. Turned out she was pregnant, so they eloped.

In retaliation, I heard her father cut her off without a penny. Maybe it's because I'm going to have a baby of my own, but I can't imagine treating my child in such a coldhearted manner."

Abby couldn't either. She and her parents might have disagreements at times, but they would never have abandoned her. "What about her mother? How did she feel about her husband's actions?"

"I never knew Mrs. DiSalvo. As I recall, she was a quiet woman who kept a pretty low profile. I can't imagine her standing up to the man. Regardless, she passed away a few years back, and he's never remarried."

It all added up to a puzzling picture. "It does sound odd that Mrs. Denman would be so upset about her father if they weren't on speaking terms."

Bridey shrugged. "Maybe they reconciled, and I just haven't heard about it. It's not like I move in the same social circles as Mr. DiSalvo. He stopped in my shop a couple of times right after I opened for business to see what I was up to here. I've heard from other small business owners in town that he never hesitated to express his displeasure if he didn't approve of their operations."

"I know he complained about Owen Quinn's food truck, saying it was driving down property values in the area." Honesty had Abby adding, "I can't say he was completely wrong on that score. For certain, he wasn't the only one who has commented on how bad that thing looks, me included. Truthfully, though, it's only ugly on the outside. Owen keeps the inside immaculate."

She finished the last bite of her gooey butter cake. "Even if Mr. DiSalvo's intentions might've been good, his manner rubbed some folks the wrong way."

Bridey laid her hand on Abby's arm. "You're thinking

about the Pratt brothers, aren't you? I knew you'd take the news hard that they arrested Gary for the murder. Are you doing okay?"

"I'm fine, but I am concerned about Gil. He's worried sick about his brother and wants to help him, although there's not much he can do. Mom, Tripp, and I met him for dinner at Owen's the other night. Owen even sent him home with extra food so he'd have a meal or two that he didn't have to cook."

"That was thoughtful of him and a good idea. In fact, I'll put together a lunch basket for Gil tomorrow and have Seth drop it off at the garage. Do you know if he has anyone else working there? I'd want to send enough for everybody."

"He's had another guy coming in to help while we were working on the race. He hasn't mentioned if Casey was going to keep coming now that Gary is in jail, but I hope so. It's not good for Gil to be alone all the time right now."

"Well, I'll pack enough to make sure there's enough to go around."

The bell over the door rang, followed by the sound of teenagers excited that school was over for the day. Although Bridey's assistant was already at the counter ready to take orders, she stood up. "I need to get back to work. Let me know if there's anything else I can do to help Gil."

"I will."

Actually, there was one thing Abby could think of, but she wasn't sure she should ask. On the other hand, Bridey could always say no. "If you happen to think of anyone else who had big problems with Mr. DiSalvo, would you let me know?"

Her friend gave her a narrow-eyed look. "You're not thinking about investigating the murder on your own again, are you? That hasn't always worked out well for you."

She knew Abby too well. "No, at least not exactly. I'd just like to know if there are other people who would have had good reason to want the man dead. It's true that Gary and DiSalvo had a big argument the morning of the race, but they'd had the same kind of confrontation before. There's no reason to think that this time was so much worse that it would've driven Gary to such violence. I also know he walked away after Gil separated the two men. It also doesn't make sense that Gary would've used one of his own tools. He's smarter than that."

At least she hoped so.

Bridey pointed out the obvious. "Gage must have thought differently since he arrested the man."

"Maybe I'm just grasping at straws."

Bridey looked as if she wanted to say more, but then she saw the line to the counter was now out the door. "Oops, I'd better get going. I'll let you know if I think of anyone who might have had an ax to grind with you-know-who."

"Thanks, I'd appreciate it."

Abby slipped past the teenagers crowding in the door, careful to protect the bag with the treat she'd promised Tripp. She really wished she'd learned more useful information that could potentially help Gil and Gary, but at least she'd tried.

On the other hand, she had learned that Mrs. Denman's reaction to her father's death was a bit over-the-top, especially if their relationship had remained broken all this time. Like Bridey had said, there was always a chance they'd made peace at some point. It was equally possible that the woman had been knocked sideways by the realization that any chance for a reconciliation was gone now that the man had died. Either could account for her grief.

Something to ponder, anyway. For now, she needed to get home and put away the groceries before taking Zeke for his walk.

Tripp wasn't back from class yet, so she left him a note stuck to his front door explaining where he could find his treat in her kitchen. Zeke plunked down on his buddy's porch and whined when she tugged on his leash.

"Sorry, boy, Tripp isn't home. I'm sure we'll see him later."

The dog begrudgingly heaved himself up to his feet and let her lead him down the driveway. From the way he trudged along, clearly her company wasn't good enough. "Sorry, Zeke, but he can't always accompany us on our outings."

Although she wouldn't mind if he did. "Maybe he'll be home when we get back. For now, what do you say we take the loop through the national forest?"

That perked him right up. She never knew how much Zeke actually understood when she spoke to him, but there were definitely words that he reacted to. When they reached the sidewalk, he immediately headed in the right direction for the path that would lead them on a meandering route through the forest. It was one of her favorite places to walk, and she loved the spicy scent of the towering cedars and Douglas firs that lined the trail.

Zeke set the pace, with Abby patiently waiting whenever he stopped to thoroughly check out any bushes or tree trunks that caught his attention. She figured dogs had their own kind of message board that they posted on whenever they passed through the area. It must make for interesting reading, because Zeke clearly found it all fascinating no matter how often they walked through the woods.

They'd pretty much had the trail to themselves, but now they were almost to where it ended in the city park. Rather than reverse course, she decided to cut through the park over toward Main Street to head back home.

They'd only gone a short distance when she regretted that decision. Headed straight for them was one of the ladies from the parking lot outside Owen's restaurant. Although not the one who'd made the snarky comment to Gil, she also hadn't objected when her friend had shot her mouth off. Abby kept walking, hoping to slip by her without incident, but no such luck.

The power-walking lady came to a screeching halt right in front of them. Planting her hands on her hips, she frowned at Abby. "It's you."

It was tempting to ask who else she would be, but giving in to snark herself wouldn't help the situation. "I'm sorry. Have we met?"

"Don't play cute with me, young lady. You're the reason my friends and I were turned away from that barbecue restaurant. I might not be able to prove it, but I know I'm right. You made a call as we passed by you on our way to the door. The next thing we knew, Owen Quinn informed us that he reserved the right to refuse service, and he was absolutely refusing us."

Although Abby couldn't have foreseen running into one of the women again this soon, she didn't regret her decision to call Owen. "That was his right as owner of the restaurant."

That had the woman huffing in outrage. "Even so, we hadn't caused him any problems. Or you, for that matter."

Rather than continuing bobbing and weaving to avoid admitting the woman was right about what she'd done, Abby decided to just own up to it. She stepped closer to use her height advantage to stare down at her shorter adversary. "Your friend went out of her way to insult a friend of mine, one who had done nothing at all to deserve that attack. He's going through a rough patch right now, and we had taken him out to dinner to cheer him up. Her thoughtless comment probably erased all of our hard work. That's on your friend, lady, not me. All I did was give you and your friends a taste of your own medicine. How did it feel to have your evening spoiled?"

When the woman started to speak, Abby held up her hand. "Never mind. I don't care." Then she sidestepped around her, taking Zeke with her. They hadn't gotten far when the pitter-patter of a speed-walking senior citizen announced that even if Abby was ready for the encounter to end, the other participant wasn't. Worried the woman would walk herself into a heart attack, Abby reluctantly slowed to a stop. "What now?"

To her surprise, the woman looked uncomfortable rather than angry. "As much as I hate to admit it, you're right. Georgia was out of line. When you see your friend again, please apologize for me. I don't know what she was thinking. We should all know better than to judge people by their appearance or who they're related to."

Then she dropped her gaze to the ground as she waited for Abby to respond. What could she say? Everyone did things they regretted.

"I'll tell him. Gil is a good man who just spent weeks organizing the Salmon Scoot to raise money for programs at the high school. He served in the navy, and he's a member of the local veterans group. That's how I came to meet him in the first place."

That information left the woman looking even more distraught. "Now I feel worse than ever. My late husband was in the navy, too. Leo wouldn't be at all pleased that I was involved in an undeserved attack on a veteran. Please tell him how much I regret it."

"I'd like to tell him whose apology I'm conveying." Abby found herself holding out her hand. "I'm Abby McCree, and this handsome fellow is Zeke."

"I'm Sheila Sorrell, Ms. McCree." She patted Zeke on the head. "Sorry, big fella, I don't have any treats with me today."

Abby pulled a pawprint cookie out of her pack. "Zeke will love you forever if you want to give him this."

Sheila laughed as she held out the cookie to Zeke. He used his best mooching manners as he gently took it from her fingers. The small connection with the dog vanquished the last of the woman's tension. She seemed to recognize Abby letting her spoil Zeke a little as a peace offering.

It also spurred her into explaining the reason her friend had gone on the attack the previous evening. "I had no idea who that man was at the time, but Georgia said afterward that she recognized him from some encounter in the past. I don't know any details, but she wasn't at all surprised his brother had murdered James DiSalvo. She even called the police to tell them about that incident."

She wrinkled her nose and shook her head. "She had 'a

thing' for James DiSalvo. I never understood it myself. He was a bit of a cold fish, but there's no accounting for taste. Georgia has acted as his plus-one for the past couple of years and held out hope that one day he'd make their relationship permanent. She's taking his death very hard."

That didn't excuse her rude behavior, but Sheila obviously knew that. "It's a trying time for all concerned."

"It is indeed. She's also upset that his daughter is being particularly difficult. Georgia contacted her to learn about the funeral arrangements and even offered to help. Francine told her it wasn't any of her business and then hung up on her. Georgia has been watching for an obituary, but there's been nothing in the paper."

"Perhaps the police haven't yet released the remains."

That thought clearly distressed Sheila. "If so, I hope they get their act together. Dragging all of this out makes it so hard on everyone concerned."

True enough. She and Zeke needed to get moving, but something Sheila had said raised a red flag. It couldn't hurt to ask a few questions.

"So did Georgia happen to mention if she'd ever been with Mr. DiSalvo when someone other than Gary Pratt had been upset about something? Maybe because of a stand he'd taken on an issue that the city council was dealing with? I understand he was a land developer. That can sometime cause tempers to flare hot."

At least the woman gave the question some serious thought before answering. "Well, anyone who knew James was aware that he had strong opinions when it came to Snowberry Creek. He believed that if people were allowed to let their property get run-down or the wrong kind of businesses were allowed to come in, it would have a detrimental effect on everyone."

"Can you think of any specific incidents that were problematic?"

"Well, there was that mobile-home park on the south side of town. The person who originally owned the land passed away. Evidently, the heir lived somewhere in the Midwest and wasn't doing a good job of managing the property from such a long distance. James contacted her and offered to purchase the place. Once the transaction went through, he informed the residents that they had to bring both the spaces they rented and their mobile homes up to snuff."

"What happened?"

"From what Georgia told me, he also raised the rents to cover the cost of the new landscaping and other upgrades. Some of the residents got upset. They even went to the city council meeting and claimed they couldn't afford the increased costs and didn't need all the fancy changes. In the end, some of them had to move."

"I imagine moving their homes was expensive, too."

Sheila winced. "That was part of the problem. Once those homes are set in place and the wheels taken off, they're not that easy to move. If the owners couldn't sell them in place, they had to just walk away."

Well, wasn't that interesting?

By that point, Sheila was looking a bit uncomfortable about the entire discussion. It was time to get going.

"Well, Zeke needs to get back home for his nap. I hope you enjoy the rest of your walk."

Sheila laughed and patted him one last time. "You too."

As the older woman resumed her power walking, Abby and Zeke made their way over to Main Street. It was hard to quit thinking about all those folks at the mobile-home park. Being forced to abandon a home because a new landlord hiked the rents beyond his tenants' ability to pay was bound to make some people angry.

The question was, had one of them been angry enough to kill?

CHAPTER 14

Knowledge was power, and Abby knew exactly where to go to educate herself about life in the dirty underbelly of Snowberry Creek. Well, technically, she didn't actually have to go anywhere. The local founts of knowledge could be easily lured to her house with the promise of fresh apple-walnut bread, a pot of English breakfast tea, and the chance to watch Tripp Blackston while he worked in the yard.

The doorbell rang right on time. Zeke was supervising Tripp out in the backyard, so she didn't have to shoo him out of the way as she shepherded her three elderly friends in the front door. Along with her, they made up the quilting guild's board of directors. As luck would have it, they'd already had a meeting planned that morning, so she hadn't even had to make up an excuse to invite them over.

"Come on in, ladies! I tried a new recipe for the apple-walnut bread today, and I'm anxious to see what you think."

Glenda led the way, and then Jean maneuvered her walker through the door with Louise bringing up the rear. As she passed by, she handed Abby a casserole dish, rolling her eyes as she did so. No explanation was needed. Evidently Jean had decided that Tripp needed another one of her tuna casseroles. Abby smothered the urge to laugh. The poor guy wasn't all that fond of tuna, but he was too nice to tell Jean the truth about the situation. Still, her intentions were good, and Abby gave her full kudos for her generosity. "I'll stick this in the fridge until I have a chance to give it to Tripp."

Jean wasn't the only one who looked decidedly disappointed by that statement. Nothing made the three ladies' day like an in-person encounter with Tripp. He tolerated their geriatric flirting with good grace and often offered them his arm to assist them down the steps. She was pretty sure that those encounters with a handsome young man gave them bragging rights at their Friday night bingo games.

Finally taking pity on them, she said, "I'll text him that it's here. He's in the middle of a big project in the backyard, but maybe he can pop in to say hi if he reaches a stopping point."

Jean brought you a casserole, and the other ladies would love to say hi if you get a chance to stop in.

More likely he'd declare there was something critical he needed at the hardware store, a paper to research at the university library, or even an emergency game of pool at the bar with his buddies. When her phone pinged seconds after she got her friends settled around the dining room table, she carefully schooled her expression before reading his reply. There was no way she'd want to risk hurting Jean's feelings if Tripp's response was anything other than polite.

Zeke and I will be by in a few. The good news is that you won't have to cook dinner tonight.

That announcement was followed by a series of evil grin emojis. Surrendering to the inevitable, she kept her answer simple. **I'll make a salad.**

And a dessert . . . that doesn't mean defrosting cookies you already have in the freezer. I want pie.

Sighing, she conceded the battle. **Fine. I'll make a pie, although I don't understand why you getting another tuna casserole is my fault.**

His final response was rather rude, but at least it made her laugh. Aware that three pairs of eyes were watching her every move, it was time to shut down the conversation with Tripp. She stuffed the phone in her pocket to make sure that no one would "accidentally" pick it up to check out what she'd been laughing about.

After the tea and treats made the rounds, she passed out the agenda for the day and dove right in. She pushed right through all the items in record time, to the point she was a little breathless by the time they reached the bottom of the page.

"Did I miss anything or did any of you have something you wanted to talk about?"

The three women exchanged glances and then turned to face her more directly with puzzled frowns on their faces. Glenda, the unofficial leader of the trio, finally spoke up. "Abby, dear, what's wrong?"

Well, that wasn't the response she was expecting. "Why would you ask that?"

"You've been talking a mile a minute, and we've never covered the entire agenda in less than fifteen minutes. If you had something else to do this morning, you could've simply rescheduled the meeting. We would've understood."

Wow, no wonder Abby was out of breath. "Sorry, ladies. I didn't mean to rush us quite so much, and I don't have any other errands this morning. However, I do have something on my mind."

Always the first one to scent trouble in the air, Jean went on point. "Abby, do you need our help again?"

"Yes. Well, maybe." She mustered up a small smile. "It's more like I need to pick your brains."

Louise reached over to pat Abby's hand. "This has to do with the Pratt brothers, doesn't it?"

Abby appreciated the gesture of sympathy. "Well, yes. I'm worried about Gil. Gary, too. The whole situation is terrible, and it's killing Gil that Gary is locked up for a crime he didn't commit."

"Are you as sure about that as Gil is?"

Glenda's question was a legitimate one, but Abby didn't even have to think about her answer. "Yes, I am. The more I think about the situation, the more sure I am that Gary is innocent. Nothing makes sense about what happened."

Jean chose another piece of the walnut bread and then passed the plate over to Louise. "How so, Abby?"

"There's no reason that Gary would've gone so far out of control. He and DiSalvo have had arguments about the motorcycle repair shop before, and it was likely they would have again. Gil can't figure out why this particular argument would've pushed his brother over the edge from angry to homicidal, and Gary swears he never got near DiSalvo again after they argued. I know both men started the race right on time."

Louise looked unhappy. "I heard from a friend that Gary didn't finish on time, though. He came in pretty far back in the pack, a lot later than he was expected to finish."

That was true, but there was another explanation for that. And if Abby wanted her friends to share their knowledge, the least she could do was the same. "Gary took longer to finish because he had a fall, which irritated a chronic problem with his knee."

Jean frowned. "If so, wouldn't the police have found that out when they talked to Zoe and the others who manned the first aid tent?"

Another good point, but one that was more difficult to disprove. "He didn't go there. Since he'd had the same problem before, he knew what was wrong and that all it required was rest and ice."

"Hmmm."

Abby turned to face Louise. "What does that mean?"

Louise's late husband had been a huge fan of the true crime genre, and she claimed she'd picked up a lot of expertise through osmosis. What she really meant was that the man would share particularly gruesome or at least interesting tidbits with her, whether she wanted to hear them or not. While not an expert on the subject, Louise sometimes offered insight that the others missed.

"Simply that his explanation for the delay sounds a bit convenient." She held up her hand to head off Abby's objection. "I'm not saying that isn't what happened. Speaking as someone with a few cranky joints of my own, I know full well how an old problem can flare up. It also makes sense that he would know best if it would pass or if he needed medical care."

She paused to draw a slow breath, maybe to buy herself time to frame the remainder of what she wanted to say. "But you have to understand why the police might not accept his explanation at face value. After all, even if people did see him come limping across the finish line, all we have is his word that that his knee hurt, and that it slowed him down. That's not an ironclad alibi."

Jean decided to play devil's advocate. "That's true, Louise. However, if he didn't kill the man, he had no reason to know that he needed an alibi in the first place. I'm sure all he could think about was finishing the race so he could go home and get off his knee. Under any other circumstances, no one would've questioned his actions."

Abby conceded that both sides of the argument had merit. "That's true, but we have to play the cards we were dealt. Well, Gary does, anyway. Which brings me back to what I wanted to talk to you three about. You've been a great help to me in the past when I needed more information about someone here in town."

Now all three women looked bright-eyed and eager to help. Glenda peered at her over the rim of her teacup. "So are you asking us what we know about Gary and Gil? By now, I'm sure you know them better than any of us."

"No, not them. It's James DiSalvo I'm curious about." Not knowing how her friends felt about the man, she needed to tread lightly. "I'm sure he had everyone's best interests at heart, but I'm guessing his efforts to maintain certain standards might have stepped on a few toes along the way."

Glenda gave a very unladylike snort. "Stomped on a lot of toes was more like it. Some truly awful arguments used to break out at the city council meetings until Mayor McKay came down hard on folks. She said that anyone who couldn't control their tempers would be escorted out the door. It took that actually happening a couple of times before people took her seriously."

"What were the arguments about?"

"As I recall, one or two were because of a couple of people who couldn't get the zoning variances they'd need to operate their businesses. James was often quite vocal on the subject. To be honest, I can't say that I was at all upset that they turned down a few of those applications."

"Can you give me an example?"

"Well, let's see . . . yes, there was one young man who wanted to open a microbrewery and do tastings in his backyard. Since the area he lived in was zoned residential, having a commercial enterprise like that wasn't allowed under the code. Parking would've been a nightmare."

That made sense even if the man was disappointed. If the city council made one exception, they'd have to do it for everybody. "Anything else that people might carry a major grudge about? Maybe to do with his business interests rather than something to do with the city council."

Nothing but silence for maybe a minute. Finally, Jean came up with one example. "He was a land developer. I don't fault him for buying a piece of property to build on, but I heard there were a few instances when he snapped up parcels that he had no real use for. He just bought them to keep someone else from using them in a way he didn't like. For instance, the guy who owns that hamburger stand out by the river wanted to build another one here in town. I understand he had his eye on a corner lot that was rumored to be coming on the market. I heard later that James convinced the owner to sell it to him directly without the bother of listing it. His excuse for interfering was that the drive-in would have a negative impact on traffic on Main Street."

At least a pattern was forming that proved the Pratts weren't the only ones DiSalvo had targeted. "Do any of you know anyone who lived in the mobile-home park on the south end of town who had to move out after DiSalvo took over?"

Louise exchanged glances with Glenda before answering. "Well, there was Ginger Walsh. At one point, she mentioned the increased rent might force her out sooner than she wanted to leave, and she wasn't sure where she could go on such sudden notice. She'd been waiting for a low-income apartment to become available."

Jean went from interested to distraught. "She never mentioned that to me. I have an extra bedroom she could've used in the interim. I thought the only reason she considered moving at all was because the mobile home was getting to be too much for her to take care of by herself."

Glenda hastened to reassure her friend. "That was true, Jean, but she needed to stay there until an apartment opened up. Between the mobile home not selling and the rent on the space going up all the time, money was becoming a problem."

"Did she say why the rents were increasing?"

Louise looked disgusted. "Right after DiSalvo bought

the place, he slapped some new paint on the manager's office, put up a few fancy signs, and scattered some planters of petunias here and there around the place. None of that justified the much higher rents he was charging allegedly because of the so-called upgrades. Besides, a lot of the folks who live there are on limited incomes."

It sounded exactly like the kind of situation Abby had been looking for, but it was difficult to imagine their elderly friend sneaking off with one of Gary's tools to murder her landlord in the woods.

"What happened after that?"

"Well, as I understand it, a member of her family—a nephew, I think—moved in with her for the short term, not that he had a lot of money, either. However, together they managed. The good news is that Ginger got her new apartment about three weeks ago, so everything worked out for her."

For Ginger, maybe, but what about her temporary roommate?

"What's the current situation with her mobile home?"

Her questions were met with silence and frowns. "It's okay if you don't know. At least you confirmed a story I'd heard from someone who . . . well, let's just say I wouldn't put much credence in her word alone. You've never steered me wrong yet, and your instincts are impeccable."

Okay, that was laying it on a bit thick, but at least they were smiling again. She knew they got a vicarious thrill from aiding her in her little private investigations. Not that she'd ever admit to Tripp or Gage that's how she thought of her efforts to ensure people she cared about were proven innocent.

"Would you have Ginger's old address at the mobile-home park? I might want to take a drive through there to see this place for myself."

A deep voice laced with a heavy dose of gravel entered the conversation. "And pray tell, Abby, why would you want to do that? Well, unless you're poking your nose where it doesn't belong again."

Rats! Busted!

CHAPTER 15

Abby really wished she'd noticed how Jean's eyes had suddenly lit up right before she said that last part. It would've warned her that Tripp had finally put in an appearance. Her suspicions were confirmed when a big hand came down on her shoulder. His grip stopped shy of painful but still managed to convey his current mood all too clearly.

The smile he offered each of the ladies in turn was friendly enough, but there was a definite thread of hot temper simmering right below the surface. She doubted her friends noticed. They were too bedazzled by the manly magnificence standing right behind her. Not that she blamed them. She wasn't immune to his smile either, not when he unleashed the full power of it.

Sadly, though, his smile didn't extend to her. He gently

increased the pressure on her shoulder, an unspoken reminder that she'd yet to answer his question. They said confession was good for the soul. Maybe so, but she was pretty sure right now it wasn't going to be good for anything except getting her into trouble.

Might as well fess up and get it over with.

"Fine, Tripp. I'd heard that Mr. DiSalvo was involved in an effort to force people out of their homes in a mobile-home park here in town. I was going to drive through the place just to see it for myself. I wasn't going to stop and talk to anyone. That's all. I swear."

When his hand finally dropped away, she resisted the urge to rub her shoulder. It didn't even hurt, and she didn't want to draw attention to the momentary tension between the two of them. Tripp leaned past her to snag a piece of the apple-walnut bread.

Jean immediately tugged on the empty chair next to hers. "Come sit down by me, Tripp. We've finished our meeting early, so you're not interrupting anything. Can Abby get you some tea or coffee?"

He smirked at Abby as he settled in the chair. "Actually, I would love a glass of iced tea."

Waiting on her friends was one thing, but she wasn't really in the mood to play waitress for her tenant right now. Refusing would only upset the ladies, and they'd never understand why she'd choose to be rude to their favorite guy.

"I'll get right on it."

She made it back in record time, hoping to head off any more discussion about their friend Ginger and her rent woes. Too late. Louise was busy filling him in on all the details that he'd missed out on from their conversation before he'd walked in. Although he kept his expression perfectly calm and pleasant, no doubt there'd be heck to pay after her friends left. What could she do to mitigate the damage?

To keep their dinner as simple as possible, she'd been planning on making a pumpkin pie with a store-bought crust, but now she'd have to up the ante. As the ladies chatted away, enjoying having a handsome man's attention focused solely on them, she did a mental inventory of her larder. She had the necessary ingredients for both a Dutch apple pie and coconut cream. As the ladies prattled on, she tried to decide which flavor would do the best job of soothing the troubled waters.

To be safe, she could always make one of each, but that was overkill. It wasn't as if she had actually done anything wrong . . . or dangerous, which was what he was really worried about. She'd make either coconut cream or Dutch apple and call it good. Of course, if he decided to blow the whole situation out of proportion, she could always defrost cookies instead.

The sound of a phone beeping like crazy dragged her scattered thoughts back to the moment at hand. She finally identified it as the alarm Glenda set to signal it was time to bring the meeting to an end and head off to the diner in town. The Creek Café did such a brisk lunch business that the ladies liked to get there early to get a booth before they were all taken.

Louise immediately began gathering up the plates, but Abby stopped her. "You don't have to do that, Louise. Tripp can help me clean up this time."

The smile she shot in his direction was as sweetly sincere as the one he gave her in return. "I'd be glad to, Abby."

Before touching a single dish, though, he brought Jean her walker and made sure she was steady on her feet before stepping away. It was hard to stay mad at a man who did things like that. Because he towered over the diminutive woman, he leaned down closer to say, "I hear you brought me dinner again. You know you don't have to do that, but it's nice of you to think of me."

When he gently kissed her on the cheek, Jean flushed rosy and smiled. She patted his arm. "At my age, cooking is one of the last pleasures I have left. Let an old lady have her fun, Tripp."

"Yes, ma'am."

After that, there was a flurry of activity while he helped Jean down the steps to the sidewalk and then returned to do the same for Glenda and Louise. Abby waved at them from the porch, waiting until they drove off before returning to clean up the dining room. At least Tripp helped as he'd promised. He whistled a tuneless melody as he washed the dishes, slowly driving Abby nuts as she waited for what she was sure was going to be an epic lecture.

She watched as he neatly folded the dish towel and hung it on the stove handle to dry. With his chores done, he looked around the kitchen with a slightly puzzled look on his face. "There was something else I needed to do. Now, what was it? Oh, yeah, now I remember."

Then his dark eyes zeroed in on her with such intensity, she actually backed up and almost fell over Zeke.

The poor dog yelped when she stepped on his paw. She immediately dropped to her knees to cuddle him close and apologize. "I'm sorry, boy. I didn't mean to hurt you."

Always generous of spirit, he gave her a big sloppy lick across her entire face. Or maybe the resulting slobbery mess on her skin was just his way of getting even for bruised toes. There was no way to know. Deciding to give him the benefit of the doubt, she hugged him again before shooting a nasty look at his buddy for laughing when she used her sleeve to wipe off most of the doggy love.

Tripp wasn't in the least intimidated. "That's the least you deserved for plotting a way to get involved in another murder investigation. I swear you don't have the sense that God gave a goat."

Kneeling left her at a distinct disadvantage. She lurched back up to her feet and put her hands on her hips, refusing to be intimidated by Tripp and his superior height. "I told you that I just wanted to drive through the mobile-home park. The woman that Jean and the others knew doesn't even live there anymore. The man who apparently owned the park is dead. The bottom line is that there's no one there for me to talk to even if I did want to ask questions. What could go wrong if all I did was drive through the place?"

He glowered right back at her. "Are you telling me that one quick cruise past a bunch of mobile homes will be enough to satisfy your curiosity? Because I'm telling you right up front, I don't believe it. Not for a second. If this adventure doesn't pan out, if it doesn't clear Gary's name, we both know you'll go looking for something else."

She wanted to deny it, but her conscience wouldn't let her lie to Tripp. "It's the only thing I've heard about that might mean someone else other than Gary had a major problem with James DiSalvo."

Then she realized that wasn't exactly true. "Well, I also learned that he and his daughter Francine didn't get along and haven't for years. And before you get all bent out of shape over that, I didn't go looking for her. I was on my way to Bridey's to get your treats yesterday when I saw Gage coming out of the shop. He smiled at me right as Francine jumped out of her car and tore into him right there on Main Street. Everybody and their brother passing by would've heard her yelling at him. When she ran out of steam and left, I offered to buy Gage a new cup of coffee."

That was as much as she wanted to tell him. Talking to Gage was one thing. Interrogating both Bridey and Sheila Sorrell about Francine was another matter entirely. She must have done something to make Tripp suspicious because he leaned against the counter, crossed his arms over his chest, and settled back as if he'd stand there as long as it took to get at the truth. "And?"

The single-word question puzzled her. "And what?"

"And what did you learn about DiSalvo and his daughter? I don't imagine Gage filled you in on all the nitty-gritty details, but Bridey would have."

She had to wonder if members of the Special Forces got trained how to ferret out information or if it was talent that Tripp had been born with. There was no way to know, and it didn't matter.

"Bridey asked me why Gage had needed a new cup of coffee so soon after he'd just bought one. I told her he'd thrown it away, claiming it had gotten cold. The truth was that Mrs. Denman had accused him of whiling away hours in the coffee shop instead of doing the job her taxes paid him to do. Evidently, the police and the prosecutor aren't moving fast enough to please her. She's wanting to get into her father's house, but it's still being considered part of the ongoing investigation. They also haven't released the body, so she hasn't been able to make funeral arrangements."

"I think it's understandable that she's upset about that."

"True, but I hated hearing her rip into Gage about it."

To lessen the tension in the kitchen, she sat down at the table and did her best to look relaxed as she filled Tripp in on everything Bridey had told her about the strained relationship between Mr. DiSalvo and his daughter. "Bridey said it was always possible they'd healed the breach at some point, even if she hadn't heard that had happened."

Deciding to go for full disclosure, she added, "We also talked about how DiSalvo treated some of the business owners in town. He checked out Bridey's place a couple of times when she first opened. She always got the impression he wasn't there because he loved coffee and muffins. He stopped short of doing a white glove test, but he was definitely deciding if her shop was worthy of being on Main Street. She never heard any complaints from him, so she must have passed his self-appointed inspection."

By that point, Tripp had joined her at the table. "It was like his complaints about Owen's food truck."

"Yep, and the motorcycle repair shop and the bar. I don't know that last part for sure, but that's what Gil told me."

"Sounds like DiSalvo didn't know how to keep his nose out of other people's business. That's a recipe for trouble, especially if he poked the wrong sleeping bear with a stick."

That image made her laugh. "True enough. So, are we good?"

"Promise me that you'll do your best to stay off everyone's radar when it comes to this case. I know people tell you things even when you're not trying to unravel a mystery, and you can't help but ask more questions when they do. But I want you to remember something when it comes to this case. If you're right about Gary being innocent, the real killer is still out there. He framed another man for murder and did it well enough that the police think they've got their guy. You don't want someone that cold-blooded to learn you're out to clear Gary's name."

She shivered, knowing he was right. "I'm not sure I can live with myself if I let an innocent man go to prison. That would make me a coward on so many levels."

Tripp stared at her long and hard. He finally sighed and stood up. "Yeah, I get that. Just be careful. Call Gage if you learn anything solid and let him take over. And for goodness' sake, if you decide to go haring off to look at that mobile-home park, don't go alone. At least wait until I can go with you."

She could live with that. "It's a deal. I have one question before you leave."

He was already halfway out the door. "Which is?"

"Dutch apple, coconut cream, or pumpkin?"

His answering smile was every bit as dazzling as the one he'd bestowed on the ladies earlier. "Dutch apple."

Then he was gone, leaving her stewing over what to do next. There was nothing more she could do to figure out who had hunted down and killed James DiSalvo during the race, but maybe she could do something for Gil. It was really not much harder to make two pies instead of one. She had plenty of apples, and there was plenty of time to get the pies baked and deliver Gil's before Tripp came back over for dinner.

And if Gil happened to bring her up-to-date on the case while she was there, so much the better.

CHAPTER 16

Two hours later, Abby drove into the parking lot in front of Gil's repair shop. There were several motorcycles parked out front, which gave her pause. Suddenly one of Gage's past lectures started playing on a repeating loop in her head. He'd been real clear the Pratts presented no threat to her, but she needed be wary of their clientele. What should she do? Go in or go away? And why hadn't she brought Zeke along for moral support?

She could text Gil and ask him to meet her outside and give him the pie from the safety of the parking lot. He probably wouldn't think anything of it if she did. But no, she wouldn't do that. Even if pragmatic, it was cowardly. Instead, she'd make a quick trip in just to drop off the pie. If he asked why the hurry, she could truthfully say that she was expecting company for dinner. Taking a deep breath, she retrieved the pie from the back seat and started toward the garage.

Before entering the work bay, she pasted what she hoped was a cheerful, not fearful, smile on her face. She could hear two men talking in the dim interior. One voice she recognized as Gil's, and the second sounded familiar even though she couldn't quite place it. At least it didn't sound like an entire bike gang had taken up residence inside.

Feeling better about the situation, she picked up speed before she lost all momentum and drifted to a complete stop. That would be even more embarrassing than shoving the pie at Gil from her car window like she was an ATM for desserts.

Her sudden appearance cut off the ongoing discussion between one word and the next. Gil was perched on a tall stool next to a workbench. He looked surprised to see her, but not unhappy. He grabbed another stool and pulled it close to where he'd been sitting. "Abby, come on in and take a load off! Have you two met?"

She immediately recognized Gil's other visitor as the bartender from the bar up the street. "We've not been officially introduced, but our paths have crossed. I'm Abby McCree, and you work at Beer."

He cringed a little at her use of the nickname Tripp's friends had given the place. Glowing in cheerful red neon script, that single word was the only sign on the place. If it had another name, she'd never heard it. Regardless, he rose to his feet and held out his hand. "Actually, I'm the owner, Liam Grainger. It's nice to put a name to the face, Ms. McCree."

"Please, call me Abby. Any friend of Gil's and all that."

Gil glanced at her hands and asked, "So what brings you here?"

She held out the box containing his pie. "I got the urge to bake and thought I'd share."

When she took the lid off the box, the combined scents of cinnamon, nutmeg, and baked apples wafted out to perfume the air. Both men leaned in close to draw in deep breaths, their expressions turning both greedy and hungry.

Gil took the box and set it on his workbench and started to put the lid back on when Liam protested. "Hey, don't tell me you're not going to share. That would be all kinds of rude."

Abby tried not to laugh as Gil pretended to consider doing exactly that. "Fine. I wouldn't want Abby to figure out what a selfish jerk I really am. For some bizarre reason, she actually thinks I'm a nice guy."

When that assessment sent Liam off into gales of laughter, Abby joined right in. So did Gil after a second. "Okay, she's smarter than that, but she likes me anyway. Give me a minute, and I'll grab a couple of plates and forks from the back."

When he was out of sight, she lowered her voice to ask, "How's he doing?"

Liam shrugged. "As well as can be expected. He's cut back on the number of jobs he's taking on right now. He'll do any emergency repairs, but no new custom work. At least Casey is doing as much as he can to help out. He's up at the bar having a late lunch right now. When he came in alone, I walked down to see why Gil wasn't eating with him. Turns out friends have been dropping off enough food that he doesn't have to cook. I think he's been surprised by the show of support."

"At least it lets him know he's not alone in this."

Liam studied her for a few seconds. "I take it you're in the 'Gary is innocent' corner."

"Firmly. It just doesn't make sense why he'd use his own tool. And someone would've surely noticed him carrying a torque wrench in the race. Even if he finished farther back in the pack than expected, it wasn't long enough for him to sneak off the route, get the tool, and then track down the councilman."

The bar owner gave her an approving look. "You've been giving this a lot of thought. From what I understand, Gary restrained himself well enough not to take a swing at DiSalvo during their argument before the race, even though the man had deliberately provoked him. I'm not sure I would've been able to do that myself. DiSalvo had a habit of trying everything he could think of to cost me my liquor license. I also take it pretty personally when holier-than-thou types start telling me that my business will be the ruination of the town."

"Seriously? He actually said that to your face?"

"Yep, and on more than one occasion."

Now she felt indignant on his behalf, too. "What was wrong with that man? You offer great burgers, the best microbrew selection in the area, and high-quality pool tables."

His eyes lit up. "So I'm guessing you're the lady pool shark Tripp Blackston mentioned when he and his buddies were in not too long ago."

Her mother would be horrified to know Abby had earned that reputation, but that didn't keep her from taking pride in it. "Yep, that's me. Poor guy, I'm not sure he'll ever get over the way I cleaned his clock the first time we played. I don't know what Tripp's been saying about me, but even Gage Logan swears he's afraid to take me on."

By that point, Gil was back with plates, forks, and a black combat knife with at least a nine-inch blade. He held it out for her inspection. "Sorry, but this was the best thing I could come up with to serve the pie. I cleaned it real good, though."

She laughed. "Far be it from me to question a man's choice of cooking utensils, Gil."

He deftly cut two huge pieces. Before he could cut a third, she stopped him. "I'll just take a sliver to see how it turned out. I baked a second one for dinner tonight."

He nodded and cut her a smaller wedge. "All the more for me to have later."

As far as she was concerned, there was no bigger compliment than having two men maintain complete radio silence for the time it took them to devour one of her creations. Liam finished ahead of Gil and was already reaching for what was left of the pie. Gil immediately gave him the stink eye and shoved the pie plate back out of his reach. "Abby is *my* friend, not yours. It's only right that I get to eat the rest of this very excellent pie by myself."

When Liam looked as if he was waiting for her to intervene, she held up her hands and shook her head. "Don't look at me. I just baked the darn thing. He doesn't have to share it if he doesn't want to, even if it makes him look like an ungrateful jerk to his friends."

Gil protested, "Hey, now! I already gave him a big piece. I was trying to save one for Casey when he comes back."

Liam snorted in disbelief. "Yeah, right. Dollars to dimes the rest of that pie disappears into your office as soon as the two of us turn our backs."

That inspired Gil to plunk the rest of the pie back in the box and shove the lid back on to cover it. "There, out of sight, out of mind. That should keep you from getting your sneaky mitts on it."

Not to be outdone, Liam said, "Don't think I will forget this the next time you ask for extra cheese on your burger at my place."

Their antics had her laughing. She hadn't seen this level of mature discourse since the second grade when she'd accidentally broken the red crayon she'd borrowed from Jennifer, the girl who sat next to her in class. After several days of snippy comments and hurt feelings, Abby had begged her mom to buy Jennifer a new box of crayons just to make peace.

When she shared that little tidbit from her past, Gil stared up at the ceiling for several long seconds before cutting another, much smaller, wedge of pie for his friend. "There. I hope you're happy now."

"Perfectly." Liam immediately dug right in and didn't look the least bit guilty about it.

Meanwhile, Gil took the pie back to his office, muttering under his breath that Casey better get his backside back soon if he hoped that there would still be any pie left for him. How he was supposed to know that the pie even existed was beyond Abby, but she didn't bother to ask.

Liam finished the last bite in record time. "Well, I should get back to the bar. That pie was amazing, Abby."

"Thanks, Liam."

He leaned in closer and slipped her a business card. "If

you think of anything I can do that will help Gil or Gary, don't hesitate to call me."

"I will."

Then he headed for the door, calling out, "Gil, I'm out of here. I'll nudge Casey back along if he isn't already on his way."

Gil stepped out of his office. "Thanks, Liam. I appreciate you coming by even if you did your sneaky best to eat my dessert."

He returned to his stool. "So, what's up, Abby? As much as I love apple pie, I suspect it was just an excuse to check on me."

She wrinkled her nose at having been caught out. "Maybe a little. I promised Tripp a pie to make up for laughing when Jean brought him another tuna casserole." She sighed. "None of which you needed to know, but I did want to make sure you're doing okay."

"I'm fine. I got the loan on the house and hired a better attorney. Gary isn't happy about me doing that, unappreciative idiot that he is. Neither of us is sure how much she's going to be able to help in the end, but I have to try."

"Is she also pushing him to take a plea deal?"

"Not so far. She hoping they'll let Gary make bail, saying they can clap one of those monitor things on his ankle. We're still waiting for word on that."

The dark tone in his voice made it clear that he didn't hold out much hope of seeing his brother outside of jail anytime soon. Her heart hurt for him. All of this was so wrong.

"Do you know if Gage is looking at any other suspects?"

When Gil picked up the combat knife, sticky apple pie

residue and all, and sent it flying past her to stick in the wall, she knew that had been the wrong question to ask. "Sorry, Gil, I didn't mean to upset you."

She didn't know which one of them was more surprised that she was still sitting there instead of bolting for the door. Gil blinked, his anger fading away almost as quickly as it had appeared. "No, it's me who should be sorry. You've done nothing but be nice to me, and here I go scaring you like that."

He walked over to pull the knife out of the wall and tossed it into his office and closed the door. While she was glad the knife was now safely out of reach, that little display of temper wasn't enough to drive her off.

"So about Gage . . ."

Gil ran his fingers through his hair in frustration. "Even if he had an open mind about the case, the prosecutor doesn't. He's got the murder weapon with both DiSalvo's blood and Gary's fingerprints on it, witnesses that say Gary was out of control angry at the victim the day of the race, and a documented history of problems between the two of them. As far as he's concerned, it's a slam-dunk conviction. He can't understand why Gary hasn't leapt at the chance to cut a deal."

"Allowing for that, was Gage even looking at anyone else at all?"

Gil shook his head, looking even more dejected. "If he was, he hasn't told me. Not sure why he would."

Then he perked up a little. "Why? Have you heard anything along that line?"

"No, but everyone I've talked to who had to deal with DiSalvo had the same opinion about him. He was the self-appointed judge and jury when it came to the suitability of small businesses here in Snowberry Creek.

Even the ones who managed to pass muster felt like they'd dodged a bullet when he didn't try to run them out of town."

"Well, I appreciate that you tried. It was a long shot at best."

Once again he drifted off into an unhappy silence. While he stewed, she was at a loss for what to say that would offer any comfort. She took the opportunity to check out their surroundings. She'd sort of expected the garage to be a greasy mess, but instead she found herself impressed. The room, while not enormous, was well lit and airy. The painted concrete floor was nearly spotless and the workbenches clean and tidy.

But it was the enormous array of tools that she found intriguing. They were all either hung in orderly rows on pegboard lining the walls or neatly tucked away in one of the large rolling toolboxes. She didn't know what all the different tools were for, but both Gil and Gary did. What's more, they also knew where each and every one of them belonged.

So if something . . . say a torque wrench, for example, had gone missing, why hadn't they noticed? It seemed unlikely they would've tolerated someone wandering around the shop unattended long enough to steal anything. Well, except for maybe Casey. Even then, surely Gary or Gil would have noticed. She suspected that normally the brothers wouldn't have left him alone very often. Regardless, she bet the prosecuting attorney planned to argue that the only person who could've taken Gary's wrench was Gary himself. The fact that no one had seen him with it the day of the race meant nothing. He would've had any number of opportunities to hide the darn thing in the park, days before the actual event.

Feeling as if she were channeling the prosecutor's mindset, she suspected that scenario fit the textbook definition of premeditated murder.

Maybe she was naïve, but she refused to believe that was what happened. Even if Gary had hidden his alleged weapon of choice ahead of time, why wouldn't he have done something equally clever to get rid of the darn thing? He could've thrown it into the river or stashed it some distance away from the scene of the crime to be retrieved at a later date. It was only bad luck that the body was found so quickly. If that hadn't happened, he would've had plenty of time to come back for the wrench.

Gil shifted on his stool and leaned toward her. "Your mind is going a mile a minute right now. Do I want to know what's going on in that head of yours?"

Maybe not, but she wasn't going to lie to him. Not about something this important.

She waved her hand around in the air to point out their surroundings. "First of all, this is the first time I've been in your shop, and I honestly didn't know what to expect. No offense, the outside of the building is pretty much a cinder block eyesore, but it's amazing in here. Neat, clean, and everything in its place. Professional and impressive to the nth degree."

He grinned a little at her assessment of his place of business. "I'd thank you, but I sense there's a big 'but' coming."

"Yeah, there is." She pointed to the row of torque wrenches hanging on the far wall, not that she'd actually known what one looked like until she'd googled images of them. The row on what she assumed was Gil's side of the shop was complete. However, there were several telltale spaces toward the end of the identical row that must belong to Gary. She figured one of the missing wrenches was the murder weapon and the others were the ones Gage's men had confiscated.

"How did the two of you not notice one of Gary's wrenches was missing?"

He grimaced. "To be honest, I don't know. I wasn't in the shop all that much the last week leading up to the race, but I have no idea why Gary didn't notice. Well, maybe because he was having trouble keeping up with the work. We'd deliberately not taken on any major projects for a week or two before Founder's Day, but one of our best customers managed to wreck his bike and had it towed here. Gary felt like he had no choice but to fix it. Between that and doing everything else while I was missing in action, maybe he just wasn't paying attention."

"But who could've come in here and waltzed out with a tool? I can't imagine either of you ever leave the place undefended when strangers are around."

He took a long, slow look around the room. "No idea. We have a lot repeat customers. Some we trust and some not so much. As a rule, we don't let anyone hang out in here if we're actually working. After hours, sometimes friends stop by to drink a few beers and shoot the breeze. I could ask Gary if any of our regulars were around the week before the race. For sure, the wrench couldn't have disappeared much before that without one of us noticing."

That was something she had been wondering about. "When will you get to see him again?"

"The new attorney is going to set up another appointment for us to meet with Gary at the jail in the next day or so. If I learn anything, I'll call you."

"That's good." She held up her hand with the first two

fingers crossed. "I hope he can think of something that will create some 'reasonable doubt' issues in his case."

Gil glanced toward a motorcycle he had up on some kind of rack that was designed to raise the bike off the floor. His unspoken message came through loud and clear. She glanced around the shop and finally spotted a clock on the far wall that featured a huge motorcycle being ridden by a hot chick in black leather. It was definitely time for her to be going.

"Well, I'd better hit the road."

He walked Abby out to her car. "Thanks again for the pie and the company."

"Anytime." She got in the car and rolled the window down. "Share the pie with Casey and tell him I said hi."

The mention of his assistant's name had Gil frowning. "I'll have to call Liam to see if Casey said if he was heading home or what. Of course it's always possible he managed to get lost between here and the bar. It wouldn't be the first time. It's a good thing we're not all that busy right now. Casey does good work when he's here, but I swear sometimes he's part ghost with the way he can up and disappear with no warning."

There was nothing Abby could do to help Gil with his employee problems, so she waved and headed home.

CHAPTER 17

Dinner went well. At least Jean had donated another of her gourmet tuna casseroles to the menu—the one with Gruyère cheese, water chestnuts, and fresh dill. In addition to the pie, Abby's other contribution was a spinach salad. Tripp had gone the extra mile by picking up a six-pack of one of their favorite microbrews. If he hadn't, she would've had to offer him wine, and that would've been problematic.

Tripp gave her a suspicious look. "I don't know what to make of that expression on your face, but it's unsettling."

She held up her drink. "I just realized why I'm glad you brought beer. I learned a lot from Aunt Sybil about entertaining, but she never told me if canned tuna calls for white wine or red."

His eyes held a glint of humor. "Everyone knows tuna delight requires a good rosé."

"I'll make special note of that, especially considering how often Jean likes to surprise you with another of her creations."

He reached for another beer and popped the top. "I really wish she'd stop, but there's no way to convince her that I'm perfectly capable of cooking for myself."

Abby feigned surprise. "Really? If you're such an accomplished chef, how come I end up feeding you so often?"

Not that she minded. She'd grown tired of cooking for one shortly after she and her ex-husband had separated. That didn't mean she wouldn't give Tripp some grief whenever the opportunity presented itself.

For a second she was pretty sure he looked a little guilty, but his expression quickly shifted gears to a superior sneer. "As the man who occasionally has to save your cute . . . uh, hide, it's imperative that I stick as close to you as possible. I can't be around twenty-four seven, but I do try to check on you as often as possible."

She rolled her eyes. "I thought your self-assigned duty was to eat as many of the things that I bake as possible. You know, to protect me from eating too many of my creations myself."

He sat up proudly. "I do that, too. Unlike most people, I'm a talented multitasker."

There was no winning with this man. Time to change the subject. "Pie now or later after we get back?"

He'd been about to take another drink, but he set the bottle back down on the table a little harder than was necessary. "And where might we be going?"

"You said if I wanted to drive through the mobile-home park that I had to take you with me. I'm more than happy to go by myself, but you seem to operate under the mistaken impression that I can't handle a simple drive-by without you riding shotgun."

He drained his beer while he considered her invitation. "Fine, we can go. Are there any other stops you want to make on this tour?"

Come to think of it, there was. "Yeah, I'm going to look up the address for James DiSalvo's house."

Tripp heaved a big sigh. "And why would you want to do that? It's not like you're going to find him at home."

Lord, she hoped not. She didn't believe in ghosts, but he was exactly the kind of person she could imagine coming back to haunt the town. She shuddered at the idea of his specter prowling the streets to make sure the place didn't fall to pieces without him there to keep an eye on things.

"I wanted to see if the police have finished up their investigation there. I know his daughter was anxious to take control of the estate as soon as possible."

"Fine, we can make a side trip there, too." Tripp frowned a bit. "But if she and her father hadn't actually reconciled somewhere along the line, what makes her think she was still in the will? Nothing I've heard about DiSalvo makes me think he was a forgiving kind of guy. It seems more likely he'd cut her out of the will to teach her some kind of a lesson."

Abby had been in the process of standing up to get started clearing the table, but Tripp's observation had her dropping back into her chair. "Wow, I never thought about that. Even if they weren't talking, they were still family. No one has mentioned him having any other kids. You'd think he'd want his estate to go to his daughter or his grandson."

"Not everyone has a close-knit family, Abs. You and I are lucky that way. Our respective mothers might drive us crazy once in a while, but we've never had to doubt that they'd come running if we needed them. They also know it's a two-way road."

He had that right. If DiSalvo had cut his daughter not just out of his life, but his estate as well, Francine would have nothing to gain by his death. Well, except for revenge, always a powerful motive. Besides, maybe she didn't know the terms of his will and had decided it was worth a throw of the dice.

All of this was useless speculation, especially since she had no concrete evidence to indicate Francine had been involved in his murder. Wanting someone other than Gary Pratt to be guilty of the crime was hardly a good reason to suspect someone. Deciding she was spinning in circles, Abby put her revved-up energy to better use and cleared the table.

Half an hour later she slowly turned into the Snowberry Creek Mobile Home Park. The paint on the carved wooden sign that divided the driveway down the middle looked fresh, even if a bit sloppy. Someone definitely needed to take a kindergarten refresher course about coloring within the lines. The royal blue background was streaked with drips of white paint from the raised lettering. Several random holes in the wood looked as if they'd been badly patched and then repainted.

Once they were past the entrance, she turned right and

followed the narrow road that wound through the complex. As they drove over the third speed bump in less than a hundred feet, she groaned. "Sorry, Tripp, this quick cruise is going to take a lot longer than expected. I get that they don't want people racing through here, but this is ridiculous. I've never seen speed bumps this big. It's like they're on steroids."

Tripp didn't seem perturbed by their somewhat jarring ride. "In the next stretch of straight road, you could always try to build up enough speed to use one as a take-off ramp and see how many you can clear before we crash back down to the ground. You know, like daredevil motorcycle riders jumping over busses but on a smaller scale."

"Cute image, but I can't afford the repairs on the car."

They continued on their bumpy way. At least at the speed she was driving, she had plenty of time to look around. It wasn't hard to spot the pots of rather shopworn petunias haphazardly scattered throughout the park. Her friends had been right about the so-called upgrades not warranting a huge increase in rent.

The homes themselves varied a lot in condition. Most were the smaller, single-width style homes with a few double-wides located on large spots along the outer edges of the park. Some tenants kept the area around their home immaculate, the flowerbeds free of weeds, and the grass neatly edged and mowed. Others, not so much.

At last they made the final turn leading back to the entrance. Tripp frowned and sat up taller. "Have you noticed how many of these places have a FOR RENT sign in the yard? And there's almost no one out and about around the ones that are apparently still occupied."

"Yeah, I have. It's weird. Almost too quiet, considering the number of homes."

On impulse, she coasted to a stop. She pointed to a plexiglass box nailed to a four-by-four stuck in the ground by the next home with one of the rental signs. "Can you get out and grab one of the information flyers from that box? Let's see if it tells us what's going on."

At least Tripp didn't argue. He grabbed a couple of the photocopied brochures and handed one to her after he got back into the car. She skimmed hers before starting off again. "I don't know about you, but it left me with more questions than answers."

Tripp tossed his up on the dash. "Has this place always been limited to people over sixty?"

"Jean and company would probably know. Their friend who moved out of here would definitely have met that criteria."

"The owners' covenants are interesting. I get that they want people to keep their places up, but saying you can't have more than one vehicle or that guests can't stay for more than a week seems pretty intrusive. What if two people live in the home and both of them drive? That hardly seems fair. And who has the right to tell folks they can't have barbecue grills? That's almost unpatriotic."

"Well, Glenda or Louise said that DiSalvo seemed intent on driving some of the existing tenants out of the place. If raising rents didn't do the trick, maybe making the rules worse and worse would."

"Messing with people's lives like that is just wrong."

She couldn't disagree. All in all, it was a pretty depressing place, and it was a relief to ease her sedan over one of the last jumbo speed bumps on their way to the exit. "Not sure I learned anything important, but the people who lived here didn't care about painted speed bumps and petunias. This was home. Moving because they want to or because they couldn't take care of the place by themselves anymore is one thing. Being forced out had to be heartbreaking."

"And most likely infuriating. Maybe even dangerously so."

"Why do you say that?"

Tripp pointed toward the sign at the park entrance. "Did you notice those dings in the sign that had been repaired and then painted?"

"Yeah, I did. Why?"

"They're bullet holes. Either someone's been taking potshots at it on a regular basis or else they went on one big shooting spree."

Abby hit the gas, ignoring the way her car groaned and shimmied as she hit the last speed bump faster than was wise. At least Tripp laughed as they both bounced up off their seats as far as their seat belts allowed. "Sorry, Abs, I didn't mean to freak you out."

"I would claim that I'm just speeding things up so you can get back to your pie, but that would be a lie." She handed him her phone once they'd reached the safety of the road outside of the park. "I programed DiSalvo's address into my GPS. Let's cruise by and then head back home."

As it turned out, his house was surprisingly close by. The edge of his neighborhood backed up against the mobile-home park, but the contrast between the two places couldn't have been more stark. The mobile-home park skated just barely on the right edge of shabby, but the area surrounding DiSalvo's home was its polar opposite. The houses were upscale, and the yards were manicured to perfection and the flowerbeds landscaped to within an inch of their lives. Not a single weed or drooping petunia to be seen anywhere.

Oddly, the driveways were all empty. Considering it was early evening, it seemed unlikely that no one was home. She bet there was another set of stringent homeowner association rules responsible for all the cars being tucked out of sight and that James DiSalvo had written or at least approved all of the regulations the residents lived by. When she shared her theory with Tripp, he nodded. "That would be a sucker bet. With him gone, I'm thinking that by this time next year these yards will be awash with dandelions and those plastic pink flamingos and garden gnomes."

She snickered. "Lovely image. Another nice touch would be a giant motor home parked in the front yard or, better yet, a car up on cinder blocks."

"Perfect. Personally, I'd drag a bunch of lawn chairs around to the front, fill a cooler with beers, invite my rowdiest friends over, and park the biggest barbecue grill I can find by the front porch."

"Yeah, you'd fit right in here, I'm sure."

"Well, at least I'd wave at the neighbors. That's friendlier than DiSalvo probably ever was."

She eyed her companion. "Remind me to never get on your bad side. I'd hate to think how miserable you could make my life if you really set your mind to it."

He rubbed his hands together like an evil cartoon villain about to indulge in a little mayhem. "Don't say you weren't warned."

As they turned the corner onto DiSalvo's street, Abby hit the brakes. After the quiet elegance of the previous homes they'd passed, she gaped at the stark contrast of the view ahead. Tripp leaned as far forward as the seat belt would allow, as if those few inches would make all the difference in making sense of the chaos at the far end of the block.

There were several police cars parked along the street at all kinds of weird angles, effectively blocking traffic from both directions. "What on earth is going on?"

"I don't know, but that's Gage standing on the front lawn." Tripp pointed at the address on the nearest house and began counting off the houses. "I'm guessing all the activity is centered right in front of DiSalvo's place."

Abby shivered. "Suddenly I'm flashing back to the night when Jada's house was broken into and Gage asked us to come pick her up."

That had happened a while back to one of Owen's employees. Someone had kicked in Jada's front door in the middle of the night, and she'd been too scared to stay there alone. Just like then, the neighbors were standing out in their front yards to watch the drama play out. It was probably the biggest excitement this quiet neighborhood had experienced, well, maybe ever.

"Uh-oh."

It took a lot to worry Tripp. Whatever had spooked him had him sliding down farther in the seat, so she did the same. Feeling foolish, she whispered, "What's wrong?"

"We've been spotted."

That had her popping up to look around, a decision she immediately regretted. Yep, Gage was already marching toward them. He was still too far away for her to get a good look at his face, but there was enough anger in his gait to make his mood perfectly clear. No matter how they tried to play this, it wasn't going to turn out well.

"Think I can do a U-turn fast enough to avoid the

storm headed this way? You know, before Gage finds out for sure it was us."

"Don't even try." Tripp sighed and settled back to wait for whatever was to come. "Even if you could, there's nothing to keep him from tracking us down later. It's not like he doesn't know what kind of car you drive."

So much for making a discreet exit, so that left option B. Back when she was a kid, she got in less trouble if she owned up to whatever infraction that had her parents upset. Gage wasn't going to be happy with them, but he'd be a lot more angry if he had to hunt them down. Bracing herself for the tirade about to be unleashed on them, she sat up straighter and rolled down her window.

Her pulse picked up speed up as he got within shouting distance. It didn't help that some of the requisite nosy neighbors were tracking Gage's journey, following him down the street to get a better handle on the situation. Great, she lived to provide entertainment for the people of Snowberry Creek.

By that point, Gage had come to a halt a few inches from her door, his arms crossed over his chest and his mouth set in an angry line. She supposed she should be grateful that he waited until he stood within inches of her car to speak. They could indulge in some mature adult conversation, maybe a brief reminder that they shouldn't be anywhere near James DiSalvo's house, and then she and Tripp could apologize before slinking off in shame.

Unfortunately, she and Gage had been given different scripts for this little scene. After glaring at her for several seconds, he marched around to the other side of the car and tapped on the glass. Tripp muttered one of the words he rarely let slip in her presence and hit the button that lowered the window. Gage leaned in to get right up in

Tripp's face, or at least as close as he could with the car door between them.

"I would ask how the two of you just happened to be driving by DiSalvo's house, but I can guess." He jabbed a finger in her direction. "Abby got curious about where the man had lived, and you decided to ride shotgun on her little outing. What were you thinking?"

"I was thinking she was going to do it no matter what I said. Rather than waiting to see what kind of trouble she'd get into on her own, I came along to do damage control."

Boy, she really hated it when Gage and Tripp talked about her as if she wasn't there. They already knew how she felt, so she didn't bother to remind them. It was time to go. She revved the engine, hoping Gage would take the hint. He didn't even glance in her direction as he kept his attention focused on Tripp.

"So why did she want to take a scenic drive through here? And more importantly, were there any other stops on your grand tour?"

It was too much to be hoped Tripp wouldn't rat her out. "Abby heard that DiSalvo had bought out the Snowberry Creek Mobile Home Park a while back and then raised the rents in order to drive out some of the less desirable residents. She wanted to check it out for herself. Our intentions were to do a quick drive-through, but the jumbo speed bumps meant we had to keep it to a crawl."

"And what did you learn from the experience?"

Abby shot him a snide look. "For starters, to never drive through mobile-home parks if you want to protect the suspension on your car."

Whoops, maybe she should have resisted the urge to smart off to him. Rather than finding her quip amusing, it had ramped up the tension in the tight set of his jaw by a factor of ten. Before she could apologize, he made a grumbly noise that rivaled one of Zeke's growls when a squirrel invaded the backyard. "Abby, in case you haven't noticed, I'm not in the mood."

"I was about to apologize when you growled at me."

He clamped his hands down on the door frame hard enough to turn his knuckles white. "I don't growl."

She turned to Tripp for confirmation. He leaned back as far as the headrest would let him so that he wasn't trapped between them. Trying to play the role of neutral bystander, he said, "Gage, you growled. Abby, give the man a straight answer."

When Gage made the same sound again, Abby struggled to keep a straight face as she tried to come up with an answer that wouldn't set him off on another tirade. "I learned that a whole lot of the mobile homes have signs in the window saying they are available to rent. I had been told that DiSalvo did some superficial upgrades as an excuse for increasing the rents. The people who couldn't afford the higher costs either had to sell their homes or abandon them. From what we could see, it appears likely that's what happened."

Tripp raised his eyebrows as he looked at her and then jerked his head in Gage's direction a couple of times. What was he trying to tell her? He repeated the gesture, this time holding his hand as if it were a gun and shot it in Gage's direction. Oh, now she understood. "The sign in the entrance looks as if it's been shot at a few times. The holes were the right size for bullets, and they'd been patched and painted recently."

Gage glanced down the street and then back at her. "Interesting. I'll check to see if the vandalism has been reported and when."

"Well, if that's everything, we should get going."

Tripp brightened up. "Yeah, she baked me an apple pie, but she wouldn't let me have any until after our little outing."

Gage brightened up at the mention of pie. "You two can go now, but I think I'll stop by when I get done here. You know, to see if you've thought of anything else that you've learned that might pertain to the case."

Abby had to give the man credit for sneakiness. She would never thought of using official business as an excuse to force a friend to share his dessert. If Tripp minded, he didn't show it. "Sure, I'll be over at Abby's."

She put the car into gear, still watching all the activity at the house down the street. With the mood Gage was in right now, there was no way she was going to press for details. Maybe later, when he was mellowed out by apple pie and coffee, he might be more approachable. But to her surprise, it was Tripp who decided to ask questions.

"So what's going on down the street? Did something happen?"

Gage was still crouched down, putting him at their eye level. His expression morphed from really crabby to something approaching bleak. "Yeah, something did."

Then he stood up and walked away without a backward glance.

CHAPTER 18

"Do you think Gage changed his mind about coming?"

Tripp checked his phone before responding. "He wouldn't just blow us off without saying something, and I haven't gotten any texts from him. Have you?"

"Not unless it's been within the last two minutes."

The two of them were sitting out on the back porch enjoying the evening air. Granted, Gage hadn't given them any specific time to expect him, but it had now been over two hours since Abby had turned the car around and slunk back out of DiSalvo's neighborhood. If Gage had told them what was going on there, they might have had a better feel for how long he was going to be tied up.

If it had been a simple case of vandalism, that big of a police response would've been a bit over-the-top. There'd been three squad cars besides Gage's, so her gut feeling was that it had been something pretty serious. Maybe someone had taken advantage of the place being vacant to break in and help themselves to a bunch of valuables. DiSalvo struck her as someone who would've showcased his superior taste and financial status in his home. In short, a burglar's ideal target.

"Think it was a break-in?"

Tripp gave it some thought. "Maybe, but I can't imagine Gage shows up every time someone breaks into a house here in town. That's not exactly in the job description of the chief of police. He only gets involved in homicides because he has more experience in dealing with that kind of case than most of the people who work for him."

Abby reached down to scratch Zeke's head. He immediately rolled over and offered up his belly, which required her to lean down over the arm of her chair to reach him. Not exactly the most comfortable position for her, but her furry friend didn't ask much out of life. She picked up the threads of her conversation with Tripp. "So you're thinking the only reason Gage was there himself was because it involved DiSalvo's house."

"That would be my guess."

"Good point."

The sound of a car in the driveway derailed their conversation. Tripp stood up to verify Gage had finally put in an appearance. "He's here. I'll go pour him some coffee and cut him some pie."

A few seconds after Tripp disappeared through the back door, Gage rounded the corner of the house. Noticing how tired he looked, she pointed toward the third Adirondack chair on the porch. "It's a nice enough evening to sit out here, but we can also go inside if you'd prefer that."

His answer was to trudge up the steps and drop into the empty chair. "I'll go wherever the pie is."

"Tripp is inside cutting you a slice."

As they waited, Gage tipped his head back to rest against his chair and closed his eyes. "Have you got anything for a headache? Mine is pounding."

Knowing Tripp would have his hands full with a tray containing pieces of pie plus coffee for all three of them, she got up to help. Standing back out of the way, she held the door open for Tripp. "I'll be right back. Gage needs something for a headache."

By the time she returned, both men had already made serious inroads into their gigantic slices of pie. She handed Gage a small glass of water and a bottle of aspirin. Pointing to his plate, she said, "Judging by the way you're wolfing down that pie, I'm guessing you skipped dinner."

"Yeah, I did, but this hits the spot."

"Not exactly a balanced meal, though." She was already reviewing the contents of her refrigerator in her head to see what she could put together in a hurry. "We have some of Jean's best tuna casserole left from dinner, along with some salad. I can fix you a plate."

"Maybe just the salad."

Tripp was about to take another bite of his pie but stopped midmotion. "If I can eat Jean's casserole, you can."

Gage chuckled. "I actually don't mind tuna casserole, but I've already had more than my daily allotment of carbs for the day."

She made a second trip inside to fix him a bowl of the spinach salad, adding a hardboiled egg and some extra cheese so he got at least some protein with his meal. Back outside, the two men had lapsed into silence. She handed Gage the rest of his meal and left him to eat in peace.

Gage wasn't the only one enjoying the quiet. Tripp relaxed and stretched his long legs out as he stared out toward the back of the property. The only sounds came from the breeze stirring through the row of enormous cedars and firs along the side of the yard and the rough rumble of Zeke snoring as he dozed at her feet.

But all good things come to an end. Gage set his empty bowl on the porch railing, took off his hat, and ran his fingers through his hair. "So tell me again why you felt the need to check out the mobile-home park and DiSalvo's house."

He sounded serious, a little tired, but surprisingly not at all angry. He already knew she was worried about both of the Pratt brothers, so there was no use in rehashing that part of the discussion. Instead, she repeated what she'd already told him about the mobile-home park. Then she added, "I don't have any specific information that would indicate anyone who lived there or maybe still does ever made any direct threats at Mr. DiSalvo. But if Gary Pratt didn't kill him, then somebody else did. If so, there has to be a reason someone was angry enough at the man to commit murder. Being forced out of your home seems like a pretty strong motive."

Gage flexed his hands and then cracked his knuckles. "And you think you're more qualified than the entire police department, not to mention the prosecuting attorney's office, to investigate the crime."

Since he didn't exactly word that as a question, she decided his comment didn't require a response. Plunging ahead, she moved on to why she wanted to drive by the councilman's house. "We were going to drive by DiSalvo's house to see if it was still taped off as a crime scene."

"And why would you care about that?"

"Mostly just curiosity. I also wondered if his daughter had finally been allowed inside and if she was going to be able to schedule his funeral. I know his lady friend was pretty upset when his daughter refused her offer of help. If what I was told was correct, Francine hung up on the woman."

Something she said had Gage sitting up straighter as if he'd just gotten a new influx of energy. "What girlfriend? No one's mentioned him having one. How did you hear about it?"

Well, wasn't that interesting?

Still, having to admit that she'd gotten Owen to refuse service to those three ladies felt a lot like when she was seventeen and had to tell her father that she'd dented the bumper on his new car. Cringing, she launched into the story. "Tripp, Mom, and I invited Gil to join us for dinner at Owen's restaurant the other night. He left just ahead of us, and we'd stepped outside as he walked by three women in the parking lot. One of them made sure he heard her describe him as a thug who belonged in jail with his murdering brother and that the restaurant would obviously serve anyone."

Thankfully, Tripp picked up their tale from there. "So to prove the woman wrong about that, Abby called Owen and told him what had happened. He met the trio at the door and told them they weren't welcome in his restaurant."

But then Tripp frowned. "Nothing they said that night indicated any of them knew DiSalvo, though."

"No, they didn't. I found that out when I took Zeke for a walk through the national forest and ended up at the park in town. One of the other ladies was out power walking when she spotted me. Evidently it hadn't taken them long to figure out that I was the reason they missed out on Owen's barbecue. She and I made peace, and she explained why her friend was taking Mr. DiSalvo's death pretty hard. She's been his plus-one for some time and had hoped their relationship would develop into something permanent. When Francine refused to let her help with the funeral, she took it pretty hard."

Somewhere in her dissertation, Gage had taken out his spiral notebook and started writing. "Did you get her name?"

Abby thought back. "Sheila Sorrell is the woman I talked to, and I'm pretty sure she said her friend's first name was Georgia. I don't think she mentioned a last name."

"Well, it's a place to start."

She had so many questions now, but none that she thought he'd appreciate her asking. But to her surprise, he offered up some answers anyway. "To save you another trip by DiSalvo's house, we hadn't taken down the crime tape yet, but we would have in the next day or so. Now we have a break-in to investigate. I can't share many details about what happened."

"Was anything taken?"

He let out a big sigh. "No way to know because the place was wrecked. His daughter hasn't been in his house for years as far as I can tell, so she won't be much help. That's one reason I'm going to try to track down his lady friend. Maybe she'll be able to tell."

The aspirin must have kicked in because the deep lines

bracketing Gage's mouth had softened, and he was no longer squinting as if the sunlight hurt his eyes. He tucked his notebook back in his pocket and picked up his hat. "I'd better head out. I don't want my daughter to think I've abandoned her."

Tripp offered him a commiserating look. "Or to think that it's safe to have the boyfriend move in to keep her company while you're not around."

Gage did a spit take with his coffee. After wiping his mouth with his sleeve, he glared at his friend. "What boyfriend? What have you heard?"

By that point, Tripp couldn't hold back his laughter. "Sorry, Gage, I was just jerking your chain. I don't know anything about Syd's social life, but she's pretty and smart. You have to know some guy is going to be all over that. I was just thinking back to how I would've viewed that opportunity when I was in high school. You know you would've jumped on a chance like that when you were that age."

"Geez, I don't need you putting images like that in my head. I trust my daughter." That didn't keep him from immediately dialing her number. "Hey, kiddo. Just wanted to check in to see how you're doing."

Abby couldn't make out what Sydney was saying, but she sounded cheery and chatty. Gage relaxed back into his chair, still occasionally glaring at Tripp, who looked totally unrepentant. Finally, when Sydney paused to draw a breath, Gage jumped back into the conversation. "I'm going to head home in a few minutes. Do I need to pick up anything on the way?"

He listened for another few seconds. "Okay, text me the list. For now, go ahead and order pizza for your friends. See you soon."

Abby just had to ask, "Friends, as in plural?"

Gage looked considerably calmer. "Yeah, her political science teacher assigned a group project. Syd invited all of her team members over to work on it. I think she said there are six counting her."

"Any of them boys?"

Gage opened his mouth as if to respond to Tripp's question, but then didn't say anything. Instead, he picked up his dishes and carried them into the house. When he came back out, he patted her on the shoulder. "Thanks for the aspirin, pie, salad, and good company. Also for the information about the mobile-home park and DiSalvo's plus-one lady."

He glared at Tripp. "Thanks for nothing, jerk."

As Tripp laughed and held up his hands in surrender, Gage shook his finger in Abby's face. "Stay out of my case. It's not your job. It's mine. Besides, I hate listening to your idiot tenant complain about all the gray hair he's sporting now from trying to save you from yourself."

Then he patted Zeke on the head and left. Abby waited until she heard his car back down her driveway before speaking. "So, who do you think broke into DiSalvo's house?"

Tripp shook his head and sighed. "Seriously? Did you not hear what Gage just said?"

"About what? You don't have any gray hair." Not that she could see from where she was sitting.

"Don't be cute. He told you to stay out of the case, and I'm pretty sure that edict applies to me as well."

She leaned closer to him, studying his dark hair. "Oops, I was wrong about the no-gray-hair thing. Sorry if those are my fault."

He immediately rubbed his hand over the side of his

head as if he could pick out the offending hairs by touch alone. "Where? How many do you see?"

When she snickered, he realized he'd been had. "There's that mean streak again."

He glared at her as he picked up his dishes. "I'm out of here."

Still giggling, she followed him into the kitchen. "Sorry, Tripp. I promise I'll behave if you want to stay."

"I've got homework to do, not to mention laundry."

Disappointing, but understandable. "Well, if you get bored, I'll be here. I think Zeke and I will watch a movie."

"Have fun."

Instead of walking away, he stepped toward her. "Do me a favor. I know you're not going to give up on proving Gary innocent. I figure Gage knows that, too. But do you think for one night you could promise to behave? I mean it, no poking around or asking any questions, no matter how tempting it might be. It's hard to concentrate on my studies when I'm worrying about what you might be up to."

"Yeah, I can do that." She raised her right hand. "Scout's honor."

He rewarded her promise with a kiss that drove all thoughts of crime solving right out of her head. Then he smiled and headed back to his place. On the way out, he called back over his shoulder, "My alleged gray hairs and I thank you."

With Gage and Tripp both gone, the house seemed too quiet. Even Zeke seemed unhappy to have been deserted by two of his favorite people. Maybe a short walk would help.

"Come on, Zeke, I need to work off that big piece of pie I ate."

And while they strolled down the sidewalk, she decided there was nothing wrong with mentally reviewing everything she'd learned about James DiSalvo and the events before and after his death. Right? After all, it was all information she already had, so it wasn't as if she was out turning over new rocks to see what crawled out.

She was pretty sure Tripp wouldn't see it that way, but what he didn't know wouldn't hurt him . . . or hopefully her.

CHAPTER 19

Abby started off the next morning by texting Tripp that she needed to go to the library. Not that she normally felt obligated to keep him posted on where she was at all times. But after their conversation last night, she figured he'd appreciate knowing that she wasn't planning any nefarious adventures to hunt down a murderer on her own.

Feeling proud of herself, she strolled into the lobby of the city hall building, which housed the mayor's office, the police department, and the library. Abby waved at the desk sergeant as she headed directly for the library to pick up the books that she had reserved.

She'd almost made it through the library entrance when a loud commotion erupted behind her, at the police desk.

Determined to ignore whatever it was, she kept her gaze firmly on her destination and continued on her way. Unfortunately, checking out books only took a couple of minutes. When she walked back out into the lobby, the ruckus had only gotten worse. Two women were arguing loudly and waving their hands around as poor Sergeant Jackson Jones did his best to referee. His position blocked her view of the two combatants, but she didn't care who it was. She was more concerned with how to get past them without being noticed, since her car was parked right outside the front door of the building.

She froze in place, not sure what the wisest course of action might be. The library would offer a temporary sanctuary, but she had other stops to make before returning to the house. She also didn't like leaving Zeke home by himself for any longer than necessary. The door that led to the parking lot behind the building was in the wrong direction to reach her car, but right now it was the safer choice.

Deciding to err on the side of caution, she turned away from the ongoing argument and made her way across the lobby toward the rear door. It was tempting to hurry, but she figured that would increase the likelihood of drawing attention in her direction. Keeping to a slow pace, she made steady progress toward her target. But as she walked, she couldn't help but overhear bits and pieces of the ongoing argument.

The first voice was shrill and angry. "I don't care what you want, lady. You have no place here. He was my father . . . and you, well, we can all guess how you spent your time with him."

That comment resulted in a huge gasp of outrage from

the other woman. "At least I had a cordial relationship with James. You, his own daughter, couldn't even be bothered to send him a card on his birthday."

Throwing her good intentions to the wind, Abby turned around to see if her suspicions were on target. Sure enough, it was Francine Denman and her father's plus-one screaming at each other. At this point, Sergeant Jones had his phone in his hand, talking fast and furiously to someone on the other end of the line. She backed toward a convenient corner and watched as the drama continued.

The conversation had ratcheted up to an even higher volume. "My relationship with my father is none of your business, so stop embarrassing yourself by playing the role of martyr. Dad may have taken you to a few fancy dinners and maybe bought you a few shiny baubles along the way. He could be charming, but the only two things that ever mattered to him were his self-image and money."

Francine paused to draw a deep breath before launching right back in. "The bottom line, lady—and I use that term loosely—was that you're only fooling yourself if you honestly thought a few steaks and gaudy trinkets translated to any kind of emotional attachment on his part. If you don't believe me, ask the gaggle of other women who had the great misfortune to be his arm candy since my mother passed. Lord knows there's been enough of them."

Then she sneered and gave the other woman an assessing look. "Most were a lot better-looking than you, not to mention younger."

Georgia looked as if she were about to have a stroke. She charged toward Francine, her blood-red nails arched and heading right for Francine's face. Before she could make contact, Gage charged out of the door behind the sergeant's desk. The two men did their best to wrestle the two women back out of striking range without anyone getting hurt.

Gage planted himself between the two and roared, "That's enough! If you two don't want to end up in adjoining cells, I'd suggest you settle down right now."

Francine wasn't having it. "Don't threaten me, Chief Logan. If you'd done your job in a timely manner, I wouldn't have to come down here every day to see what the holdup is. I still haven't gotten into my father's home, which means I don't have access to his legal papers. His attorney claims he only handled Dad's business affairs and doesn't know anything about a will or trust or whatever Dad had set up. I have no idea who handled his personal stuff."

Georgia rolled her eyes. "If you're thinking he left you a dime, you're wrong. He quit thinking of you as his daughter years ago. He told me that in no uncertain terms."

From the way Francine flinched, Georgia had succeeded in landing a cruel blow. Rather than acknowledge the comment, Francine kept her focus directly on Gage. "I need to find out what kind of final arrangements my father wanted. My phone keeps ringing day and night with people wanting to know when the funeral will be."

Georgia immediately inserted herself back in the conversation. "I heard someone broke into James's home. Ask Francine where she was. I bet she did it."

Francine snapped back, "Me? Why on earth would I have to break into my father's house? Once the police are done fiddling around, I should be able to take possession of the place and everything in it, including my mother's jewelry. By the way, lady, if any of it is missing, I'll make sure the police know you're the one they should be looking at for the theft."

She shot a nasty look at Georgia. "I've heard from several people you talked him into letting you wear my mother's triple strand of pearls to some dinner dance."

Having made her point, she turned back to Gage. "Right now, all I'm worried about is the funeral."

Then she pointed at him and then at Sergeant Jones. "And you two are my witnesses when I tell this . . . this woman that she is not welcome to attend. If she dares show her face there, I will expect you to arrest her for trespassing."

The older woman hissed in outrage, and neither man seemed to know how to respond to that bombshell. Could she really be charged with trespassing at a funeral home or cemetery? Abby thought that was pretty iffy, but she had no idea who she could ask. Not Gage, that was for sure. Even though the situation was getting more interesting by the minute, it was past time to make a break for the door.

She sidled along the wall, timing her movements to when Gage was focused on the other two women. Escape was almost with her grasp when she risked one last glance back over her shoulder. Great, Gage was staring right at her, his eyes narrowed in suspicion. She held up her library books to show him why she'd been there. Rather than wait to see if he understood, she bolted out the back door and hustled around to the front of the building.

The rest of her errands would have to wait until tomorrow. If either of those women learned she'd witnessed their outrageous behavior, neither of them would take the news well. She didn't want to risk running into them right now.

Luck was with her, and she made it back to her car with no problem. As she drove, Abby replayed what she'd seen and heard. It was obvious Francine had no use for her father's lady friend, and apparently her father had burned through several different relationships since his wife's death. Had that come as news to Georgia? Had he dumped someone in order to date her? If so, there might be someone else Gage hadn't even considered as a suspect out there who had it in for the man.

If she took both women at their word, neither of them had been inside DiSalvo's house since his death. So, had the break-in been random, just someone hoping to make a quick buck by robbing the place because the owner had died? Until Gage learned what, if anything, had been taken, that would probably remain an open question.

Had DiSalvo really let other women borrow his late wife's jewelry? Even if he'd had the right to do so, she could understand why that would upset Francine. Who had she been talking to that had told her about Georgia's alleged interest in her mother's pearls? It had to be someone close to her father or Georgia herself to have heard about it. Well, unless he and Francine had been talking more than most people realized.

When she pulled into her driveway, she could hear the weed trimmer running in the backyard. Considering Gage might be upset she'd witnessed the altercation between the two women, it might be a good idea to give Tripp fair warning about what had happened. She'd rather he heard it from her first. After parking her car, she took a deep breath and headed over to where Tripp was working. He had on protective headphones because of the noise, so she touched his arm to get his attention.

She waited until he shut off the machine and took off the headphones to speak. "We need to talk."

He frowned as soon as he got a good look at her face. "What's happened now?"

She held up the library books. "I went to the library just like I said I was going to do. It's not my fault that it shares the lobby with the police department."

He pinched the bridge of his nose and sighed. "Again, what's happened now? Or maybe I should be asking what you did to tick off Gage this time."

Did he have to assume that this was her fault? Biting back her irritation, she launched into her explanation. "I walked into the city hall through the front door. Although I waved at Sergeant Jones, I didn't stop to talk to him or anything. I went straight into the library, picked up these books, and walked out."

"And then?" he prompted when she didn't immediately continue.

"As I headed into the library, two women started hollering at Sergeant Jones. It wasn't until I was on my way out that I realized DiSalvo's daughter and his alleged girlfriend had decided to get into a shouting match right between me and the front door. I was parked out on the street, but I was understandably reluctant to walk past them to get out."

He set the trimmer down on the ground and crossed his arms over his chest to give her his undivided attention. "That was the smart thing to do, but I'm guessing there is more to the story."

"Well, I might have gotten distracted by their conversation for a short time." Feeling a bit defensive, she tried to justify her actions. "I should have kept going, but you would've stopped and stared, too. When DiSalvo's lady friend tried to claw his daughter's face, it took both Gage and Sergeant Jones to separate them. I've never seen anything like it. Seriously."

Before he could interrupt, she rushed to the finish. "I tried to make it to the back door of the building before anyone noticed me, but I know Gage spotted me. I left and didn't look back. I have no idea what happened after that, but I decided to come straight home rather than run the rest of my errands. I didn't want to risk running into either one of them once Gage kicked them to the curb."

"So you're telling me this in case Gage finally decides to lock you up for your own safety? You know, so I can bring Zeke for visits and sneak you cookies. And by the way, they'd be store-bought. Unlike you, I don't think people who get themselves thrown in the slammer deserve strawberry shakes or homemade baked goods."

She couldn't help but laugh. They both knew he'd feel obligated to bring her the good stuff because that's what she'd done for him. "I don't believe you. At the very least you'd show up with a giant slice of Frannie's coconut cream pie."

His smile turned wicked. "Yeah, but I'd sit right outside your cell and eat it in front of you. I might even bring a piece for Gage, so he could join in."

She mimicked his stance by crossing her arms over her chest. "I think that would constitute cruel and unusual punishment."

"More like tough love."

That last word seemed to hover in the air between them, leaving her speechless and him looking as if he wished he could press rewind and take it back. Abby stammered, "Tripp?"

She wasn't sure what she was going to ask him, but he didn't give her a chance to figure it out. "Look, I need to finish up here and then head back to school for a late class. If Gage comes hunting for you, tell him to let me know when visiting hours are."

Then he put his headphones back on, cranked up the trimmer and started edging the flower beds along the back of the house. She stared at his back for a long moment, watching and wondering what was going on in his head right now. Telling herself he'd meant nothing special by what he'd said, that it was just a figure of speech, she gave up and took her books inside.

She slipped Zeke a couple of his favorite treats. It was nice to have one uncomplicated male in her life. "Come on, boy. We'll go out on the front porch and enjoy the sun for a while. You can doze in the shade while I read."

After fixing herself a cold drink, she pondered the two books she'd brought home from the library. The decision about which one to read turned out to be easy. She wasn't in the right frame of mind to enjoy the romance. All things considered, figuring out "whodunit" would be a whole lot simpler than "what was Tripp thinking."

CHAPTER 20

Dinner was a sad affair. She finished off the leftover tuna casserole along with a small salad. Rather than sit at the kitchen table with all those empty chairs reminding her she was alone, she'd taken her plate to the living room to read while she ate. After giving the book a solid try, she gave up on the mystery after two chapters. There wasn't anything wrong with the story, but she couldn't seem to focus on the plot. At any other time, it would've been fine, but she couldn't help but be jealous of the way the amateur sleuth managed to stumble over the perfect clue at the exact best time. Too bad solving real-life mysteries didn't seem to work that way.

Rather than sitting there feeling sorry for herself, it was time to do something useful. "Zeke, I'm going to go upstairs and work on the baby quilt. You're welcome to join me if you'd like, but I won't blame you for giving me a wide berth right now. I'm not exactly fun company."

He took her at her word and stretched out in the middle of the living room floor with a satisfied sigh. She envied his simple life sometimes. All it took was a bowl of kibble, a few extra treats, and a sunbeam to sleep in to make him happy. He also had a few people to love and loved him back. Who could ask for more than that?

That thought had her flashing back to Tripp's offhand comment about tough love. Part of her insisted it was just a common expression, that it meant nothing. But for a moment when they were standing there face-to-face, that one word had left her flustered and wishing . . . well, she wasn't sure for what exactly.

Again, she needed to put that behind her and focus on something else. When she reached the sewing room, she paused outside of the door long enough to center herself. Doing her best to leave Gil's problems as well as her own out on the landing, she stepped across the threshold and turned on the light.

As always, Abby felt surrounded by her aunt's presence. Everywhere she looked she saw something that her aunt had touched, had loved. The day she'd cut out the baby quilt, Abby had left a pile of fabric scraps and her aunt's rotary cutter lying on the cutting table, which made her feel a bit guilty. Her aunt had always insisted that workers should respect their tools and keep their work area neat and clean. The bottom line was that Aunt Sybil couldn't abide clutter. She said it wasn't just a matter of protecting the tool itself, but that it also made things more efficient.

Hunting through a mess to find the right tool every time something needed to be done only made the job take that much longer. It was a habit that Abby hadn't quite mastered, but she was trying. In her mind, this was still Aunt Sybil's work space, and she wanted to honor that. Abby tossed the scraps in the trash and then glanced up at the ceiling as she slipped the cutter back into its box. "Sorry, Aunt Sybil. I'll do better."

She made quick work of straightening the rest of the room before settling in to sew more of the squares together. After each one was completed, she pressed the seams and then added it to the row of strips on the cutting table. It was gratifying to see the quilt gradually coming together. She was sure that Bridey and Seth, both artists in their own way, would appreciate her efforts.

After pressing the last strip, she debated whether to start sewing them together or let that wait for another day. Glancing out the window, she realized quite a bit of time had passed while she'd been working. Dinner had been hours ago, and she could use a snack. Some cheese and crackers along with a glass of wine would hit the spot.

It was also surprising that Zeke hadn't been up to check on her. While he enjoyed his naps, he didn't much like being ignored for this long. Knowing he'd forgive her anyway, she made a point of adding a couple of his favorite cookies to her plate. They could sit outside and watch the sun go down.

They'd just stepped out on the back porch when her phone rang. When she saw the name on the screen, she really wished she'd left the darn thing inside. As tempting as it was to ignore the call, she couldn't do that to Gage. Considering she'd been expecting to hear from him ever since he spotted her at city hall, it might be a relief to just get the discussion over with.

Trying to sound curious rather than worried, she swiped the screen and chirped, "Hey, Gage, what's up?"

"I was wondering if you were up to a game of pool at Beer. Gil is already here, and we were thinking you and Tripp would be the perfect suckers . . . I mean worthy opponents to play against. Losers buy the next round, so don't forget to bring lots of money."

Her spirits immediately brightened. "Sounds like fun, but I think Tripp had to study tonight."

Gage snorted. "He'd never turn down a chance to play pool."

"So why didn't you call him first?"

A couple of seconds passed before Gage answered. "Because I figured if I called to invite you directly, you'd know I understood you were at the library this morning and only accidentally walked into that disaster in the lobby."

The last vestiges of the dark cloud that had hovered over her all day finally dissipated completely. "Well, I guess I'll be seeing you soon. Better check the available balance on your credit card, Mr. Lawman, because you're going to need it tonight."

"Dream on, lady. I'm not sure how much credence to give Tripp's claims about your skills. Personally, I think it was his way of downplaying his embarrassment over being beaten by a—"

Abby cut him off right there. "You better not have been about to say he was embarrassed about being beaten by a girl, Gage. Because I'm telling you right now, that's insulting."

His amusement came through clearly. "I'd never be that stupid, Ms. McCree. I was going to say he was beaten by a pool hustler. As a Special Forces soldier, he should have known the enemy can take on many forms, some quite surprising ones. Feminine wiles are a particularly devious form of pool warfare."

By that point, she was laughing. "Enough, enough. I'll go roust out my partner in crime and be there inside half an hour. If he can't come for some reason, I'll call you back."

Feeling much better about life in general, she called Zeke back inside, grabbed her purse and headed across the backyard. As it turned out, she didn't even have to knock. Tripp stepped out on his porch with a beer in his hand. "What's up?"

"Dump your drink and put on some shoes. We've been challenged to a round of pool by Gil and Gage, and I'll want you clearheaded and sober when we get there. Gage has impugned my pool skills, implying you only said I was good at the game to avoid admitting you were taken in by my feminine wiles."

Rather than pour the beer out, Tripp guzzled it down. "So we're out to avenge your honor?"

"Well, that and to avoid paying their bar tab if we lose."

"Challenge accepted. I'll be right out."

An hour later, Gage was frowning big-time as she ran the table for the second time in a row while his partner glared at him. Gil gave up chalking his pool cue and leaned it against the wall. "Tell me again how I got stuck with you as a partner? I feel like this was a setup of some kind, and I've been had."

Gage gave him a disgusted look. "What kind of idiot would I have to be to set up my own partner to lose? Do you think I really wanted to buy this many drinks for Tripp and his pool-hustling girlfriend?"

That last bit almost caused Abby to screw up her shot, but she drew in a deep breath and slowly let it out. When the last ball rolled into the corner pocket, Gage slapped a twenty-dollar bill onto Tripp's palm. "I cannot believe she did it again."

Gil wasn't nearly as upset since he wasn't the one forking out money this time. When Tripp returned, the bar owner was with him. Liam had a pool cue in his hand. "I'm hearing rumblings that there's a good game to be had at this table."

He motioned for Gil, Gage, and Tripp to step back. "Gentlemen, I think it's time for someone to offer the lady some real competition. How about it, Abby? You up for a good game?"

She had a feeling her winning streak was about to come to an end, but it would be cowardly to refuse the challenge. "What kind of stakes are we playing for?"

Liam set up the table while he considered the question. "If I win, you owe me a dance. If you win, I'll make you one of the burgers you like so much and even throw in onion rings and fries."

"Make it burgers for my whole posse."

"Fine, two dances and burgers for you and these idiots. Best two out of three."

"You're on."

The only one who didn't look particularly happy about the situation was Tripp, but he didn't say anything. When Gage tossed a quarter high in the air, she called out, "Heads!"

"Heads it is. The lady goes first."

Abby lined up her shot and the game began. As it turned out, she and Liam were pretty evenly matched. She took the first game, and he took the second. While Gage racked up the balls for the third and deciding round. Gil patted her on the shoulder. "Stay loose, Abby. Don't even think about how this poor biker friend of yours will go to bed hungry tonight if you lose."

Gage gave her an equally sorrowful look. "And don't forget your favorite police officer, Abby, and how much he loves Liam's onion rings."

She made a show of looking around the bar. "I didn't know Deputy Chapin was here, too."

Clapping his hand over his heart and staggering back a step, Gage tried his best to look devastated. "That hurt."

Tripp joined in, but he kept his voice low enough that Abby was pretty sure she wasn't supposed to hear what he said. "Get over it, Gage. The lady came with me. If she loses, I have to watch her dance with someone else."

Ignoring Tripp's complaint, she pointed at Gil and Gage. "Thanks for the added pressure. Now get out of my way and let me concentrate."

Her three companions drew up stools and settled in to watch the final game of the match. They applauded and hooted when she sank a ball and booed with extra enthusiasm when Liam did. Their ridiculous antics drew the attention of others in the bar. She wasn't used to being in the spotlight, but she did her best to ignore the press of the crowd. When she missed the shot, her supporters groaned.

She stepped back from the table to give Liam room to move in for the kill. There were only a couple of balls left on the table, none of them in a great position for an easy score. As he circled the table looking for the best shot, she glanced at Tripp. He looked decidedly grim. Was Tripp really upset about the prospect of her dancing with someone else? She wasn't sure what to make of that. Lost in thought, she missed Liam's shot. Well, technically, it was Liam who missed the shot. Half the people watching applauded while the others groused about it.

She studied the table and smiled. His mistake had resulted in the remaining two shots being far easier ones. Seconds later, the bar erupted in applause. Liam joined in and then bowed in front of her.

"The burgers will be along shortly. Good game, lady. One of these days I'm going to want a rematch."

"Fair enough, and don't forget the onion rings."

He'd already started back toward the bar, but called back over his shoulder, "I wouldn't dare."

Abby returned her cue to the rack on the wall. When she turned around, Tripp was waiting for her. "Gage and Gil staked out a booth for us over in the corner. You played a good game. Congratulations."

"Thanks. I did it for the sake of starving bikers and favorite cops everywhere."

Then she glanced toward the already crowded dance floor on the other side of the bar. "I'll enjoy my winnings, but dancing would've been fun, too."

As soon as the words left her mouth, Tripp grabbed her hand and dragged her in that direction. "We've got time for a quick one before the burgers arrive."

He led the charge through the other dancers until he found a big enough opening in the crowd. Luck was with them, or at least she thought so, when a new song started, this one slow and romantic. Tripp pulled her into his arms and held her close as they gently swayed to the old R & B song. This wasn't the first time they'd danced together, and she hadn't forgotten how much she enjoyed the experience.

"Did you see the look on Gage's face when we beat him and Gil tonight? I can't believe they thought I had exaggerated how good you are."

"Maybe they fell victim to those feminine wiles that Gage mentioned earlier."

Tripp grinned. "And don't forget about Liam. He almost never loses a match."

"My mom would be so proud to know her daughter has earned herself a reputation as a pool shark."

She felt his laugh rumble through his chest. "Wait until she hears about all the challenges you'll start getting from the local talent."

"Seriously?"

"Yep, they'll all want to see if you're for real the next time there's a tournament, especially since you managed to beat Liam. Maybe Jean and the ladies can be your cheerleaders. I bet the three of them would love hanging out here watching their girl playing for burgers and beer."

Now she knew for sure he was jerking her chain. "I'll probably need some muscle to protect me from sore losers."

"No doubt."

"Are you up for the job? Or should I see if Gil has some free time? He can be pretty scary."

Tripp ignored her question as the song came to an end. After spinning her out and back into his arms, he kissed her. It felt like a claiming, especially when he finally answered her question. "I know you're joking about needing some muscle. I also know you were kidding about asking Gil, but I don't like the idea of you depending on anyone else to pull you out of the line of fire."

When he released his hold on her, her knees went all wobbly for a second. It was both a relief and a surprise that she managed to reach their booth and slide into the seat without mishap. As soon as Tripp joined her, Liam appeared with a big tray loaded down with food. He handed out burger baskets, which were followed by cold beers.

He gave Tripp a wary look before speaking to Abby. "Never let it be said that I don't pay off on my bets."

Then he grinned at Gage and added, "Not that I condone or allow real gambling in my fine establishment. This was just a friendly wager between friends."

Gage waved him off. "No problem, Liam. Besides, I can't exactly run you in, considering I had to buy a few beers for my friends here tonight."

He held up his drink and they all clinked bottles. Abby set hers down and tried not to look smug, although she suspected it was an epic fail on her part. "The good news, gentlemen, is that by the time we walk out of here, all evidence of any bets will have disappeared."

To illustrate what she meant, she picked up one of the onion rings and took a big bite. "The cops here in Snowberry Creek don't arrest people unless they have hardcore evidence of guilt."

As soon as the words were out of her mouth, she wanted to kick herself for being so thoughtless. She met Gil's gaze across the table and mouthed, "Sorry. I wasn't talking about your brother."

He shrugged it off. "It's okay."

No, it really wasn't, but there wasn't much more she could do right now. Hoping to redirect the conversation in a safer direction, she asked, "How are things at the garage? Are you keeping up okay with Casey's help?"

"More or less. At least he's someone to talk to, even if he does make a mess of things at times."

She understood that attitude. She loved the house her aunt had left her, but the three-story Victorian was way too big for just one person. At least she had Zeke for company. Well, and Tripp, too. Gil and his brother not only worked together, they shared their family home. Having Gary in jail left Gil alone on two fronts.

"Why don't you come over for dinner tomorrow night? Zeke misses you."

Gil rolled his eyes. "Yeah, right."

"Seriously, he's still sulking because we had dinner with you at Owen's, and he wasn't invited."

Tripp joined in. "He's also upset Owen sent extras home with you and didn't even send him scraps. That dog lives to mooch, which is hard to do when we eat at a restaurant. He carries a grudge, too. You'd be doing us both a favor if you came over."

Gil gave Abby a hopeful look "Will there be dessert involved? I'm having dreams about that pie you brought me."

That startled a laugh from Gage, who had been following their conversation with interest. "Do you even have to ask, Gil? This is Abby we're talking about. You can't walk in the door at her house without her shoving sugar in some form at you."

Even if it was true, she hadn't been force-feeding him all those cookies. "I hadn't realized it was such a hardship having to consume fresh baked goods, Gage. Next time, I won't bother making the effort. Serving carrot and celery sticks is so much healthier."

Then she gave Gage an evil look. "Better yet, I'll send your daughter a note telling her how often you end up at my kitchen table gobbling up cookies, pie, and coffee cake."

Gage winced as Tripp shook his head sadly. "Tsk, tsk, Gage. You've really blown it now. I can't imagine how you've forgotten about how mean Abby gets when she's riled. You'd better do some hardcore groveling pretty quick or it will be a cold day in you-know-where before you see another snickerdoodle, much less one of her apple pies."

"Fine, fine. Abby, I apologize. I didn't mean to offend you. I think I was just jealous that you were inviting Gil over, but not me."

She winced. That had been rude. "Sorry about that, Gage, but you're always welcome."

He laughed. "That's okay. As often as you've fed me, I've got no cause for complaint. Besides, I promised Sydney I'd go to the play at the high school tomorrow night."

"Is she in it?"

"Only behind the scenes, but she helped design the sets and wants me to see them."

He checked his watch. "I'd better get going. I hadn't planned on making an evening of it when I stopped by here for a cold one on my way home. Glad we did, though. I needed a night out."

After standing up, he offered Gil a rueful smile. "Thanks for being my partner, even if we did end up on the losing end of the deal."

"I enjoyed it, Gage." Then Gil pointed at Tripp. "Next

time we draw straws to see who gets to partner with Abby."

Tripp leaned back in the seat and put his arm around her shoulders. "Fat chance, biker man."

Gage left some money on the table as a tip. "I'll leave you folks to fight it out. Drive safe."

As she watched him make his way through the crowd, it occurred to Abby to wonder if it had been a bit weird for Gil to spend the evening with the police chief who had arrested his brother. When she asked him, he didn't seem bothered by it, at least not much. "This isn't the first time Gage and I have been on opposite sides in a situation, and he's always treated me fair. Can't fault the man for doing his job."

He gathered up their empty burger baskets and stacked them on the end of the table and lined up their empty bottles in a neat row beside them. She figured it gave him a way to keep his hands busy. "He did say that he's investigating whether the break-in at DiSalvo's house is connected to his murder."

Abby perked up at that bit of news. "That sounds encouraging. At least Gage seems willing to consider the possibility that the case isn't as cut-and-dried as the prosecutor thinks it is."

Gil looked slightly happier. "Actually, that's why he asked me to meet him here. He wanted me to hear about what was happening directly from him but away from his headquarters. Not sure why, though."

He pulled out his wallet and laid a ten on top of Gage's. "What time should I show up tomorrow?"

"Six o'clock would be good, but my schedule is flexible. What would work best for you?"

"I normally lock the doors at five and then straighten

the place up and put the tools away. Most days I'm on my way home by five thirty, but lately it's been taking longer. Casey does good work, but he's nowhere as organized as Gary is. Even when he tries to put everything back, he's more hindrance than help. Most days, it's easier to leave it and come in early the next day to straighten up before he comes in." He shook his head and added, "That's a roundabout way of saying that one way or another, I'll be at your place around six."

"Perfect. See you then."

She and Tripp followed Gil out into the parking lot and waved good-bye before they got into her car. As she drove home, something Gil had just said kept niggling at her mind. His comment about straightening up the garage and putting the tools away reminded her of her aunt's attitude about such things. She suspected Aunt Sybil and Gil would've hit it off had they ever met.

But that wasn't what had stuck out about the conversation. What if Gary had also waited to clean up when Casey wasn't there? That might explain why he hadn't noticed right away that one of his tools had gone missing. Maybe Gil—or better yet, Gage—could ask him if he'd also left the garage a mess the night before the race. If so, that would've given the killer a chance to steal a tool. They'd just have to find out who had stopped by the garage that day. They'd have a list of customers in their records, but one of their friends might have stopped by to visit, too.

By the time she pulled around behind the house to park, she'd decided to think about the possibility a bit more and then try to find a way to mention it to Gage. That was a problem for tomorrow. Right now, she wasn't sure if she might not have another one on her hands. With her own mind whirling with the possibility of an explanation why neither Gary nor Gil had noticed the wrench had gone missing, she hadn't noticed how quiet Tripp had been the entire way home.

Not sure what to make of it, she said, "Well, we're home."

When he didn't immediately respond, she was at a loss what to say next. Maybe if she opened her car door, the sound would jar him out of his reverie. It was a relief when it worked, because she wasn't sure what she would've tried next. He joined her on the short stroll across the yard to her back porch, still not saying a word.

As usual, Zeke was waiting to bolt outside as soon as she opened the door. As he charged out into the yard to patrol and take care of business, she waited to see if Tripp would volunteer whatever was on his mind. When he finally made a move, it was to back her up against the side of the house, his hands settling on her waist in a gentle hold.

"Tripp? What's going on?"

"I'm wondering if I should apologize for not being happy that you were willing to dance with Liam Grainger. Or for telling you I don't like the idea of you turning to anyone else for protection. I can't help that I feel that way, but I'm not sure I have the right."

He brushed a lock of her hair back from her face. "Honestly, I'm a bit confused. Are we friends or something more? Sometimes it's hard to tell."

If he could be that truthful, she should own up to her own feelings on the subject. "I've been wondering about that myself. The other day Gil offered to take me for a ride on his motorcycle just because I've never been on one. He was worried about how you'd feel about him taking your girl for a ride. I told him I wasn't sure you thought of me that way."

"And if I'm thinking I might want to do exactly that?"

She didn't want to say anything that would damage their friendship long term, but "might" wasn't going to cut it. "I'd say you need to make up your mind and let me know what you decide."

"Fair enough. Until then, you think about us, too." He stepped closer. "And this."

Then he kissed her, taking his time and doing a thorough job of it. When he finally broke it off and stepped back, he said, "I'll bring the beer for dinner tomorrow night. Gil doesn't strike me as a guy who drinks much wine."

It took her a few seconds to catch up with his abrupt change of subject. "Sounds good. See you then."

Zeke was back and ready to go inside. She opened the door and followed him in. As usual, Tripp waited until she threw the dead bolt before walking away. She watched from the kitchen window until he reached his own door. He stopped shy of his door to wave one last time before finally disappearing inside, leaving her confused and yet hopeful at the same time.

She patted Zeke on the head and sighed. "I've gotta tell you, boy, this has been a strange evening. What do you say we head up to bed?"

He didn't need to be told twice. By the time she finished locking up and trudged up the stairs to her room, the dog was already asleep and snoring away. What she wouldn't give for her own life to be that simple. Instead, she had one friend who was worried about his brother never getting out of jail, another one who didn't want her help solving a murder, and a maybe boyfriend who didn't seem all that sure he wanted that title.

Since there wasn't anything she could do to change any of it right then, she just headed into the bathroom to get ready for bed herself. Maybe after a good night's sleep, things wouldn't seem quite so complicated.

But then again, all things considered, probably not.

CHAPTER 21

Abby couldn't believe her rotten luck. Up until then, her day had been off to a great start, and she'd really hoped to preserve her good mood for as long as possible. She'd worked all morning polishing the updated procedures and suggestions she and Gil had come up with for Connie Pohler's notebook on the annual Salmon Scoot. There was no time like the present to turn it in, so she and Zeke had driven downtown to drop it off.

As soon as she'd walked into city hall, Sergeant Jones had greeted Zeke and offered him one of the dog treats he kept on hand. Leaving Zeke with him, she had headed into the mayor's office and set the notebook on the counter. After giving the notebook a quick skim, Connie thanked her profusely for all the work she and Gil had done to make the race such a huge success. Abby made a quick escape after Connie promised to call if she had any questions about any changes they'd suggested.

Considering Connie hadn't hinted even once that she was now on the short list for some other major project, Abby decided to celebrate with a quick stop at Something's Brewing. It should have been obvious that things were rolling along far too smoothly. She'd been too busy gloating over her successful escape to notice who was walking out of the shop just as she was about to walk in. Sadly, James DiSalvo's lady friend was far more observant.

"It's you!"

Who else would Abby be? This wasn't the time for snark, but it might very well be time to turn and run. Instead, she stood her ground. All she wanted was some coffee and maybe a peach muffin. Her plan had been to do a quick grab-and-go since Zeke was waiting for her in the car. Now she'd be lucky if she made it out of the place alive.

Georgia blocked the door, preventing Abby from going inside. "Sheila tried to tell me I shouldn't be angry over what you did at the restaurant that night, but I'm not quite so forgiving. I don't care if that biker is a friend of yours or not. His brother murdered my James, and I wouldn't be surprised if he was an accomplice."

That did it. Uncomfortably aware that they were drawing attention from both the people inside Something's Brewing and those out on the sidewalk, Abby fought to keep her voice low and calm. "Lady, you don't know squat about me or him. I know you're upset about DiSalvo's death, but he wasn't a saint, either. Now, if you'll excuse me."

By that point, the older woman had worked up a full head of steam. "Actually, there's no excuse for you, young lady. How dare you speak ill of James! He was dedicated to this town."

That pragmatic little voice in the back of Abby's head began chanting, *Just walk away. For Pete's sake, just walk away.* Proud of herself for being the calm one in the crowd, Abby simply said, "Let's agree to disagree. After all, I didn't know Mr. DiSalvo, and you definitely don't know either me or my friend."

Obviously Georgia's own little voice was on hiatus or else it was as pushy and obnoxious as she was, because she didn't back down an inch. "You and your friend are exactly the kind of people that James feared would be the undoing of our lovely town. That's why he was so proud of being elected to the city council and all the good work he did there despite other people's efforts to thwart him."

That did it. "You're right, lady. Snowberry Creek is a lovely town, but that's due to the hard work of all kinds of people, not just one man. Again, if you'll excuse me. You're blocking the door."

"Abby, is there a problem here?"

She turned to face the newcomer to the conversation. "Hi, Chief Logan. I was just agreeing with the lady here that Snowberry Creek is a lovely town even if we might disagree on what that means."

If Gage was surprised that she'd addressed him by his title, he gave no sign of it. "Mrs. Froman, it appears you're blocking the door. I'm sure Mrs. Kyser would appreciate it if you ladies moved this discussion down the sidewalk so her customers can get out."

That's when Abby noticed that several people were hovering just inside the shop and looking pretty put out. She immediately stepped back to give the other woman room to clear the doorway. As soon as she did, Georgia charged past, bumping into Abby and knocking her back into Gage in the process.

It was impossible to know if she did it deliberately, but Abby was pretty sure either way that Georgia probably hadn't meant to drop her own purse in the process. When the large tote-style bag hit the ground, its contents spilled all over the sidewalk. It was tempting to walk into the coffee shop and let Georgia deal with the mess she'd made on her own. Cursing the manners her aunt had drilled into Abby from a young age, she made herself at least make a token effort to gather up a few items while Gage did the same.

After picking up a couple of lipsticks and a hairbrush, she spotted a soft gray drawstring bag. When she reached for it, Georgia snapped, "Don't touch that!"

Too late. Abby straightened up and held it out on the palm of her hand. Georgia was about to take it from her when she noticed the panicky look on the woman's face. What was so special about the pouch? Instinct had her closing her fingers around it. As soon as she did, she realized the contents felt like beads of some kind, most likely a necklace.

"I hope your necklace wasn't damaged when it hit the ground, Mrs. Froman." As she spoke, she tugged open the drawstring at the top of the bag and spilled the pearl necklace out onto her palm. Giving Georgia an innocent look, she said, "These are lovely. I'm so glad they appear to be unharmed."

She held up the triple strands of lustrous pearls to give Gage a better look at them. "You don't see pearls like these very often anymore. But, you know, I seem to recall someone mentioning recently that her mother had a necklace like this."

His eyes widened as he made the same connection. When Georgia immediately made another try to snatch the necklace, Gage put his much longer reach to good use and grabbed it first. "So, tell me, Mrs. Froman. What are the chances that these are the pearls Francine Denman mentioned in that little discussion the two of you had in the lobby at city hall?"

The woman retreated until she bumped into the building that housed the coffee shop, her back literally against the wall. "I don't know what you're talking about, Chief Logan. Those pearls were a gift from a friend."

His smile turned positively predatory. "Well, let's say I'm a bit unconvinced. I'll apologize if I'm mistaken, but I think I should hold on to these for a while. You can have them back when your friend comes in to make an official statement about them being a gift. I'll also need to know where he or she got them. You might let them know a receipt wouldn't go amiss, either."

Abby handed him the pouch and watched as he slipped the necklace inside. After tying it shut with the drawstring, he tucked it into his shirt pocket and gave Georgia another hard look. "On second thought, I need you to come with me down to headquarters so we can discuss this situation in more detail. Considering the recent break-in at Mr. DiSalvo's house, I'd feel better if I took an official statement from you."

The woman sputtered in indignation. "Are you seriously suggesting that I broke into James's house?"

"That's definitely part of the discussion we'll be having. If you give me your word that you'll follow me down to city hall, I'll let you drive yourself there."

"And if I choose not to do that?"

He shrugged and pointed toward his cruiser. "Well, if you'd prefer to ride through town in the back of my police car, I'm fine with that. So, given your options, what's your decision?"

Georgia drew her ragged dignity around herself like a shroud. "I'll meet you there, but I will be calling my attorney. Any discussion will have to wait until he gets there."

"Fine."

Figuring it was time to make herself scarce, Abby quietly walked away. Zeke would be wondering what was taking her so long, and Gage knew where to find her if he wanted to talk. She really hoped he didn't, but she'd deal with it if he called. She was more upset about missing out on the latte she'd been looking forward to. There was nothing preventing her from buying one, but she didn't want to face either the curious stares or the barrage of questions that would be leveled in her direction if she went into Something's Brewing now.

As she walked past the front window, though, Bridey knocked on the glass. She held up one finger as if asking Abby to wait, and then mouthed, "Drive around back."

It only took a couple of minutes for Abby to reach her car and then drive down the alley that ran behind Something's Brewing. Bridey was waiting for her with a to-go cup of coffee and a paper bag.

Abby rolled down her car window and started to dig her wallet out of her purse. Bridey protested. "You don't owe me anything, Abby. You deserve a peach muffin and a latte after having to deal with that woman. She was being a pain even before you arrived, going on and on about how the entire town should be in deep mourning over the death of DiSalvo. Near as I can tell, she's furious that we haven't put on a state funeral for the man."

Bridey practically shoved the coffee and bag into Abby's hand, as though she thought she might refuse to accept them. As if that would ever happen.

"Thanks for this, Bridey. It's much appreciated."

"No problem. And don't you go feeling bad for her. If she hadn't left on her own, I would've kicked her out because she was upsetting my other customers. I don't know what her problem is, but you had the patience of a saint dealing with her as well as you did."

It wasn't a good time for Abby's conscience to stir to life, but she found herself confessing how she'd prevented Georgia and her friends from eating at Owen's restaurant. "So, honestly, she does have a legitimate reason to not be happy with me."

Instead of being shocked, Bridey looked delighted by what Abby had done. "Lady, that was absolutely diabolical. I like it."

She stepped back from the car. "I'd better go back inside. Enjoy your coffee, and I stuck in some treats for Zeke and an extra muffin for Tripp. I didn't want you to have to wrestle him for it if he sees you get out of the car with the bag in hand. No offense, but I don't think you could take him in a fair fight."

That image had Abby grinning. "You're assuming I'd fight fair in the first place."

"True, but I'd hate to see him beat up over a muffin. Even retired soldiers have pride."

"Considering peach is my favorite kind, I'd do it in a heartbeat. I'll tell him that your thoughtfulness saved him some bumps and bruises. He'll appreciate that."

Bridey waved one last time and disappeared back into her shop. Zeke woofed softly as if to demand his share of the goodies. Abby reached back over the seat to offer him a doggy cookie before driving off.

Unfortunately, her good mood lasted only a short time when she realized that Georgia having the late Mrs. DiSalvo's necklace might have answered the question of who had broken into the councilman's house. She'd really been hoping that the murder and the burglary had been done by the same person. Considering Gary Pratt had been in jail at the time of the theft, he couldn't have committed the second crime.

Even if Georgia turned out to have "borrowed" the necklace, there was no way that petite woman could have swung a torque wrench hard enough to kill a man, especially one she had such obvious strong feelings for. It was also impossible to imagine a scenario where she could somehow have gone skulking around in the motorcycle shop to steal Gary's wrench without someone noticing. So much for pinning both crimes on her.

Well, unless it turned out that the necklace really was Georgia's, and not the late Mrs. DiSalvo's at all. If that were the case, then there was still at least some possibility that whoever broke into the house had also killed its owner.

She didn't plan on mentioning the confrontation to Gil when he came over for dinner. But if he heard about it from someone else, she wouldn't lie about it. Barring that happening, she would avoid telling him anything until she managed to find out from Gage how his discussion with Georgia turned out.

For now, she'd go home, enjoy her coffee and muffin, and then work on dinner. And while she did that, the rest of the world could just take care of itself.

CHAPTER 22

It turned out that Bridey had been right on target about the muffins. Tripp was sitting on his porch steps reading when Abby pulled into the driveway. As she got out of the car, his eyes zeroed in on the bag in her hand, which had him up and prowling in her direction. Clearly he assumed, or at least hoped, there was something in the bag for him. Considering how often she brought him something from Bridey's, it wasn't really his fault for thinking that way. That didn't mean she couldn't make him suffer a little bit.

Thinking Zeke might derail his buddy long enough for her to make it to her own porch, she let him out of the back seat, but her ploy failed miserably. The wily beast hadn't forgotten the bag held treats for him, too. He parked his backside on the ground right in front of her, trapping her against the car, his eyes pinned on the bag.

Surrendering to the inevitable, she set her coffee on the hood of the car while she gave him a cookie and muttered, "Traitor."

Meanwhile, the other hungry male in the vicinity continued to circle closer. Trying to act oh, so casual, he asked, "Hey, Abby, what's in the bag?"

"Doggy treats."

To prove she wasn't lying, she dug through the bag for one of the small cookies and offered it to her always hungry dog. "Bridey tucked a few of these in the bag for Zeke along with my muffin. Wasn't that nice of her?"

"It was." Tripp inched forward. "But that bag looks pretty heavy for just one muffin and a few Zeke treats."

"Not really. You know Bridey bakes really big muffins. She had peach today, my favorite. Yours, too, as I remember." She picked up her coffee, sidestepped Zeke, and gave Tripp a sugary-sweet smile as she waltzed past him. "I plan to enjoy every crumb."

"You're right about the size of the muffins. They're plenty big enough to share with a friend."

Taunting him with the bag, she smiled. "That's not happening, soldier boy. She gave it to me. I had a rough experience right outside her shop, and she felt sorry for me."

He fell silent as he trailed along half a step behind her. Not about to mistake his silence for surrender, she tightened her grip on the bag and sped up. That lasted for all of three steps before Tripp made his move, startling her into dropping the bag. Zeke was only too glad to join their game. He grabbed the sack and took off running. He made a wide loop around them, staying just out of reach.

"Dog, drop it now!"

The note of command Tripp injected into his order only served to confuse Zeke. He stopped moving long enough to give them a questioning look. Was this a game or not? Finally, he lay down and dropped the bag between his huge front paws. With his tongue lolling out in a doggy grin, he watched Tripp as if telling him the next move was his.

Pitching his voice low and calm, Tripp apologized for the confusion. "I'm sorry, boy. I didn't mean to yell, but we should give the bag back to Abby."

Zeke looked toward her for verification, so she smiled and nodded. "That's right, big guy. You've had your treats, and now I'd like mine."

Provided the mastiff's slobber hadn't soaked through the paper to defile the muffins. Surely he couldn't have contaminated both of them in that short amount of time. But if only one was edible, she definitely had dibs on it. To make sure she got first choice, she walked over to Zeke, crooning compliments and promises of back scratches and future treats if he surrendered the bag to her.

When it was safely back in her custody, she patted his head and started for the porch. Her coffee had also ended up on the ground, so she picked up the empty cup on the way and gave Tripp a crabby look. "You made me spill my drink."

He looked only marginally sorry. "I'll make a fresh pot."

"You bet you will."

She tossed him her keys so he could let himself inside while she made herself comfortable on the porch. Zeke kept her company, his eyes still on the bag as she checked out its contents. Luckily for him and Tripp, the muffins had survived in relatively good shape. So had the one remaining bone-shaped cookie. Once she had her replacement coffee in hand, she would dole out the goodies.

It wasn't long before Tripp stepped back out on the porch with two steaming mugs and a couple of napkins in his hand. She could only chuckle at his optimistic belief there was a muffin in his immediate future. He wasn't wrong. After setting her cup of coffee up on the porch railing, she tossed him the bag after claiming her peach muffin.

"Thanks, Abs."

"Don't thank me; thank Bridey. She figured I'd have to fight you for it if she only sent one. It was a little unclear who she thought would come out on top if that happened."

He'd been in the process of peeling the paper off his muffin, but he paused long enough to give her an amused look. "Seriously?"

"Okay, she did say you could take me in a fair fight. I, however, pointed out that when defending a peach muffin, I make no promises to fight fair in the first place."

"I stand forewarned." He went back to unwrapping the muffin. "So what happened that convinced Bridey you needed a dose of caffeine and peachy goodness to recuperate?"

Abby filled him in on the details. He was frowning by the time she was done, so she tried to reassure him that all was well. "Georgia might have fired the opening shots, but Gage finished the battle. She's the one who had to make a trip to the police department to explain how she came by the necklace. Even if she can prove it was hers to begin with, she has to know her trip to the pokey will get around town. I'm betting she'll hate that."

"That's probably true, but I'm not worried about her. You shouldn't be, either." Suddenly there was a wicked gleam in his eyes. "Nope, if I were you, I'd be far more worried about what trickery Connie Pohler has up her sleeve."

Uh-oh. What had she missed? "Care to explain?"

"Well, don't you think you got off a little too easy?" He gave her a few seconds to think about that before continuing. "That woman has never hesitated to saddle you with a new job as soon as you finish one. Why is she behaving differently this time? That makes me think whatever project she and the mayor have lined up next must be huge. They've clearly decided to give you some time to let down your guard before springing it on you."

What a horrible thought! She wished she could say he was way off base with his assessment of the situation. Darn it, couldn't Tripp have let her bask in the glow for a little longer before bursting her balloon?

"I can always say no."

He almost choked on the bite he'd just taken. "Seriously? When did you suddenly develop that particular skill? It must be pretty darn recently since I've never known you to be able to do that in the past."

Just because he was right, that didn't mean he had to rub it in. "Jerk."

He arched a brow. "Sorry if the truth hurts."

"Well, now that I'm aware of the potential problem, I can be ready to duck and cover."

"Yeah, good luck with that. But moving on to a happier subject, what are we having for dinner tonight?"

"A different take on lasagna made with corn tortillas and taco spices. It's already put together in the fridge, so all I have to do is bake it. We're having slaw as a side dish. I've already made the dressing, so I just have to toss it with the cabbage right before we eat. The only thing left to do is make the pie, but I'm going to start that next."

"That sounds good."

"I thought so, too. I texted Gil and asked him to let me know when he's headed our way. That way I can wait until I hear from him before I stick the casserole in the oven in case he gets a later start than he was expecting."

"Good idea." Then, after a short pause, Tripp gave her a somber look. "What are you going to tell him about what happened this morning? If that lady was the one who broke into DiSalvo's house, it won't do anything to clear Gary's name."

Leave it to him to get right at the heart of the problem. "Nothing, if I can help it. There's always a possibility he's already heard about it since everything played out right in front of Something's Brewing. If he asks me, I won't lie. Barring that, though, I'd rather not say any-thing until I find out from Gage how it all turned out. Well, if he bothers to tell me anything at all. But if the necklace is hers, it won't affect Gary's case one way or the other. Even if she did steal it, I can't see her actually killing DiSalvo. In some ways, her involvement just confuses things."

Tripp leaned down to pet Zeke. "I really feel for Gil. You feel so helpless knowing in your gut that someone is innocent but you can't prove it."

He'd actually been in that painful no-win situation twice since she'd met him. She wadded up the empty bag, venting some of her frustration. "There has to be something we're all missing."

Then she winced. "Not that I'm investigating or anything, but there has to be something the police have missed. If Gary didn't do it, then obviously someone else did. So far that person has been able to evade detection, but I have to believe eventually he or she will slip up. When that happens, Gage and his men will pounce."

Tripp sounded pretty grim. "Not to rain on your parade, but you know that doesn't always happen."

True, but she hoped it would this time, for Gil's sake. And with him in mind, she dragged herself up out of her chair. "Well, I've got a pie to bake."

Tripp took the hint. "I'm going to hit the books for a while. Zeke can come hang out with me if he wants to."

The dog immediately lumbered to his feet and followed Tripp down the steps, abandoning Abby to go snooze on his buddy's love seat. She'd miss him, but she'd also get more done without him underfoot. "See you both later. I'll text when Gil is on his way."

And while she rolled out the pie crust, maybe she could figure out who else had a vested interest in seeing James DiSalvo sleeping six feet under.

When Tripp returned, six-pack in hand, Abby had just finished setting the table. Gil had texted her twenty minutes ago that he was on the way. He should arrive any second, but she had something she wanted to run by Tripp before then. "So, I've been thinking."

He stuck the six-pack in the fridge and then leaned against the counter. "I'm listening."

"We know that DiSalvo bought the mobile-home park, but we don't know the identity of who he bought it from or the exact circumstances of the sale. Glenda, or maybe it was Louise, said the previous owner had died and the heir lived out of state. If so, then it would be another dead end. But what if DiSalvo found a way to force them to sell? You know, leveraged it somehow."

Tripp didn't look happy, but at least he wasn't yelling at her for even bringing up the subject. "And how would you go about finding out? You know, without actually investigating on your own?"

She opened the oven door to peek at the casserole, mostly to buy herself a little time to come up with an acceptable answer. When it came to Tripp, it was always better to go with the truth. "I'm not sure. It would help if I knew someone who actually lived there, but I don't. Jean's friend moved out not long ago, so she might know something. I'd really hate to bother her unless I have no other choice."

"That's considerate of you."

There was no missing the sarcasm in his voice. Fine. And he wondered why she didn't like talking to him about this stuff. Fortunately she was saved from having to continue the conversation when the doorbell rang. "Looks like Gil's here."

When she started for the entryway to let him in, Tripp matched her step for step. "Just so you know, this conversation is not over, just postponed."

"Fine."

For once, she didn't look out the window beside the door before opening it. To her surprise, it wasn't Gil standing on the porch. Her welcoming smile drooped a bit, but she managed to revive it with some effort.

"Gage, what's up?"

He looked past her to where Tripp hovered just behind her. "Sorry to interrupt your evening, but I wanted to talk to you about what happened today. I should've called first."

The rumble of a motorcycle drew everybody's attention to the street. A few seconds later, Gil turned into her driveway and maneuvered his bike around Gage's cruiser to park in front of it to avoid blocking him in. While he dismounted and took off his helmet, Gage let out a low whistle. "Well, that complicates the situation. Maybe I should come back tomorrow."

"If you think that's best."

Although she really hoped he'd stay. She got that he might not want to talk about the situation with Georgia in front of Gil. But if he did postpone the discussion, she'd probably be awake a good part of the night wondering what was going on.

Finally, he shook his head. "Well, I'm guessing you've already told Tripp about what happened, and half the town witnessed the situation with Ms. Froman. I don't want to mess up your evening, though, so I won't stay long."

Tripp tilted his head in Gage's direction and raised his eyebrows. Realizing he wanted to know if Gage should stay for dinner, she nodded. He winked at her and issued the invitation. "Abby made a big casserole and baked a pie, so there would be plenty to go around if you don't have other plans for dinner."

By that point, Gil had joined him on the porch. "Sorry I got here a little later than expected. I was locking the door when Casey showed back up. He'd already left for the day, but evidently he missed his ride. Anyway, he needed me to drop him off at the grocery store. He said he could catch the bus from there."

Abby shrugged. "You're not late. Dinner is just now ready."

Gage directed his next comment directly to Gil. "I won't take offense if you'd rather I didn't hang around for dinner, Gil. Just say the word, and I'm out of here."

Gil studied Gage for a second or two before turning to Abby. "The more the merrier as far as I'm concerned. Well, as long as I still get my fair share of whatever dessert you made."

That had everyone laughing, the small thread of tension gone. The four of them filed down the hall to the kitchen. Tripp got out another place setting for Gage while Abby started putting the food on the table. By unspoken agreement, they kept the conversation light as they ate. She had a single serving of the casserole, but all three men had seconds and Tripp briefly considered a third before deciding he'd rather leave more room for pie.

She made coffee and cut huge wedges of pie and passed them around, making her own half the size of the ones she gave her three guests. Gage studied his with a small smile on his face. "I really shouldn't eat this, but I don't care. It's been one of those days, and I deserve a little something for my efforts."

Which brought them back to his reason for being there.

Gage fiddled with his coffee cup, his forehead furrowed. Finally, he gave Gil a considering look. "What I'm about to tell you stays between us for now, Gil. I'm not asking you to hide anything from your brother's attorney long term. I just need another day to get everything locked down. If it got out that I told you anything before I go to the prosecutor with this, it could cost me my job."

Gil didn't even hesitate. "You've always played fair with me, Gage. As much as I hate it, you had no choice but to arrest my brother. I also know you haven't stopped looking for the truth even if the prosecutor thinks he has everything all locked up. If you need me to keep my mouth shut, I will."

"Fair enough. So to bring everybody up to speed, I want to review what happened today. Abby, if I missed something, don't hesitate to jump in."

Then he gave Gil a quick overview of the situation with Georgia, and who she was in relationship to James DiSalvo. Abby then explained to Gil that Georgia was the one who had been rude to him in Owen's parking lot before adding in a few details of what had happened outside of Bridey's before Gage happened upon the scene. "When Gage and Georgia headed for city hall, I came home."

Gage leaned back in his chair and sipped his coffee. "As it turns out, the necklace that fell out of her purse did belong to James DiSalvo's wife. All things considered, it was smart of Ms. Froman to bring her attorney into the discussion. She says she 'borrowed' the necklace from DiSalvo's house. Allegedly, she wanted to wear it to honor him at the funeral. I'm not buying that explanation, at least not completely, and his daughter could insist we press charges."

Abby wasn't a big fan of DiSalvo's daughter, and it wouldn't surprise her if Francine insisted on Gage throwing the book at the woman. "I've got to say I'm having a hard time picturing Georgia breaking into the house. Although imagining her in all black spandex and a ski mask is pretty funny."

All three men grinned at that image, but then Gage got serious again. "Imagine my surprise when the lady informed me that she had a key to his house. Evidently, DiSalvo gave it to her so she could water his plants and bring in his mail whenever he was out of town. In short, she didn't have to break in, even if her reason for being there this time wasn't exactly legitimate."

Well, wasn't that interesting? "So if it wasn't her, who was it? And why? I know Francine was pushing to be allowed into her father's house, but she knew it was only a matter of time before she would be given permission."

Gage shrugged. "Right now, your guess is as good as mine. And we don't know how much say Francine will have about what happens to DiSalvo's estate. So far no one has been able to track down any legal documents. In the absence of a will or trust, she would be the next of kin, but we're still working on that."

Tripp finished the last bite of his pie and pushed his plate to the side. "So, if this Georgia woman is to be believed, that leaves you two different perpetrators—her and someone so far unidentified. I guess this also means you don't have any idea if anything else besides the necklace is missing from the house."

"That's true, but that's not the interesting part. Ms. Froman swears she picked up the necklace the day after the murder. When she left, the house was in perfect order, not so much as a dirty dish in the sink or a wet towel in the bathroom."

Gil fiddled with his napkin, slowly tearing it into strips. "I can't say that I'm surprised. DiSalvo always struck me as what my mother used to call a fussbudget, the kind of guy who wouldn't tolerate anything out of place. But I can't exactly imagine him doing a bunch of house-work himself. Didn't he have a maid service or some-thing?"

"Yeah, he did, but he'd put a pause on them coming in. Evidently, he was planning to leave on a business trip right after the race was over. The deal was for them to wait until he contacted them before resuming service, so the maids hadn't been in since right before he died."

By that point, the note of excitement in Gage's voice had them all hanging on his every word. Even so, Tripp interrupted him to ask a question. "Did DiSalvo have a security system?"

"No, actually he didn't, which I found a bit odd. Most people in that neighborhood do, but evidently he was ei-ther too cheap to pay for the service or else thought no one would dare break into his home."

"So, how did you find out someone had broken into the house? Did they break a window or something?"

"DiSalvo stopped the maid service but not the land-scaper. Lucas Gregg and his crew come once a week to maintain the lawn. They use the yard waste container to empty the bag on the lawn mower and for any branches they trim or weeds they dig up. But when one of his men went to do that, he realized someone had been dumping garbage in the container. Mostly carryout containers and beer cans."

Gage got up to pour everyone more coffee as he kept talking. "Any other time, they might have assumed Mr. DiSalvo made the mistake. Normally, the crew would've just dumped the garbage into the right container and gone on about their business. But Lucas knew about DiSalvo's death, and the only reason they were there was the man prepaid for their service by the month. They didn't expect there to be anyone else around."

Curiouser and curiouser. Abby added cream to her cup as she thought through the implications. "So he called the police."

Even though Gage nodded, it still didn't make sense. From what she and Tripp had seen the day they'd intended to drive by DiSalvo's house, the police response seemed a bit over-the-top for a few aluminum cans and pizza boxes.

Looking back, she remembered Gage had never said exactly what they'd found at the scene, only that "something" had happened. There seemed to be one only one logical conclusion. "There's more to it than the trash being in the wrong spot, isn't there? Whatever Mr. Gregg and his people saw set off bigger alarms."

"Yep. Lucas looked through several windows before calling it in. From what he could see, it looked like someone had trashed the place. There was a lock box with a key that the maid service used, so we got the code from them to get the key. We're not exactly sure how the vandal got in. But whoever it was used black spray paint on most of the walls, writing some pretty angry things about

DiSalvo. One wall was different, though, and I found it particularly interesting."

Abby's pulse kicked up a notch, leaving her feeling as if they were all perched on the edge of a cliff and about to go tumbling over. Both Gil and Tripp must have been built of stronger stuff, since their demeanors appeared relaxed. But when Gage didn't continue after having dropped that little bomb, Gil gave up all pretense of being calm, his voice full of gravel as he leaned in close to the table and asked, "What did it say?"

"DiSalvo deserved what he got. No regrets."

CHAPTER 23

The shock of his blunt statement made it hard for Abby to focus on what else Gage was saying. She missed a few words, but what she did hear was awful enough.

" . . . was written with a brush, not a spray can. The paint was blood red, with drips running down from every letter. Not sure if that just happened or if it was planned as a special effect. Honestly, it was pretty creepy."

It would've given Abby the creeps, too. What kind of person would write that kind of message on a dead man's wall? Well, unless it was the murderer himself. Surely this would be enough to provide Gary's defense attorney with enough ammo to prove there was now reasonable doubt that he was the killer.

Meanwhile, Gage was still talking. "It would be nice to know for sure if the guy brought the paint with him or if he found it in DiSalvo's garage. It would carry more weight with the prosecutor if we could prove the would-be artist bought the paint with the specific intent to vandalize DiSalvo's house. Of course, it could've also been some nutcase just stirring up trouble for the heck of it or maybe as a show of support for whoever actually killed the man."

"Will you go to the prosecutor with what you've found?"

"Yeah, most likely tomorrow afternoon. He won't be happy that I've waited this long, but he's been tied up in a trial. That will be the excuse I give him, anyway."

He rolled his shoulders and stretched. "I also got the county to send out their crew to dust the place for fingerprints and look for other evidence that will lead us to whoever has been squatting in that house. It's way too soon for them to have gotten any results, so we'll all have to be patient."

It was no coincidence that he aimed that last comment directly at Gil. The message got through even if Gil didn't look particularly happy about it. "And I'm making no promises that we'll learn anything that will help your brother. Right now all the hard evidence we have points straight at him, and the prosecutor isn't going to be inclined to cut him loose anytime soon."

Up until that point, Gil had been handling the situation pretty well. But now, he rose to his feet, his hands clenched into fists. "So you're telling me that you and that idiot in the prosecutor's office will let my brother rot in jail even though you suspect the real killer is still out there roaming free? I thought you had some sense of honor left, lawman."

Gage stood up and mirrored Gil's angry stance. It wouldn't take much before they did more than simply glare at each other.

Abby looked from one to the other and back again, gauging their mood. It didn't take a genius to know this was bad. Real bad. Both men were poised on the verge of violence. Tripp had remained seated, but there was nothing relaxed about him, either. She wasn't sure which man he would side with. He and Gage had been friends for years, but Gil was a guest. This might not be Tripp's house, but she knew he considered it his territory to protect. Even Zeke was on high alert with his attention focused on the threat presented by the three men.

She had to calm the idiots down. Didn't they realize they all shared a common goal to see justice done, even if it was for different reasons? Tripp had spent twenty years serving a higher cause. Gage had done the same, both as a soldier and as a cop. It would go against everything he stood for to let an innocent man go to prison for a crime he hadn't committed. Gage was doing everything he could to get to the truth. And Gil, well, he wanted to protect his younger brother.

Slamming her hands down on the table, she lurched to her feet. Feeling as if she were channeling Aunt Sybil, she snapped, "That's enough. Sit down, both of you."

To her surprise, they did exactly that. That was good, but she wasn't done. "This is my home, and you are my guests. If you can't be civil to each other, leave. Gage, you first."

He didn't like that. Not one bit. "Why? Correct me if I'm wrong, but I thought we were friends."

Really? That's where he wanted to go with this? "Yes, Gage, we're friends. The reason I want you to leave first is that you're parked behind Gil. Simple as that. No ulterior motive involved."

She had her gaze pinned on Gage, so she wasn't sure whether it was Gil or Tripp who tried to disguise a laugh as a cough. Right now it didn't matter. Rather than take offense, Gage looked amused, the corner of his mouth quirking up just enough to signal the danger had passed.

He picked up his hat and retreated toward the nearby door. "Sorry, Abby. Thanks for dinner. Gil, I'll be in touch."

The other man nodded. "You know where to find me."

Turning his attention toward Tripp, who still looked poised for action, he said, "At ease, Sergeant. I'm leaving now."

As soon as he disappeared, Abby sat back down, exhausted by the brief conflict. She really, really hated fighting with people she cared about. With some effort, she glanced up at Gil, who had resumed standing. At least he looked more resigned than angry now. "Are you all right?"

"No, but don't you worry about me." He shuffled his feet and frowned. "I apologize for losing it like that. The last thing I would ever want to do is scare you."

She hadn't liked it, but she did understand it. "Don't worry, Gil. We're good."

"On that note, I'll be leaving."

Just as Gage had done, Gil saved his last words for Tripp. "Apologies to you, too, Tripp. I'll see myself out."

She and Tripp sat in silence until the rumble of Gil's bike had faded away in the distance. Forcing a note of cheeriness into her voice that she certainly didn't feel, she said, "Well, this turned out to be an interesting evening."

Tripp didn't immediately respond, but he didn't seem

to be still upset about the brief confrontation between Gage and Gil. Leaving him to stew about whatever he had on his mind, she began clearing the table. It was unlike Tripp to leave all the work to her, but he made no move to help.

She'd finished loading the dishwasher and moved on to the few things that needed to be washed by hand before he finally stirred. Without saying a word, he got a clean dish towel out of the drawer and started drying everything. After that, he wiped down the table and the counters while she set the timer on the coffeemaker so she'd wake up to a fresh pot in the morning. With that done, she was ready to call it day.

Trip hung up the towel to dry and then asked, "Want to take Zeke for a walk?"

That wasn't something they usually did this late in the evening, but she couldn't bring herself to refuse the invitation. "Sure. Let me get a jacket and my keys."

Outside, the evening air was cool, which it often was in the Pacific Northwest. The moon was nearly full and surrounded by twinkling stars. She breathed deeply and let the day's tensions slowly fall by the wayside.

Tripp had continued to be largely silent, but he seemed to be gradually loosening up. At least he wasn't marching down the sidewalk as if heading into battle. When they reached the point where the trail through the national forest met up with the sidewalk, he hesitated. "I don't suppose you want to take the path through the forest this late."

Although the trail officially closed at sundown, she didn't reject the idea out of hand. "The last time I did that, I got momentarily kidnapped by your buddy."

Tripp flashed her a grin. "That was your fault for deciding to follow me in the middle of the night. If you'd have stayed in bed like a sensible person, you wouldn't have ended up scared half out of your wits."

That was nothing less than the truth, so she took his hand and laced their fingers together.

"I'm game, if you are."

He tugged on Zeke's leash. "This way, boy."

Only a short distance in, the trees crowded in close enough to the trail that their intertwining branches blocked most of the night sky and the silvery light offered by the moon. It didn't seem to bother either of her companions, so she just held on tight to Tripp and trusted him and Zeke to keep her safe.

Tripp flexed his hand a little, maybe a hint that she was gripping his hand a bit too hard. "Just so you know, I stole the flashlight out of your kitchen drawer. If it gets too spooky out here for you, let me know."

She laughed. "Thanks."

They let the peace of the night surround them. After a while, Tripp spoke again. "I'm sorry dinner turned out the way it did. I don't know what Gage was thinking by telling Gil, much less us, about all of that. He had to know the man wouldn't take it well."

"I know, right? I was hoping they'd learn something to clear Gary's name. But it sounds like even if Gage thinks he didn't do it, the prosecutor may go ahead with the case unless Gage can come up with equally strong evidence that points at someone else. That makes no sense that the guy wouldn't listen to Gage's instincts. There has to be something somebody can do."

"I'm all for that as long as that somebody isn't you, Abby. I hate you getting sucked into another murder case. It was bad enough that you were one of the first people on the scene. But now it seems as if you keep getting drawn in closer and closer."

"I don't mean to. I really don't."

He just sighed. "So, what are you going to do next?"

"Nothing. Even if I wanted to, everything seems to be a dead end."

Another long silence. Finally, he said, "Go over it all with me. Tell me what you're thinking."

She pondered where to start. "I think James DiSalvo was the kind of man who made enemies, no matter how good he thought his intentions were. You don't mess with people's homes and businesses without getting some pushback. Then there's the way he cut off ties with his daughter because he didn't approve of the man she married."

"Yeah, he sounds like he was a real prize. That doesn't mean he deserved to die."

"I never said he did. But how could he not realize that what he was doing might have consequences?"

Tripp squeezed her hand. "I can't speak for him specifically because I never met the man, but there are people who think the world revolves around them. If they want something done a certain way, they don't understand why anyone would disagree with them. Maybe he legitimately thought the people in the mobile-home park would appreciate his efforts to improve things there, even if the changes were only cosmetic. He also probably thought that his efforts to make sure only the right kind of businesses were encouraged in town would benefit everyone."

She could hear the smile in his voice when he added, "I bet if you try hard enough, you could think of a few types of businesses you wouldn't want on Main Street, especially next to Something's Brewing, where all the high school kids hang out in the afternoon."

Okay, she had to give him that much, but it still shouldn't be left up to just one person to make those decisions. "Good intentions aside, you've got to wonder how many people were hurt by his actions, especially if they were collateral damage. It's only going to get worse for Gil and Gary if Gage isn't able to find out who really did kill the man."

And they were back to where the discussion had begun. Tripp tugged her in closer to his side and wrapped his arm around her shoulders. "Tomorrow will be soon enough to worry about everything again. What do you say we just enjoy our walk?"

"Good idea."

Their resolve to put everything connected to the murder out of their minds lasted until after they returned home, Tripp heading to his house while she and Zeke went to hers. She even avoided thinking about it while she indulged herself in a soothing candlelit bubble bath before turning in for the night.

Sadly, as soon as she pulled up the covers and tried to get comfortable, the thoughts came roaring back, whirling through her mind in a nonstop dance. She even tried counting possible killers instead of sheep. There was the unlikely possibility of Georgia Froman, followed by Francine Denman, and then there was the mysterious artist who had somehow managed to camp out in DiSalvo's house.

She tried to counter all the dark thoughts with memories of how hard Gil had worked to make the race a huge success. For that matter, Gary had put in a lot of effort, too, by taking up the slack at the shop so his brother could connect with more people in the community. Then there was tonight when Gil had gone out of his way to give Casey a lift to a distant bus stop. Heck, Gil would've probably taken him all the way home if he'd asked.

But come to think of it, back when she and Tripp had given Casey a ride, he asked them to drop him off at the grocery store by the bus stop. Did he live close by there? If so, she and Tripp wouldn't have minded waiting for Casey to pick up a few things at the store before dropping him off at home. The only answer she could come up with was that he lived some distance from town and didn't like asking people to go so far out of their way.

Regardless, the effort both Pratt brothers put into working with Casey despite his quirks was just that much more proof they were nice guys under their tough-looking exteriors. Too bad more people didn't realize that about them. There had to be something she could do to help change that.

With that thought, she coaxed Zeke up onto the bed with her. As usual, his undemanding presence and the soothing rhythm of his rumbling snores worked their magic, and she drifted off to sleep.

CHAPTER 24

The next morning, Abby woke up feeling restless. Her continuing worries about Gil and Gary were only part of it. Now that the race was over, she had a lot more free time on her hands than she was used to having. In a determined effort to do something productive, she spent a solid two hours working on the baby quilt. After sewing the last few strips together, she cut out the fabric she planned to use as a border, the contrasting binding, and the quilt back itself.

At that point, she decided she'd done enough for one day and went back downstairs. She loved working on the quilt, but she really needed to do something more active. There was always laundry to do, but where was the fun in that?

Maybe Tripp would like to take a ride out to Gary's Drive-In to have lunch. Sadly, when she peeked out the back window, his parking space was empty. So much for that idea. She and Zeke could always go by themselves, but that held little appeal.

She also didn't think she should swing by to check on Gil. If he was at work, he probably wouldn't appreciate being interrupted. As always, it was tempting to head over to Something's Brewing, but she really didn't need the temptation of Bridey's creations right now. Not to mention she still had a piece of apple pie down in the kitchen.

If she ate it, she could always take Zeke for an extra-long walk to burn off both her extra energy and the calories. She picked up the plate holding the wedge of flaky crust and baked apples and considered whether to indulge herself. It took a lot of effort, but somehow she dredged up enough willpower to set it down and stepped back.

She gave it one more longing look. "Temptation, thy name is written in cinnamon and nutmeg."

To distance herself before her resolve weakened any further, she pocketed her keys and wallet. Then she grabbed Zeke's leash and called him to her side. "Let's go, boy. I think we could both use some fresh air and exercise."

From the way the dog bolted across the back porch and down the steps as soon as she opened the door, she wasn't the only one who needed this outing. She let him set the pace even if it left her a little breathless by the time they reached the sidewalk. Turning left, they followed the same route as the night before with Tripp.

Half an hour later, they reached the point where the national forest gave way to the city park. From there they strolled along the trail beside Snowberry Creek as it wound through the park. The immense Douglas firs and cedars along with the peek-a-boo view of Mount Rainier in the distance offered a postcard-perfect backdrop for their walk.

Her pleasure in their outing lasted right up until she spotted Gage and his daughter Sydney sitting at a picnic table down near the water's edge. Ordinarily, she would've been glad to see them despite the events of the previous evening. But in this case, it was more the other person approaching from behind Gage's back who had her considering doing an about-face and heading in the opposite direction. If Gage had been alone, she might have done just exactly that. But he wasn't, so she couldn't. Not in good conscience, anyway.

Because once again, Francine Denman looked as if she had every intention of reading Gage the riot act. She marched across the hillside in a straight line, building up a full head of steam as she did. With her hands clenched in fists at her sides, she appeared to be muttering under her breath as if rehearsing what she wanted to say.

At least Abby was closer to the Logans. If she hustled a little, she'd reach them in time to forewarn Gage and maybe get Sydney out of the danger zone before the angry woman got within shouting distance.

Gage happened to glance in Abby's direction and waved. When she frowned and jerked her head in Francine's direction, he glanced back over his shoulder. Understandably concerned, he immediately rose to his feet, saying something to his daughter at the same time. Abby picked up her pace until she reached them.

"Hi, Gage. Sorry to interrupt your outing."

He looked resigned to his fate. "You're obviously not the problem, Abby. Thanks for the warning. By the way, I'm not sure if you've ever met my daughter. Sydney, this is Abby McCree. She's a friend and Tripp Blackston's landlady."

Sydney managed to smile, but it was clear that she'd picked up on her father's sudden surge of tension. "Nice to meet you, Abby, but what's going on, Dad?"

"I'm going to have to talk with the lady heading in our direction. It won't be pleasant, and I don't want you caught in the middle of it."

Then he glanced around the area as if trying to figure out a safe passage for her escape. Abby held out the end of the dog's leash. "Sydney, this is my roommate, Zeke. I think he'd appreciate another stroll along the water. Would you do that for me?"

The teenager looked to her dad, who mustered up enough of a smile to reassure her. "You'll be fine with Zeke, Syd."

"And will you be fine, Dad?"

"Yeah, I'll be okay. The lady just wants to discuss a case with me."

The two adults watched as the mastiff-mix all but dragged Sydney along in his wake. At least the girl was laughing as she struggled to keep up. Gage kept his eyes on her, but spoke to Abby. "You could go with them, Abby. I can handle this."

"I never said you couldn't, Gage, but Syd will worry less if you aren't alone."

He grumbled, "I hate that you're right about that. The two of us have been so busy lately, we haven't had much time together. It was her suggestion that we grab some muffins and drinks at Bridey's and then hang out here for a little while. So much for that idea."

By that point, Francine was within earshot, so he turned to face her. "Ms. Denman, what can I do for you?"

"You can do your job, Chief Logan. I really don't think that's too much to ask."

What did Francine think he'd been doing all this time? When Abby took a step closer to the woman, Gage blocked her way. "I have been doing my job, Ms. Denman. As you well know, an arrest has been made in your father's case."

"That's interesting, but not helpful. As far as I can tell, nothing else is getting done. The bank won't allow me access to his safety deposit box without the keys, which are somewhere in the house. You can imagine my surprise when I drove by, expecting that all that tasteful yellow crime scene tape would be long gone. Then one of Dad's neighbors informed me that there'd been a break-in."

She crossed her arms over her chest and glared at Gage. "Care to tell me why I'm evidently the last person to hear about that?"

"I sent a deputy to tell you what happened, but no one was home. He was going to try again today. We also tried to reach you by phone, but the number was no longer valid."

Francine's belligerent stance shattered as if his words had landed a physical blow. Concerned the woman would collapse right where she stood, Abby slid around Gage and risked reaching out to her. "Ms. Denman, maybe we could all sit down and talk."

Looking confused, Francine blinked several times as if she were struggling to make sense of what Abby had just said. "I'm sorry, you look familiar for some reason. Do I know you?"

"Not really, Ms. Denman. I'm a friend of Gage's, and you might be thinking of when we briefly crossed paths outside Something's Brewing a while back. You were involved in a discussion with Gage out on the sidewalk as I walked by."

As she spoke, she took Francine by the arm and led her over to the picnic table. Once she was seated, Abby walked to the bench on the other side and sat down. After a few seconds, Gage joined them.

Still looking a bit shaken, Francine gripped the edge of the table, her knuckles white against her skin. "I can't pay the phone bill, but I didn't know they'd already turned it off."

Gage was good at his job because he cared deeply about people. It would've taken someone with a lot harder heart than his to not sympathize with the woman in front of him right now.

"What's going on, Ms. Denman? Is there anything I can do to help?"

Her laugh was bitter. "Not unless you have a whole lot of money you don't particularly need, but thanks for asking. My husband was diagnosed with cancer about ten months ago. He's responded well to the treatment, and the prognosis is positive. The downside is that kind of good news comes with a huge price tag. He was self-employed, so no work means no money. I've gone back to work, but I don't make enough to cover more than the most basic bills."

Tears trickled down her cheeks, but Abby didn't think Francine was even aware of them. She didn't have any tissues with her, so one of the napkins that had come with Gage's muffins would have to do. When she pressed it into Francine's hands, the woman looked a bit confused and then finally scrubbed at her cheeks with it.

"Sorry, I know none of that is your fault. It's actually

nobody's fault, but the stress has my temper running pretty hot these days."

What an awful situation. "That's understandable. You've got a lot on your plate right now."

"That doesn't mean I should take it out on anybody else." Still sniffling, Francine blotted her eyes and drew a deep breath. "I know I keep pushing to get into Dad's house, Chief Logan, and that you're doing your best to get to the bottom of things. My father would've wanted justice for his murder, but that's the least of my problems right now. No doubt you've already heard that he and I weren't on speaking terms. He thought I was ungrateful and made no bones about it. That lady friend of his probably gave you an earful on that subject."

Gage didn't bother to deny it. "There are always two sides to a story."

"That's so true. You see, Dad expected me to be the perfect daughter, one who would marry someone he thought worthy of the honor of being related to THE James DiSalvo. My role would be to produce a grandson for him to groom as his heir. I decided I'd rather marry someone I loved even if his pedigree wasn't up to Dad's standards. I've never regretted that decision."

She stared off into the distance. "That said, I foolishly thought Dad would eventually get over it and come to recognize that Curtis is a fine man, one who works hard and loves our family. Now it's too late. Dad's dead, and there's no way for us to make peace. Logically, it's highly doubtful that he would've left me a dime of his money, but I can't quit hoping."

By that point, Gage looked as if he wanted to punch something—or someone. Abby didn't blame him. If James

DiSalvo suddenly reappeared at that moment, she'd be tempted to take a torque wrench to him herself. It wouldn't accomplish anything, but maybe she'd feel a lot better.

Gage twisted in his seat to check on his daughter. Sydney and Zeke had completed the loop of the trail, but the two of them were sitting on the grass about fifty feet away. Smart girl. They were close enough to satisfy her father that she was okay but far enough away to prevent her from getting caught up in an uneasy situation.

He turned back to Francine. "Ms. Denman, I'm really sorry you're going through such a rough patch. This is actually my day off, but I'll see what I can do about getting you inside your father's house. Since we're still investigating, I can't let you in there by yourself. However, I'd be glad to act as your escort. What works for you?"

Francine looked marginally happier. "I actually have to get back home and take my husband for his doctor appointment, but maybe we can try for tomorrow sometime. I'll call you from my neighbor's house in the morning."

"Sounds good, Ms. Denman. You have my number if anything comes up before then."

In case Gage had something else to say to the woman that he didn't want Abby to hear, she decided to make herself scarce. "Gage, I'd better go reclaim my dog before your daughter gets too attached to him. Ms. Denman, I hope the doctor has more good news for you and your husband."

"That's kind of you, Abby."

"I'll talk to you later, Gage."

Having said her good-byes, Abby made her way over to Sydney and Zeke. The dog had his head on Sydney's lap while she petted his fur. Rather than reclaiming her roommate, Abby took a seat on the grass. Right now

Gage's daughter needed Zeke's undemanding company more than Abby did.

"Is that woman still there?"

"Yes, but she's about to leave. Your father is investigating her father's murder and another case that may or may not be related to his death. She wanted to know what was going on."

The explanation didn't placate Sydney one bit. "And she couldn't have called him at the office? Or, considering it's his day off, maybe talk to someone else? The man is entitled to a life, no matter what the people of Snowberry Creek seem to think. Sometimes I really hate his job."

Until that last comment, Sydney had sounded calm, as if having her outing with her dad interrupted hadn't ruffled her feathers. She might hide her anger better than most, but it was clear she didn't appreciate having to share her father's attention right now. If Abby were better acquainted with the girl, she would've put her arm around her. Luckily, comfort came in many forms, and Zeke had the situation well in hand. He lifted his head long enough to give Sydney a couple of quick swipes on her cheek with his tongue, which made the teenager laugh.

Sadly, Abby had to rely on mere words. "Gage is a good man, but you already know that. The people in this town are lucky to have him, Sydney. Most of them know that even if they sometimes forget to say so. Lord knows, he's been there for me often enough. I do try to make sure he knows I appreciate everything he does."

Sydney went back to stroking Zeke, a small grin peeking out. "I'm guessing you're the one who does all the baking. I can always tell when he's been by to see you and Tripp because he waits until I go to bed and does a long run on the treadmill. Don't tell him I said anything, though. He likes to think he's being sneaky."

Abby laughed. "Your secret is safe with me."

"I'm glad he's got such good friends. I'll be leaving for college eventually, and I don't want him to be alone."

Before Abby could come up with a suitable response, Sydney said, "Dad's headed this way. Guess he and that lady got things settled."

She gently slid her legs out from under Zeke and relinquished his leash to Abby. All three of them stood up and waited for Gage to join them. "I hope you and your dad can enjoy the rest of the day without his work interfering."

"Me too." Sydney bent down to give Zeke a quick hug. "Thanks for taking me on a walk, Zeke. We'll have to do it again sometime."

It didn't surprise Abby that's Gage first words were directed to his daughter. "You okay?"

Sydney nodded. "I had a good time with Zeke. He's a great dog."

He gave Zeke a long look. "Actually, I think he's some weird mash-up of a pony and a garbage disposal."

Funny as that was, Abby rushed to defend her pet. Covering Zeke's ears, she glared at Gage. "Hush, you'll hurt his feelings. You know very well he's part mastiff and part something else."

Gage snickered. "It's the something else that has scientists baffled."

His daughter punched him on the arm. "Dad, don't be mean. Zeke is a real sweetheart."

Gage held up his hands in surrender. "You're right, Syd. He's a great dog."

To show he meant it, he gave Zeke a thorough scratching. "Thanks again, Abby, for charging into the fray. Let's just cross our fingers that I can get permission to allow Ms. Denman into her father's house tomorrow. It would be nice if she could get the answers she needs, one way or another. I'm guessing it's the not knowing that is making things so hard for her right now. She can't make any kind of plans with everything so up in the air."

"Has she at least been able to plan her father's funeral?"

"It's scheduled for the day after tomorrow. All things considered, she decided to keep things simple and limit attendance to immediate family only. Some folks, and you can guess who, aren't happy about that, but it's Francine's decision to make. She did say she might have a life celebration party to honor him at some point in the future when things have settled down a bit."

From what Francine had told them about her personal finances, Abby had to guess that money had driven her decision to keep the funeral low-key. She felt for the woman.

It was past time for her and Zeke to be heading homeward. "Well, I'd better get moving. Zeke gets grumpy if he doesn't get his afternoon nap right on time. I also live in fear of having to carry him home if he gets tired of walking."

Gage laughed. "That's quite an image. I think I'd actually pay to see that. If I snapped a couple of pictures, maybe your buddy Riley Molitor could even print them in the paper."

"Dad, I swear I shouldn't take you out in public." Sydney shook her head, obviously praying for patience. "Seriously, Abby, would you two like a ride home?"

"Thanks for the offer, but we're good. My house isn't all that far."

Gage gave Zeke one last pat on the head. "Okay. I'll give you a call tomorrow if I learn anything interesting."

Now, that was a surprise. He didn't make a habit of sharing information when it came to his cases. Maybe he thought he owed her for helping him out today, but she didn't want their friendship to be based on keeping score.

"Till then."

One tug on Zeke's leash was all it took to have him towing her down to the parking lot. From there, they made it the rest of the way home in good time. Thank goodness, because Zeke wasn't the only one in need of a nap right now. The long walk and the stress of dealing with Francine Denman with her various problems had taken their toll.

And if the nap didn't help, maybe that last piece of pie would.

CHAPTER 25

"**W**hy are you so antsy?"

Abby shoved her phone back in her pocket and went back to trimming the rhododendrons. When it became obvious that Tripp would wait as long as it took for her to get around to answering his question, she gave up trying to ignore him. That didn't mean she had to give him a straight answer. "I don't know what you're talking about."

"Yeah, right. That's the third time you've checked your phone in the past half hour. Are you expecting an important phone call or something?"

She still didn't want to tell him. "Or something."

"Very funny. I can always tell when you're up to something you don't want me to know about. Might as well fess up now, because I won't give up until you tell me."

Nosy jerk. Well, he wasn't really a jerk, but his persistence could be really irritating at times. "Fine. Gage said he might call today, and I'm worried I might not be able to hear my phone out here."

It was too much to hope that Tripp would be satisfied with her explanation. "So, are you his unofficial consultant on homicide cases now?"

Even if it felt like that sometimes, she'd never admit it to Tripp. "How do you know it isn't about something personal?"

She hated when grown men rolled their eyes like a teenage girl. Tripp was especially adept at it, which made it even more irritating. "If it was personal, you wouldn't be looking so guilty right now."

This was a losing battle, and she knew it. Might as well get it over with. "Yesterday I took Zeke for walk to the park, and Gage was there with his daughter. I would've just waved and kept going, but I wasn't the only one who had spotted them. James DiSalvo's daughter was headed in their direction. I warned them just in time to send Sydney out of the line of fire. She walked Zeke while Gage and I talked to Francine. And before you ask, yes, I could've gone with Sydney. But Francine was so upset, she nearly collapsed. It took both of us to calm her down and find out what was really going on."

Most of her explanation poured out on one breath. She paused to refill her lungs before continuing. "So I don't know if Gage was actually able to let Francine go through her father's house, and I don't plan to call and ask him. He was the one who said that he might share what he found out."

"Curiosity is eating you alive right now, isn't it?"

He knew her so well. She had to laugh a little about

that. "Yeah, but I'm still not going to pester him. I'd think you'd be proud of my forbearance."

"I would be if I really believed you wouldn't find some other way to poke your nose in his business."

So maybe Tripp was a jerk after all.

"Well, if you'll excuse me, I need to finish up with these bushes."

And wouldn't you know it, her phone chimed just as soon as she turned her back to Tripp. Sure enough, Gage had sent her a text. He kept it short and to the point, not to mention mysterious and worrisome.

On my way over. Got news. Not all good.

She hadn't been all that concerned about whatever he and Francine found out, but she was now. There was no use firing back a demand for clarification, so she just answered **Okay**. If Gage had wanted to explain what was going on by text message, he would have. Sending the short message at least bought her several seconds to regain control before turning to face Tripp again.

Her efforts to act calm must have failed miserably. Tripp took one look at her face and immediately half dragged, half carried her over to sit down on his porch steps. It was quick thinking on his part considering she wasn't all that sure she could've made it that far on her own.

"What's happened now, Abby?"

She felt stupid when she could only say, "Nothing. Well, probably not anything important."

Realizing she wasn't making much sense, she tried again. "Gage is on his way here. All he said was that he had news, and not all of it is good."

"And he didn't say what it was about? Or, more importantly, who?"

She clenched her fingers together and shook her head. "Sorry, but that's all he said. For some reason my imagination kicked into high gear and ran wild with all kinds of ideas about what could've gone wrong. I'll be all right in a second."

Tripp sat down beside her. "The idiot should've just said he was stopping by and then told you what was going on after he got here. Anyone with half a functioning brain cell should've known that text would freak you out. Heck, it's even got me worried."

They sat there in silence watching for Gage's cruiser to pull into the driveway. Fortunately, they didn't have to wait long. Abby started to stand up, but Tripp tugged her back down on the steps. "He can come to you."

The expression on Gage's face had her wanting to take off running for the sanctuary of her house and lock the doors, shutting him and his not-good-news outside. Gage must have been a mind reader, because he planted himself directly in the middle of the most direct route to her back porch, his arms crossed over his chest. Sighing, she resigned herself to listening to whatever awful thing he wanted to tell her.

"What's up, Gage?"

"First of all, I'd like you to stay calm, and I promise Gil's going to be all right."

Really? He dropped a bombshell like that and actually expected her to stay calm? Only Tripp taking her hand in his kept her from flying apart. "What happened?"

"He's not sure. Liam walked down from the bar to check on him, something I guess he's been doing most every day. He found Gil flat out on the floor of the garage with a sizable lump on his head. He was just coming to and had no idea who hit him or why. The last thing he remembers was looking around the place for a shipment of parts that was supposed to have been delivered. Anyway, Liam called it in. The EMTs responded along with one of my people. Deputy Chapin took the preliminary report and then let Liam drive Gil to the hospital to get checked out."

For the first time, Gage smiled just a little. "Evidently that stubborn biker flat out refused to go by ambulance. Something about not needing all the fanfare for a simple trip to the hospital, thank you very much."

Tripp snickered. "I'm guessing Gil's language was a bit more colorful."

"To say the least." Gage glanced at Abby and then back toward Tripp. "The man was in pain, so a bit of salty language was understandable. He cares what Abby here thinks of him, so I thought it best to paraphrase a little bit."

She snorted. "I wouldn't fall over in shock if I heard a bad word or two, Gage."

By that point he was openly grinning. "From what I heard, it was a whole lot more than a word or two and pretty darn creative. Deputy Chapin even took notes. Like I said, Gil was really hurting."

"What did the doctors say?"

"Liam is supposed to call me when they get the results of the CT scan. That will determine if they'll keep him overnight or send him home. It might also depend on whether the doctor thinks it would be safe for Gil to be alone. The one time I got a concussion, my wife had to wake me up every so often all night long. Not sure if that's still the usual protocol, so we'll have to wait to see what the doctor thinks."

Abby couldn't stand the thought of Gil being left on

his own and hurting. "If he needs to have someone around, he could crash at my place for the night. Or I could stay at his house if he'd rather."

Both men were already shaking their heads, leaving her to ask, "Why not?"

Tripp was the one who answered. "Think about it, Abby. Someone attacked him, and Gage has no idea who it was or why. What if they decided to take another shot at Gil while you were alone with him at his house?"

Okay, she got that. "Then he can come here. The two of us and Zeke can stand guard."

At least Gage surrendered without a fight. "Okay, I'll have Liam extend the invitation, but don't be surprised if Gil turns it down. He won't risk putting you in the crosshairs of whoever attacked him."

She wanted to argue the point, but Gage wasn't the one she needed to convince. "Well, all we can do is offer. Let's hope the doctor will park Gil in a hospital bed overnight. Maybe I can convince him to be reasonable after he's been stuck eating green gelatin for dessert instead of one of my coffee cakes."

Time to move on to another subject. "You said not all of the news was good. That sort of implies you have more to tell me."

"Francine and I went through the house today. That's where I was when the call about Gil came in."

Was he really going to make her pry every detail out of him bit by bit? Evidently, since he didn't immediately launch into a more detailed report on their findings.

"And, Chief Logan?"

The jerk recognized the note of frustration in her voice and found it amusing. "And what exactly are you asking?"

She let out a long sigh. "Never mind. As I'm sure Tripp is about to remind me, what you found or didn't find isn't really any of my business. I'm just glad that you were able to help her."

It was hard to keep a straight face when confronted by two grown men looking as if she'd just hit them between the eyes with a two-by-four. After a second, Tripp covered her forehead with the palm of his hand.

"She's not running a fever, Gage, but maybe Gil isn't the only one who got hit on the head today. Or it could be sunstroke. She's been working out here in the yard for quite a while."

For his part in their little comedy routine, Gage moved in closer and held up his forefinger right in front of her face. Moving it slowly back and forth, he issued an order. "Follow my finger, Abby."

Instead, she crossed her eyes and stuck her tongue out at him.

He immediately faked looking more worried. "Tripp, this is serious. She can't even follow simple directions."

Tripp frowned big-time but with a hint of humor in his eyes as he tried to take her pulse. "Are you feeling dizzy or anything?"

Okay, enough was enough. She jerked her hand free and scooted a few inches away from him. They were joking around, but for some mysterious reason it made her crabby. "What's wrong with the two of you? How many times have you told me to stay out of police matters? And now that I'm trying to do exactly that, you're giving me nothing but grief."

Both men apologized. Neither of them meant it.

"That's it. I'm going home. Let's go, Zeke."

When the dog didn't immediately haul himself up off

the ground, she wanted to borrow a few salty words from
Gil. With her hands on her hips, she tried one more time.
"Now, Zeke."

Harrumphing a bit, he dragged himself up to his feet
but still made no effort to move. Rather than stand there
and argue with him and thereby provide additional amusement for the other two males, she threw her hands up in
the air. "Fine, stay with them. Just remember that later
when you want me to bake some more of your peanut
butter cookies."

With one last dirty look at all concerned, she added,
"'Cause I'm telling you right now, I don't see that happening anytime soon."

She made it all the way to her back porch before Zeke
rethought his decision and charged across the yard to
catch up with her. Or maybe it had been a group decision,
since both Tripp and Gage weren't far behind him. Just
because they'd finally come to their senses didn't mean
she was going to play hostess this time.

As tempting as it was to slam the door closed and lock
it once Zeke made it inside, she refrained from doing so.
She helped herself to a can of pop from the fridge,
grabbed a couple of Zeke's treats and retreated to the living room. The dog followed after her just as she knew he
would. He stopped once or twice to look back toward the
kitchen where his buddies were. However, the dog had
his priorities and staying near his treats was right up there
at the top of the list.

She was firmly ensconced in her favorite chair when
the two men finally joined her in the living room. Judging
from the noises they'd made in the kitchen, she wasn't
surprised to see they each had a cup of fresh coffee and a
plate stacked with cookies and another with cheese and

crackers. Tripp handed her a small plate and then held out the snacks so she could help herself first.

He actually looked a little worried, as if wondering how she would react. Or, to be honest, overreact. She normally had better control of her temper and her emotions, but she was worried about Gil. Francine, too, even though she hardly knew the woman. It took some effort, but she managed a small smile. "Thanks for playing host, Tripp. I'm sorry I lost my temper. Mostly, anyway."

That last bit had him grinning. "Not a problem. Considering everything that's happened lately, a little meltdown isn't unexpected."

Gage sat on the couch. He washed down a cookie with a big sip of coffee before joining the conversation. "I really was going to tell you about what happened with Francine, Abby. I shouldn't have played games with you."

Her smile came easier this time. "Let's just go with apologies all around and move on. So what did you learn?"

"I had warned her about the vandalism before we got there, but it still hit her pretty hard. She hadn't been inside the house since her mother died, so even crossing the threshold was hard for her. I guess she and her mom stayed in contact all along, but they had to be careful DiSalvo himself didn't find out. He might have viewed it as a betrayal by his wife."

That was just so sad. Family was everything, warts and all. At least Francine hadn't been cut off completely from hers. "DiSalvo seems to have been the real loser in all of this, living all alone instead of rebuilding his relationship with his daughter and her family."

Gage shrugged. "And maybe Francine was better off without him. I can't imagine he would've been any less controlling if they had tried to mend their fences."

"True enough. That seems to have been the way he treated everyone he came into contact with."

Gage sandwiched a piece of cheese between two snickerdoodles and took a bite. Evidently he liked the taste because he immediately assembled another one. Did he think the cheese balanced out the carbs in the cookies? On the other hand, who was she to criticize?

"We made a quick pass through the whole house and then circled back to do it again more slowly. I made sure we both wore gloves to avoid adding our fingerprints to any that were already there. The forensics team has already been through, but they mainly concentrated on the areas where the house had been vandalized as well as the doors and windows, hoping to see how someone got into the house."

"Was she able to find the safety deposit keys? Or his legal papers?"

"Yes to the keys, but no to the papers. We're hoping they're in the safety deposit box. I'm going to meet her at the bank in the morning. She did find the rest of her mother's good jewelry in the dresser. She was really upset to learn Georgia had taken the pearls, but she knows we have them now. We can't give them to her until we find DiSalvo's will and maybe even his wife's. Mrs. DiSalvo may have designated they should go to Francine no matter how her father felt about that decision."

"I'll keep my fingers crossed for her."

"I take it you've pretty much eliminated her as a suspect for the vandalism." Tripp reached for some more crackers and cheese. "Any thoughts about who might have been hiding out in the house or why they painted what they did on the walls?"

Gage's frustration was obvious in the tight set of his

jaw. "I just can't see Francine being the one behind the vandalism, but I wanted to be with her to see how she reacted to just being there. It wasn't easy for her, but she treated the place with respect. Can't say she was surprised that her father had incited that kind of anger in someone."

Abby leaned down to stroke Zeke's head. "So you didn't find anything useful."

For the first time, Gage looked a bit smug. "Oddly enough, we did. When she went through her father's closet, she found a sleeping bag. It was all neatly rolled up on a shelf above DiSalvo's enormous collection of expensive suits and fancy shoes."

Tripp looked less than impressed. "So? Lots of people have sleeping bags."

"Well, her father took the family camping exactly one time when she was a little girl. He only did it because it was something that people in the Pacific Northwest were expected to do. They bought all brand-new gear and appropriate camping clothing for what was supposed to be a week-long trip."

Abby tried to picture James DiSalvo in a flannel shirt, jeans, and hiking boots, but the image wouldn't come into focus.

Gage continued. "Apparently it was the worst vacation imaginable. Sleeping in a tent and cooking outside quickly lost all appeal when it rained for forty-eight hours straight. Finally, they piled all their wet gear into the back of the SUV he'd rented for the occasion and retreated to the nearest motel. It was a run-down and dingy place, so even that was roughing it by their standards."

"I bet DiSalvo was a real joy to be around." Tripp snorted. "I would've begged him to tie me to the roof rather than have to spend hours inside the car with him at that point."

Gage drained the rest of his coffee and set the cup aside. "Me too. Anyway, the bottom line is, that sleeping bag didn't belong there. When their ill-fated camping trip was over, her father donated every bit of their expensive gear to charity. The only sleeping bag he ever allowed in the house after that was the pink one Francine used to take to sleepovers."

Abby sat up straighter as all the pieces were coming together. "So the sleeping bag must belong to the trespasser."

Gage eyed the last cookie on the plate but then sat back as if putting more distance between him and temptation. "That's my theory. I called the team back to take custody of the bag and to check the bedroom area for fingerprints."

"Can they get prints off cloth?"

Before Gage could respond, Tripp answered his own question. "Never mind. I know there's likely to be other evidence they can get from the fabric, but there's a chance of at least partial prints on the zipper pull."

Gage gave Tripp the kind of smile a teacher would offer a student for coming up with the right answer. "I asked them to put a rush on it, but don't hold your breath. It could take a couple of weeks to get the results. A vandalism case is pretty low priority. Right now, there's no proof that this was anything but some transient taking advantage of an empty house. The fact that it belonged to a murder victim might just be a coincidence."

"But it might not," Abby insisted.

Gage didn't press the point. Instead, he set his plate and cup on the coffee table. "And on that note, I have to stop at the store on the way home. I promised Syd I'd cook something special for dinner tonight."

"What's the occasion?"

The lines around his world-weary eyes deepened. "Today I watched a daughter grieve over the loss of her father, a man who was gone from her life long before he actually died. As hard as it is to believe, Francine seems to have genuinely loved DiSalvo despite everything, and he's never going to know what he missed out on. I prefer to think I'm smarter than that, so I'm going to cook whatever my own daughter wants and be darn glad to do it."

Then he was gone.

CHAPTER 26

Abby glared across the small hospital room at one stubborn biker. Gil sat on the side of the bed where he'd spent the night, wincing with every move he made. It was only a little after nine, and the man was determined to be up and on his way by nine thirty.

"I know for a fact that the doctor suggested you stay here until later in the afternoon. I think you should do what she says."

Gil started to shake his head but froze as he grunted in pain. "I already signed the discharge paperwork."

Frustrated, Abby sighed. "Then tear up the paperwork. You can't be the only idiot who thought he was ready to go home when he wasn't. Isn't. Whatever. They have to have some kind of procedure for that."

He glared at her through bloodshot eyes. "I want to go home."

"You've got a concussion."

"It's not my first one. Won't be my last. There's nothing they can do for me here that I can't do for myself at home."

Moving slowly, he leaned down to pick up his boot. The effort clearly cost him both pain and energy. She considered letting him suffer, but it wasn't in her to do that. "For Pete's sake, let me get that for you."

"Stop fussing, woman."

"Stop being an idiot."

Her assessment of his behavior only made him grumpier, but she didn't care. She picked up the boot and helped him slip it on and then did the same with the second one. "They said to wait until they round up a wheelchair before leaving the room. Argue about that, and I'll add a second lump to your skull to match the one you've already got."

He mumbled something unflattering about her under his breath, but she ignored his complaint. "And since I'm driving, you get no say in where we go. I'm taking you to my house. When we get there, you'll give Tripp your keys so he can go to your house and pick up whatever you'll need to camp out in my guest room for two nights. No more, but no less."

The silence in the room gathered like a storm about to break. Gage had warned her that Gil would likely refuse her offer of hospitality, but she wasn't going to give up without a fight. She stepped back from the bed to give Gil some room, both figuratively and literally. He stared down at the floor for several long seconds.

"Abby, I appreciate the offer, but I don't know who did this to me or why."

She conceded that much. "I know, Gil, and it worries you that I might get caught in the middle of it. But it won't just be the two of us. Zeke makes for a pretty good alarm system, and he's protected me on more than one occasion. Tripp is inside and plans to camp out on the couch downstairs. You'll be safer there than alone at your house."

When that didn't move him, she tried again. "The doctor said you need to have someone with you for at least the next twenty-four hours. If you have someone else who can come stay with you, fine. Otherwise, I'm your best option."

When there was no response, she pulled out the big guns. "I made pie."

He held up his hands in surrender. "Why didn't you say that in the first place?"

Abby ignored Gil's bad mood as she followed him up the back porch steps. By the time they were inside, the biker was breathing hard and looking pale. Even so, she tried not to hover as he made his way to the kitchen table to sit down. As tempting as it was to say "I told you so," she remained silent until he was settled in place.

"What can I get for you?"

"I'd love a beer, but I'll settle for some coffee and maybe some toast. I'm due for a pain pill and don't want to take it on an empty stomach."

The coffee was already brewing, so she put two pieces of bread in the toaster and pushed the lever down. Left with nothing more to do for the moment, she joined the two men at the table. Meanwhile, Gil pulled his key chain from his pocket and shoved it across the table toward Tripp. "My room is the first one on the right. Some clean jeans, a couple of T-shirts"—he paused to glanced at Abby and then back at Tripp—"and some other stuff out of the top dresser drawer would be appreciated."

It was hard not to smile at his discomfort in talking about underwear and socks in front of her. "I've got an extra toothbrush, toothpaste, and other things you might need in the guest bathroom right next to where you'll be sleeping."

She suspected Gil appreciated her minimizing the amount of rooting around in his personal stuff that Tripp would have to do. He pointed toward a silver key. "That key is for the front door."

Tripp stuffed the keys in his front pocket. "I know you can take care of yourself, but you're running on fumes right now. On your own, you can probably make it as far as the living room where you can conk out in a chair or on the couch. However, you might need my help getting up the stairs if you'd rather stretch out in a bed. It's your choice."

"The chair. I've had enough of being in bed for now."

"Okay. I'll be back soon." Tripp started for the door but stopped. "Do you need me to go by the shop for anything?"

"Not that I can think of. Gage made sure it was locked up after his people finished poking their noses into everything yesterday."

She was surprised that he sounded amused by the prospect of law enforcement rifling through his place of business again, but maybe he was used to such things. Tripp let himself out the back door, leaving her and Gil alone. Well, except for Zeke, who nudged Gil's arm out of the way to put his head on the man's leg. Stroking the dog's head seemed to soothe Gil as much as it did Zeke.

When the toast finally popped up, she put it on a plate and set it in front of Gil, along with the butter and two kinds of jam. After pouring them both coffee, she carried the cups to the table and then made a second trip for a glass of water and his pain medicine.

He downed a pill and set the glass aside. "Thanks, Abby, and not just for the toast. I'm a bit of a bear when I'm hurt. Just ask Gary the next time you see him."

Then he winced. "I can't decide whether I should have his attorney tell him what happened or not. He doesn't need to be worrying about me, but I wonder if it might help him figure out if there's a connection between why someone set him up to take the fall for murder and the attack on me."

"Maybe it wouldn't hurt, but you don't have to decide until you catch your breath. Finish your toast, and then Zeke can help you get settled in the living room."

Gil huffed a small laugh. "You think having Zeke fuss over me is more palatable than having you do it?"

She shot him a grin. "Yep, I do."

After finishing his toast, Gil slowly pushed himself back up to his feet. "I'm going to mosey on down the hall to the living room. Give me a few minutes to get settled before you check on me. A man's entitled to some dignity."

"Yes, sir."

She hung back in the kitchen while he trudged down the hall. By the time she finally ventured into the living room, Zeke was settled on the floor beside Gil's chair.

The man himself was ensconced in the wingback chair and had even covered up with the lap quilt she'd left within easy reach of where he was sitting.

Making sure Zeke wasn't watching, she slipped Gil a plastic bag of doggy treats to dole out as he saw fit. "Unless you need anything else, I'm going to go upstairs to work on a quilt. I'll leave the door to the sewing room open, so I will be able to hear you if you holler."

"Sounds good."

She perched on the arm of the couch. "I promise to quit hovering in a second, but first I wanted to make sure there isn't anything you need me to do. Are you expecting any shipments at the shop? Do you need me to pick up the mail there or anything? And what about Casey? Was he expecting to work the next couple of days?"

"I tried calling him from the hospital to let him know what was going on and to stay away from the shop, but he never answered. He doesn't always, so no surprise there. I left a message that the shop is closed for a few days and told him to call if he had questions. Of course, that's going to be hard considering my phone is dead right now. I should have told Tripp to grab my charger."

"I'll call him. Maybe he's still at your house."

"Thanks." Gil closed his eyes and rested his head against the back of the chair. "As for the rest of it, the mail will be fine for a couple of days, and hopefully the delivery guys won't leave stuff outside while the shop is closed. In fact, that's why I was hunting for missing parts. The driver swears he carried the box inside, but I never saw it. Checking the shelf in the back is the last thing I remember."

"So no idea who hit you?"

"Nope."

"That must be frustrating."

"Yeah, it is. Usually I know if I've ticked someone off and why." He opened his eyes enough to squint at her. "I'm still not thinking completely straight. I probably should've also asked Tripp to do a quick drive-by just in case someone did drop off anything outside the shop."

"I'll give him a call about that and the charger. He won't mind making an extra stop, especially if I tell him that I'll do it if he can't."

Gil laughed and immediately regretted it. Rubbing his forehead, he said, "You are one sneaky woman, Abby McCree. Tricking your man into doing something because you know he doesn't like you taking risks."

It wasn't the first time Gil had made the assumption that she and Tripp were more than just friends. She wasn't sure what to make of that. Regardless, he was right. She shouldn't take advantage of Tripp's protective instincts.

"How about I just ask Tripp to stop by the shop with no mention of me going instead. How's that?"

"Better."

"I'll leave you alone, then."

She'd barely made the short distance to the staircase in the hallway when Gil spoke again. "If I forgot to say it, thanks for fussing, Abby."

"That's what friends are for."

Gil dozed off and on for most of the day. Once his phone was recharged, he spent a little time calling customers to tell them the shop would be closed for a few days. He also checked his messages, but still no word from Casey. Gil didn't seem all that concerned about it, saying the guy would turn up eventually. If not, it wasn't as if Casey was a permanent employee.

Tripp had been in and out. After dropping off Gil's things, he'd gone out to mow the grass. Abby caught his attention as he made another pass across the yard. "Do you need anything at the store? I told Gil I'd be back in an hour or so."

"A gallon of milk, a loaf of bread, and some eggs."

When he reached for his wallet, she waved him off. "Worry about that later."

Tripp reached out and gently brushed a strand of hair back from her face. "Okay. Let me know if you get delayed for some reason. Gil's not the only one who's worried that his problems might have followed him here."

"I'll be careful. No talking to strangers."

"And lock your car doors."

She offered him a salute. "Yes, sir. Orders received and understood."

The fact that he didn't crack a smile at her antics sent a small shiver of apprehension dancing down her spine. When he headed back to the lawn mower without saying another word, she caught up with him and tugged on the back of his shirt to get his attention again. "Tripp, I meant it. I'll be careful. Do you believe me?"

"I believe you mean it. I'm not sure I believe you will."

With that, he gave the lawn mower a hard shove and went back to work, leaving her staring after him. Did he really think she was that careless with her own welfare? As soon as she got in the car, she locked the doors and kept a wary eye on her surroundings to the point of feeling a bit paranoid as she drove through town. She wanted to believe both Gil and Tripp were overreacting, but it was hard to question their logic, especially considering they still didn't know who had put Gil in the hospital or why.

At least it didn't take her long to finish her shopping She stepped back outside to discover it had started raining while she'd been in the store. After quickly stowing the groceries in her trunk, she debated what to do next. Tripp and Gil were expecting her back in just over half an hour, so there was a little time before she needed to head back to the house. Maybe she'd take a quick drive to the small farmer's market just outside of town. Fresh corn was just coming into season, and it would go well with the hamburgers she was cooking for dinner.

Her plans made, she headed toward the turnoff onto the state highway at the far end of town. Shortly after making the turn, she passed by the entrance to the mobile-home park that she and Tripp had explored. Several new bullet holes in the entrance sign squashed any desire to drive through the place again. Wouldn't Tripp be proud of her forbearance?

A little farther down the road, she spotted a familiar figure walking along the side of the road, coming toward her from the opposite direction. Casey shuffled along, frowning at the ground as if he had a lot on his mind. Had he gotten Gil's message? If not, there was a good chance the man had no idea what was going on.

Unfortunately, the shoulder of the highway was narrow, not to mention that particular stretch was also pretty hilly with limited visibility. It wouldn't be safe for either her or Casey if she were to stop now. Maybe she'd have a better chance on her way back from the farmer's market when she'd be on the same side of the road as he was. If not, at least she'd be able to let Gil know that she'd seen him and that he looked okay.

She reached her destination a few minutes later, and once again luck was with her. The farmer's market drew customers from all over the area, and sometimes it was difficult to even find a parking place. This time, though, the gravel parking lot only held a handful of cars. Inside the rustic barnlike structure, she grabbed a basket and made a quick trip up and down the aisles, loading up on whatever looked good.

While waiting to pay, she checked her watch and realized she was really cutting it close time-wise. To avoid worrying Tripp and Gil, she sent a quick text to tell them where she was and that she was on her way back, adding that traffic was getting heavier so it might take longer than usual to get home. Considering how quickly both men responded, she was glad she'd taken the few seconds required to let them know. They'd probably both feel a whole lot better when she walked in the door.

She'd been right about the traffic heading back toward Snowberry Creek. It was most likely due to people who worked in Tacoma or even Seattle making their way back to town. As she drove, she kept a wary eye on the cars ahead of her while watching for Casey.

He was nowhere in sight, which was both curious and disappointing. There were no bus stops that she could see, but it was always possible that someone had already offered him a lift. The only road that crossed the highway in that area was the one that led into the mobile-home park. Could he have gone in there? It wouldn't surprise her at all to find out that's where he lived.

Should she do a quick drive-through to see if she could spot him? She doubted Tripp would think so, but she had no plans to stop other than to talk to Casey. At the most, it would delay her arrival home by ten minutes. If it would take longer, she could always send another text to update both Gil and Tripp.

She had but seconds to decide. Ignoring any second thoughts on the subject, she pulled into the center turn lane and waited for a break in the oncoming traffic to whip across the road into the mobile-home park.

Regrettably, there was no sign of Casey anywhere near the entrance. Maybe that was for the best. After all, it really wasn't her responsibility to let him know why the garage was closed. One thing did make her curious, though. If Casey did live in the mobile-home park, why wouldn't he allow anyone to drive him there? The bus line did go past the entrance, but the nearest stop had to be a mile or more away.

Resigned to not finding her quarry, she continued driving. It was definitely time to head back to the highway. She would've turned around, but the road was clearly marked one-way. A couple minutes later, she'd reached the point where the route through the park veered to the left for about three blocks before it took another sharp turn back toward the entrance. It wouldn't take her all that long to finish the loop, but it was definitely going to make her even later getting back home. Rather than face the wrath of two worried men, she checked the rearview mirror to make sure there weren't any cars coming up behind her. With the coast clear, she stopped to send another short text before continuing on her way.

Just as she hit the gas, though, a car shot out of a driveway right in front of her, forcing her to slam on the brakes to avoid a collision. The near-accident was partly Abby's fault for not noticing the other car, but other than the rush of adrenaline that came from the brief scare, no harm was done.

By that point the other car had reached the turn at the end of the block, giving her the first clear view of the vehicle. It looked vaguely familiar, and it took her a second to decide it looked a little like the SUV that Francine Denman drove. She couldn't see the driver from that angle, and it was raining too hard to pick out many details. Besides, the color and general shape could've belonged to any number of makes and models.

She did wonder if the driver lived in that particular mobile home or was just visiting. Curiosity had her slowing to see if there was a name on the mailbox at the end of the driveway. No luck there, just the street number. She was about to drive off when someone peeked around the rear corner of the mobile home before ducking back out of sight as soon as he spotted her. Wasn't that Casey? For sure the man was wearing the same color and style of hooded jacket he'd had on when she passed him out on the highway.

Should she drive on by? If it was Casey, he was clearly trying to avoid her. The question was why? Was he somewhere he shouldn't be? Or did he simply prefer to protect his privacy as much as he could? It wasn't as if she actually knew him all that well. They'd only spent that short time together when Tripp had given Casey a ride the day Gage and his men had executed the search warrant at Gil's shop.

Maybe if she left the engine running and only rolled down her passenger window partway it would reassure him that she had no intention of intruding any further than that.

When he peeked out again, she smiled and motioned for him to come closer. After a bit, he stepped out into plain sight and moved in her direction one slow step at a time.

When he got close enough that she wouldn't have to holler at the top of her lungs, she smiled again. "Hi, Casey, I passed you out on the highway on my way to the farmer's market. When I didn't see you on my way back, I thought maybe you'd come this way. I just wanted to let you know that Gil has been trying to reach you. He's had to close the shop for a few days, and he wanted you to know."

He jerked his head in a quick nod to let her know he understood. He shifted from one foot to the other and had a great deal of trouble keeping his attention focused on her. She knew he was easily upset, so his jittery behavior came as no surprise. Even though she'd made no move to get out of the car, his agitation continued to grow.

"Well, I'll be going. Take care, Casey."

With another one of those jerky nods, he spun on his heel and headed back around the mobile home again. Figuring she'd accomplished all that she could, she put the car in drive and started forward. As she drove, her mind swirled with questions. What was he doing back there? If this was where Casey lived, why didn't he simply go inside if he didn't want to be seen?

She glanced back to see if she could catch one last glimpse of him. To her surprise, he was using a tree stump to climb over the six-foot high cedar fence that divided the mobile home park from the neighborhood on the other side.

Okay, then. Maybe he didn't live there at all, and he just used it as a shortcut. That might account for why he was so twitchy about being spotted. But where was he headed? There was nothing in that direction except a bunch of houses. The kind that cost tons of money. In fact, if she remembered correctly, those houses were part of the same neighborhood where James DiSalvo had lived.

A shiver of apprehension ran down her spine as several pieces of the puzzle she'd been trying to fit together since the day of the race seemed to snap into place. Casey would've had access to Gary's tools. He would also have been able to slip up behind Gil if he'd been working the day he was attacked. Even if he'd just happened to stop by, Gil wouldn't have hesitated to turn his back on the man. Too bad Gil's memories of the event were so jumbled and hazy.

But even if those pieces might somehow fit together, there was no clear link from Casey to James DiSalvo. Well, unless it had something to do with the mobile-home park. It was hard to know if she was on the right track, but she really hoped like crazy that she wasn't. That kind of betrayal would hurt Gil even if it did manage to clear his brother's name. Finally, she drew a deep breath and drove on. She really needed to get back home.

There'd be plenty of time later to ponder the situation. It wasn't as if she had any hard evidence, only suppositions, and there had already been one innocent man arrested for DiSalvo's murder. She wouldn't be able to live with herself if she was responsible for a second one to end up behind bars when all she knew for sure was that he'd climbed a fence. Maybe Gil would have some idea about why Casey had been at the mobile-home park or why he'd chosen to leave it in such an odd way.

As she pulled out onto the highway, her conscience reminded her that if all else failed, she could always give Gage a call.

CHAPTER 27

By the time Abby got home, she'd convinced herself that she was seeing connections where there weren't any. At least nothing definite enough to bring up the subject to her two dinner guests, much less the chief of police. Instead, she'd put Gil to work shucking the corn, figuring it was something he could do sitting down while letting him feel useful. As he did that, she cooked the beets and made a vinaigrette dressing. Combined with fresh greens and pine nuts, they made for the perfect salad to go along with the corn and burgers.

After dinner, Gil helped with the cleanup before heading upstairs to his room, because his headache was back. After making sure Gil made it safely to the second floor, Tripp took up residence at the dining room table, saying he planned to put in several hours on his homework.

Feeling a bit at odds and ends, Abby retreated to the

sewing room to work on the baby quilt. She layered the quilt top with batting and the fabric she'd chosen for the back. After pinning everything in place, she started the quilting process. First, she outlined each of the squares and then carefully stitched along the edges of the individual hexagons. Even working at a slow pace, she made good progress. At least it gave her something else to think about.

About an hour later, Zeke showed up looking lonely. Judging by the way he kept wandering around the room, lying down in one spot for a few minutes before moving on to another, he was also restless. She knew just how he felt. Deciding she'd reached a good stopping point, she put the quilt back on the cutting table and did several stretches to relax her stiff muscles.

When Zeke let out a huge sigh, she grinned. "What do you say, boy? How about a short walk to work out the kinks? It would do us both some good."

The dog woofed and took off like a shot, thumping down the steps at an alarming rate. She could only hope that he wasn't making so much racket that he woke up Gil. She followed at a much more sedate pace and took care to avoid the creaky spot at the top of the last flight of steps. With her rain jacket and Zeke's leash in hand, she poked her head into the dining room to let Tripp know where she was going. He was nowhere to be seen even though his computer was still up and running. Most likely he'd run back over to his place to get something.

Rather than wait for him to return, she wrote him a short note to invite him to join them. She said they would be turning left at the sidewalk and added the time, so he'd know how long they'd been gone.

Zeke held still long enough for her to clip his leash to his collar and then hauled her out the front door and down the steps. She finally gave his leash a sharp tug to remind him which one of them was in charge. At least he got the hint and settled down. By that point, the rain had slowed to a soft mist that actually felt good on her face, sort of fresh and clean. Sadly, it was too dark to walk through the national forest. It might be different if Tripp had caught up with them, but she wouldn't risk it with just her and Zeke. If Tripp did come looking for them, hopefully he'd realize they wouldn't have gone that way. She really should have thought to tell him that in the note she'd left.

Instead, they would walk the eight blocks over to Main Street. From there, they could turn right and walk six more blocks before turning back toward the house. It wouldn't take them long to complete the circuit, but it should be more than enough to take the edge off. Before making the turn, she glanced back to see if Tripp was on his way, but the sidewalk was empty. It was disappointing, but she didn't blame the man for choosing homework over a walk in the rain. Well, not much, anyway.

For once, Zeke didn't stop at all of his favorite bushes and trees, which kept them both moving at a pretty quick clip. It didn't take them long to reach Main Street. Traffic was almost nonexistent, and they still had the sidewalk to themselves.

"Zeke, we must be the only ones in town with the energy for an evening walk. I think we should be proud of us."

Her furry companion must have agreed with her assessment of the situation. He held his head high as they strolled past the darkened storefronts that were already closed for the day. Only the drugstore and the diner down the street were still doing a brisk business.

A minute later, a passing vehicle slowed as it pulled

even with them, and the driver waved at her. It was difficult to make out the person behind the wheel because the streetlights were reflecting off the wet windows on the vehicle, but she finally realized it was Francine Denman. As soon as Abby waved back, the SUV sped up again.

The evening air suddenly took on a definite chill that hadn't been there only moments before. She wanted to put it down to the fact the rain had picked up, coming down in huge drops that splattered on the ground. But as Francine's taillights disappeared around the corner down the street, Abby flashed back to earlier when she'd wondered if she'd been the one driving away from the mobile home where Casey was hiding. Maybe the rain had her seeing similarities where there were none, but it wouldn't hurt to be careful.

Zeke had finally found a tree that he thought required a thorough sniffing, but Abby tugged on his leash to get him moving again. He resisted for several seconds but finally let her lead him on down the sidewalk. She patted him on the head. "Sorry, boy. I promise next time you can linger all you want. And after I get you dried off at home, I'll dig out that bison jerky we save for special occasions."

No doubt the dog understood the coaxing tone of her voice more than the specific words she said, but once again he ignored all of his usual stops in an effort to get back home sooner. Of course, maybe he didn't like the cold rain any better than Abby did.

A block before the closest street that led back toward her house there was a break in the sidewalk where a narrow alley ran between two buildings. They were about to step down off the curb when someone inched into sight. The shadows cast by the adjoining buildings made it hard to identify who it was, but the gun pointed at her was all too clear.

"Abby, leave the dog and get in the car."

There was no mistaking Francine's voice in the darkness. For his part, Zeke had great instincts when it came to sensing when someone presented a threat to Abby. His growl was deep and angry. When Francine responded by aiming the gun at him, Abby grabbed his collar to prevent him from charging the woman.

"What do you want, Francine?"

"That crazy man has my son. He said the only way he'd let us go is if I brought you to him."

"What crazy man?"

"The one who killed my father and then vandalized his house. I went there with my son to pick up a few things, but that guy had gotten back in again. He grabbed my son and threatened to hurt him if I didn't bring you to him. Something about you seeing him someplace he wasn't supposed to be. He held a knife against my son's throat and ordered me to take this gun. He said I'd need it to force you to come with me. It was only a matter of luck that I spotted you walking that monster dog of yours. Casey only gave me an hour to get back, and I wasn't sure how I'd lure you out of your house."

Was Francine really saying that Casey was the mastermind behind all of this? It was hard to get her mind around that idea. Why would he betray Gary and Gil like that? They both had offered him work and given him rides. The day the police raided the garage and Gary was arrested, Gil had gone out of his way to make sure Casey was okay.

"But why not stop and call the police?" Abby asked the question more to buy herself some time than because she really thought Francine would listen to reason. She was clearly desperate to protect her son, making it unlikely anything Abby said would make any difference.

"He specifically said no police. I won't risk my son's life on the off chance Chief Logan and his clown-car cops could save the day."

She aimed the gun in Abby's direction again. "Tie the dog to that lamppost and then get in the car."

Before Abby had a chance to move, Francine brought the gun up to point right at Abby's face. "And don't try anything stupid. Casey never said you had to be alive, just that I had to bring you to him. I don't want to hurt the dog, but I won't hesitate to sacrifice you for the sake of my son."

Feeling as desperate as Francine sounded, Abby tried to think of some way out of the situation. She wouldn't sacrifice her dog's life to save her own, and so she did the only thing she could. It took every bit of strength Abby had to drag Zeke over to the lamppost. She knelt at his side and gave him a quick hug to calm him down. When he was sitting quietly, she unfastened his leash. After wrapping it around the lamppost, she fed the hook end through the loop on the other end. Once it was secured, Abby clipped it back on his collar.

Careful to keep her back to Francine, she hugged Zeke again, using that as cover for what she was really doing. She keyed in Francine's license plate number on her phone, intending to send it to Gage and Tripp in the hopes they'd come running to the rescue. But before she could hit send, Francine was right there standing over her shoulder. "Get a move on, Abby. The dog will be fine."

It was a miracle Francine didn't see the phone before

Abby could hide it. She gave Zeke one last hug and ran her hand down his broad back. Then, placing her hand on the ground to push herself back up to her feet, she slipped the phone under Zeke as she stood. "Stay safe, boy. Someone will make sure you get back home to Tripp."

"Come on, Abby. Time is running out. Who knows what that awful man is doing to my son?" Francine yanked on her arm, eliciting another growl from the dog. Worried that he'd stand and reveal the phone, Abby hustled toward the car, drawing Francine's attention away from Zeke.

When she headed toward the passenger door, Francine blocked her way. "You drive. I'll sit in back so I can make sure you don't try anything."

Zeke started pitching a fit, fighting hard to break free. Abby blinked back tears and gave him a sharp command. "Sit, Zeke. Now!"

When he complied, she got in the car and fastened her seat belt. It took Francine longer to get settled into the back seat. Maybe it was hard to fasten a seat belt while trying to keep a gun pointed in the right direction. As scared as she was, Abby knew she couldn't make a break for it even if Francine didn't have a gun handy, not with the woman's son in danger. Maybe she'd be able to convince Casey to let everyone go if they promised to give him a head start.

She really tried to hold on to that positive thought, because someone needed to remain calm. It sure wasn't going to be Francine, not with the way she kept shifting around in the back seat and mumbling under her breath.

"So what's the plan when we get there?"

Not that she thought her captor had really planned that

far ahead. To her surprise, though, Francine answered almost immediately. "I'll exchange you for my son and leave."

Seriously? Did she really think it was going to be that easy? For Pete's sake, Casey had gone to the extreme of holding Francine's son hostage to force her to kidnap Abby at gunpoint. He'd have to be crazy to let any of them go free on the chance they'd call the authorities. Of course, Francine would promise him anything, say anything, to keep her son safe. Abby couldn't fault her for that, but neither did she want to be the sacrificial lamb.

"Are you sure you don't want to call the police before we get there? If you don't want to call Chief Logan, we could call Detective Ben Earle of the county sheriff's department. He's one of the best in the area and lives close by. I'm sure he'd help us."

"No."

The blunt refusal to even consider the idea was infuriating. "We have to do something, Francine. Casey may have said he'd let you go, but do you really think that's going to happen? The man has to be pretty desperate to have done something like this. He's already killed your father and let an innocent man take the blame. What's to keep him from killing again?"

"Shut up." As she spoke, Francine tapped the barrel of her gun against the side of Abby's face, a cold reminder that Casey wasn't the only threat. "We're almost there, so all of this will be over with soon enough."

Abby gripped the steering wheel hard enough to make her hands ache. It was tempting to swerve sharply from side to side. Maybe if someone thought she was driving under the influence, they'd call the police and report her.

That might even have worked if there was anyone around to see them, but they'd already reached the entrance to the neighborhood where James DiSalvo had lived. The street was empty, without a single car or person in sight.

Everyone must be tucked up inside staying warm and dry. Couldn't there have been one hardy soul out for a jog despite the weather? This was the Pacific Northwest, and people were supposed to pride themselves on never letting a little rain get between them and a good time.

As she drove the last few blocks to their destination, she let her mind drift back to Zeke. Had someone found him? She hoped so. The poor boy had been abused by his prior owner. Was he feeling betrayed and abandoned right now? Her heart ached for him.

"Turn into the driveway."

Abby did as ordered, taking note that the drapes and blinds were drawn on all the windows, blocking any view into the house. The porch light was off, leaving the front of the house shrouded in darkness. At least a light came on when the garage door rolled up at their approach, and Abby pulled inside without waiting to be told. After turning off the engine, she left the key in the ignition and got out of the car.

Francine was already waiting for her. She motioned toward the door into the house with the barrel of the gun. "Get inside."

It took every bit of willpower Abby could muster to take that first step forward. The second was only slightly easier. When she didn't pick up speed, Francine gave her a hard shove. "Get moving."

A second push almost sent Abby stumbling to the ground, but she caught herself before she fell. If it weren't for the gun, she would've been tempted to punch Francine right on the nose. Reining in her temper took a lot of effort, but she tried. Right now anger felt better than fear.

Abby opened the door into the house and was immediately hit with the smell of old garbage. Gross. Doing her best to ignore the stench, she stepped into a utility room that led into the kitchen. Drifting to a stop, she paused to listen. If there was anyone else in the house, they were being awfully darn quiet. While she didn't want to be greeted by a raving maniac, the oppressive silence was unsettling.

"Where to?"

Francine waved the gun in the direction of a hallway just outside the kitchen door.

"That way. Casey should be waiting for us in the family room."

Gage had told Abby about the vandalism in the house, but this was the first time she'd seen it for herself. All kinds of craziness had been written in spray paint on the wall. Obscenities alternated with insults directed at the late owner of the house. She glanced back at Francine to see what her reaction was to the graffiti, but the other woman was too focused on their destination to take notice. Of course, she'd already seen the destruction when she and Gage had gone through the house.

"I never really knew your father, but I bet he would've hated his home being treated with such disrespect. Your mother, too. Still, some paint and elbow grease, and it should clean up fine."

If she'd been hoping to establish some kind of rapport with her sympathetic comments, it failed miserably. In a chilly monotone, Francine sneered. "I'd be doing everyone a favor if I burned it to the ground. Considering the number of people my father screwed over, I bet I could make a fortune selling tickets to people who would dance while the place went up in flames."

So much for hoping that Francine had made some kind of peace with the past. By that point they'd almost reached their destination at the back of the house. The hall ended in an arched doorway that opened into the family room. The strange silence Abby had noticed back in the kitchen remained in full force.

What was waiting for them in the next room? She didn't know and for sure didn't want to find out. But the painful press of the barrel of the gun against her spine left her no choice but to find out. Struggling to draw a full breath, Abby swallowed hard and wiped her sweaty hands on her jeans. None of it helped. How had things gone so wrong?

Finally, out of choices and out of chances, she crossed the threshold into the family room to learn her fate.

CHAPTER 28

Dread of what she was about to walk into coupled with an overactive imagination had ramped up Abby's fear to the point that the serene tableau in front of her came almost as a letdown. *Almost* being the operative word. There was no sign of Francine's son, just Casey. But instead of being the rabid menace Francine had described, he was stretched out on the oversized sofa, snoring softly with his eyes closed. If he was faking being asleep, he was doing a bang-up job of it. The trail of drool from the corner of his mouth somehow made the already weird situation even scarier.

What on earth was going on? Staring at Casey, Abby slowly curled her hands into tight fists and locked her knees to stop them from shaking. It was hard to think clearly with her pulse pounding away in her head, but there had be some way to make sense of everything that had happened since the second Francine had stepped out of that alley. For starters, seeing Casey passed out on the couch was counter to everything the woman had told Abby about the situation. If the man was out of control and threatening Francine and her son, where was the boy and why was Francine the one with the gun?

With that single thought, once again all the pieces of the puzzle twisted and turned and then finally snapped together to form a coherent and complete picture. The truth was a physical blow that sent Abby staggering closer to Casey and farther from the real menace standing behind her. She took a second or maybe two to school her expression, aiming for a calm she certainly didn't feel, before she turned around.

Just as she feared, gone was any sign of the frantic woman she'd faced in the alley. In her place was a cold-eyed killer. She didn't know which was worse—the reptilian glint in Francine's eyes or the self-satisfied smirk that celebrated her convincing performance as a distraught mother.

"Francine, I take it your son isn't here."

Okay, maybe that wasn't the best opening gambit. The smirk was instantly replaced with a low growl that would've done Zeke proud. "No, he's not. His father has custody of Ryan, and I'm not allowed to come near him."

Considering the fact she was once again looking down the barrel of Francine's gun, it was time to tread softly. "I'm sorry to hear that. I can't imagine how difficult that must be for you."

That earned her a roll of the eyes and a return of Francine's smirk-face. "Don't pretend you know me at all. It won't save you and only wastes my time."

Rather than cower, Abby stood ramrod straight. "The

least you can do is explain what the heck is actually going on here. You owe me that much."

Francine blinked several times as if trying to make sense of what Abby had just said. "Seriously? Do you actually think you have any right to make demands of me?"

Abby had no idea where this bravado on her part was coming from, but it was more dignified than whimpering, her only other option. "Yes, I do. I've never done anything to harm you or anyone you care about."

The dramatic eye-roll made another appearance. "Don't be stupid. The problem is that you can connect me to Casey over there. Right now, Chief Logan is still acting like he has the right guy sitting in that jail cell, but he has to wonder why anyone would use one of his own tools to commit murder. It wouldn't take a genius to realize that Casey had access to the garage, too. I'm only surprised that they haven't come after him for breaking into this house. His fingerprints are all over the place. I made sure of that."

Abby remembered Gage saying something about that and decided to share. Anything to keep the woman talking. "Chief Logan said it could be a week or two before the results came back. Something about robberies not having the same priority as murder."

Francine looked disgusted. "That figures. But even when they do get the results, anyone who knows Casey will have a hard time believing he managed to pull off the perfect murder all by himself. Right now, the police have no idea that he and I know each other, and I want it to stay that way."

"So that was you I saw driving away at the mobile-home park."

After a brief hesitation, Francine nodded and said, "I couldn't risk you eventually telling your cop friend."

And for that the woman had seen it necessary to kidnap her? Abby wanted to kick herself. Next time she saw something, even if she wasn't sure of what she'd seen, she would go straight to Gage with it no matter how far-fetched it seemed. Well, if there ever was a next time. Right now that was looking highly unlikely.

Her only hope was to buy enough time for someone to find Zeke and then hopefully decipher the rather cryptic message she'd left typed on her phone. Would they immediately realize it was a license plate? Such a fragile thing to pin all of her hopes on. It wasn't as if she'd hung a sign on his collar outlining all the pertinent details that would immediately set Gage and Tripp on her trail.

Rather than waste energy on what she couldn't control, she jerked her full attention back to the situation at hand. What else could she ask Francine that wouldn't trigger a rash response?

"How did you come to know Casey?"

Francine leaned slightly to the side to look past Abby at the man still snoring away on the couch. "Like me, he hated my father. I saw him yelling at Dad in town and followed Casey to ask him what was going on."

The answer didn't surprise Abby, but the malevolent dose of venom in the other woman's voice did. Clearly Francine was an accomplished actress. Before that night, she'd always spoken of her father with regret and frustration, maybe laced with a hint of bitterness. But this time, her words sent a chill up Abby's spine. Francine wasn't the first crazy person she'd stood face-to-face with, but it never got less scary.

"Why, Francine?"

Despite a small laugh, Francine looked anything but amused by the question. "You already know why I hate him. Maybe that makes me a bad daughter, but I don't care. He could've helped me so many times, but he wouldn't. Oh no, there was no room for second chances in his world. He was a huge proponent of people living with the consequences of their bad choices."

When Francine fell silent, Abby prompted her to continue. "Which were?"

"My husband left me and took our son with him. Curtis even convinced the court he should have full custody of Ryan. Something about me being too unstable to be trusted with my boy, which is just ridiculous. I'd never do anything to hurt him."

Other than murder his grandfather? Because it was clear that even if Francine hadn't done the job herself, she'd participated. Then there was the fact she was planning to kill at least two more people. Right now, though, she went on complaining about her husband.

"I know Curtis bribed the judge to get that ruling, but he'll be sorry. They all will. Can you imagine anyone having the gall to call me unstable?"

Actually, Abby was pretty sure that Francine's picture was next to the word in the dictionary. She probably also had an honorable mention next to "crazy," "homicidal," and "whack job."

Now was definitely not the time to share that observation.

"And Casey's reason for hating your father?"

"He thinks my father stole his aunt's mobile home." Francine gave a dismissive wave of the hand. "As if my father would've even wanted it. Evidently when Casey's aunt moved out, the management wouldn't let him stay since he wasn't the owner. You'd have to ask him for the details. He told me all about it, but I didn't pay much attention."

A noise from behind Abby had both women turning to check on the third member of their little group. Casey was struggling to sit up. He succeeded on the second attempt, leaning forward with his elbows balanced on his knees. "Sorry, Francine, I must have fallen asleep."

Considering his grogginess and the cup and saucer sitting on the coffee table, Abby was willing to bet he'd had some help with that. He was lucky Francine hadn't decided to poison her partner in crime. When he finally looked up, his eyes were glassy and confused. He glanced around the room before finally focusing on the two women. "Abby, what are you doing here?"

Abby jerked her head in Francine's direction. "She forced me to come. As to why, you'd have to ask her."

He must have been starting to shake off the effects of whatever Francine put in his coffee, because he gave her a sharp look. "You said no one is supposed to find out we know each other or that I've been crashing here until I leave town while things cool down."

"Plans have changed." Francine gave Abby a shove. "Go sit by him."

She did as ordered while Casey made a valiant try to stand up. Failing miserably, he nearly landed on Abby as he fell back on the seat cushions. "What's with the gun, Francine?"

Francine had been holding the weapon down at her side, but now she had it aimed directly at her confederate. "Like I told you, we need to tie up all the loose ends. You were supposed to take care of that biker's brother, but I'm pretty sure you screwed that up. There's been no mention in the paper or on the news of him dying."

Casey glared at his accomplice. "I hit him as hard as I could. He was unconscious when I left."

"You should have hit him again if you weren't sure you got the job done the first time." Francine shook her head in disgust. "No matter. If he's gone to ground somewhere, I'll find him eventually. I can't risk him finally realizing you were the only one who could've stolen the torque wrench for me. Once he starts asking questions, do you really think I can trust you to keep your mouth shut?"

Casey was definitely looking more alert by this point. "That doesn't explain why Abby is here. She's never done anything to you, and she's been nice to me."

Abby felt obligated to point out that she hadn't been the only one. "So were Gil and Gary, yet you let Gary take the blame for the murder and you tried to kill Gil."

He dropped his gaze to the floor, his shoulders slumped. "I stole the wrench, and I hit Gil. I didn't—"

Francine cut him off before he could finish. "Shut your mouth, Casey. None of that matters. She saw both of us at the mobile-home park. Like I told her, up until then, no one had any reason to connect the two of us."

Abby wondered what Casey had been about to say that Francine didn't want her to hear. What if he was about to say he hadn't been the one to kill James DiSalvo? Was Casey just another tool in Francine's arsenal? Meanwhile, the woman was still talking to her accomplice, speaking slowly as if trying to explain a difficult subject to a child. "It would be a bad thing if Gage Logan learns that we know each other and that we both had reasons to hate my father. How long do you think it would take him to wonder if we might have worked together to take good old Dad out of the picture?"

Casey frowned up at the woman. "Not long?"

She rewarded him with a chilling smile. "Good guess, Casey. If that happens, I won't inherit my father's estate. I can't give you back the mobile home if I don't take over my father's properties. So now do you understand why Abby is a loose end?"

He cringed as he looked at Abby before he quickly turned his attention back to Francine. "She doesn't know nothing about what happened, Francine. If she did, the police would've been looking for both of us by now."

"She knows enough, Casey. We can't risk it."

Abby sat up straighter, angling herself so that she could keep a wary eye on both Casey and Francine. Deciding it was time to get involved in the conversation again, she reached out to touch Casey's shoulder. "What she means is that *she* can't risk it, Casey. If I'm a loose end just because I happened to see the two of you at the mobile-home park, what about you? She asked you to get her something she could use as a weapon instead of just buying one somewhere. I'm guessing she specifically said it should be a tool from Gil and Gary's shop because they had problems with her father, too. Did she have you hide it at the park after she hit her father with it? If so, did she remind you to make sure you didn't get your fingerprints on it?"

He was already shaking his head. "No, I thought of that on my own."

She smiled and patted him on the shoulder again. "That was smart thinking, Casey."

But she bet Francine didn't think so. "Did she also

suggest you hide out here in her father's house? Maybe even that you should paint the graffiti on the walls?"

She didn't need Casey to answer her questions. Francine did when she snapped, "Shut up, Abby! You're twisting things."

Casey's attention bounced between the two women. "But she's right, Francine. You said I could bunk here for a while. You also said I should make it look like some kids broke in and messed up the place. You know, to confuse Gage Logan and his deputies."

Did either of them really think Gage was that stupid? She suspected Francine did, but she was in for a rude awakening. He'd figure it all out soon if he hadn't already. Not that she should sing his praises right now when she was already skating on thin ice. The harder she pushed, the more likely the woman would strike out.

On the other hand, Casey seemed totally oblivious to the fact that Francine had scheduled two executions tonight. She might not know exactly what the woman had planned, but their imminent demise was definitely on the agenda. She didn't know about Casey, but Abby wasn't going to go down without a fight. She needed a weapon. Anything would do. Something heavy she could throw. The only thing in reach was Casey's empty coffee cup, but at least it might provide enough of a distraction for her to be able to bolt toward the back door.

She slid closer to the end of the sofa to give herself room to maneuver. It wouldn't help if she got all tangled up with Casey while trying to make a break for it. She didn't want him to get hurt. But all things considered, it was everybody for themselves.

Francine shifted her weight from one foot and then

back again as she focused all of her attention on Casey. "I need you to kill her. It's the only way we'll both be safe."

He slowly shook his head. "I ain't no killer, Francine. I already told you that."

"Yeah, well, you need to man up this time. I can't do everything myself."

Abby lost control of her mouth, blurting out the truth as she saw it. "What she means is that she wants you to kill me, so she has an excuse to shoot you. Then she'll tell the cops that you lured both of us here with a threat to her son, so she was only acting in self-defense. Too bad, so sad she couldn't stop you in time to save me, too."

"I've already told you to shut up, Abby. Don't make me tell you again."

Francine motioned with her hand for Casey to come stand beside her, but he stubbornly remained right where he was. "I'm not going to kill Abby. She's been nice to me, and she's never done anything to you. If I leave town tonight, no one needs to know any of this happened. She won't say anything. Will you, Abby?"

Heck yeah she would, but right now it behooved her to lie through her teeth. "I never told anyone that I saw you together. I see no reason for that to change. As far as anything else that I've heard tonight, I can't prove any of it was true."

Francine let out a frustrated sigh. "Fine, I'll do it. I'll just have to stage things differently than I'd planned."

As she sighted down the barrel of the gun, a low growl echoed down the hallway behind her. The noise startled Francine into looking back over her shoulder. As she did, Casey shoved Abby to the floor and then upended the coffee table. It might not stop a bullet, but it might lessen the impact if Francine managed to get a shot off. As an afterthought, Abby grabbed the coffee cup off the floor and heaved it at the woman as hard as she could before ducking down again.

Luckily, Francine had bigger problems than her two intended victims hiding behind a piece of oak furniture as ninety-five pounds of angry dog charged in and took her down hard. Gage and Deputy Chapin followed right behind, shouting for Francine to drop the weapon.

Abby was too busy trying to curl into the smallest target possible to see exactly how things actually played out after that, but the battle was short-lived. The drama was all over except for Francine's ranting and raving as Gage's men handcuffed her and dragged her out of the room.

Gage himself called out, sounding amazingly calm, "You can come out now, Abby. You too, Casey, but with your hands up."

Zeke didn't wait for her to leave the shelter of the coffee table. She'd covered her head with her arms, but he pushed his way past them to give her a drool-laden slurp of the tongue across her face. If someone had told her she'd go from cringing in terror to laughing in a matter of seconds, she wouldn't have believed them.

But that's exactly what happened. The tears didn't start until Tripp gently lifted her off the floor and held her tight.

CHAPTER 29

Two days later, Abby walked into city hall carrying two large grocery bags filled with cookies for the police department. Sergeant Jones grinned and came out from behind the desk to help her. Well, and to figure out which of the various containers was his, not that he was rude enough to ask.

"Here, Sergeant, this one is for you."

He eyed the large container with interest. "All this is for me?"

She shrugged. "I know it's a bit over-the-top, but I've been baking pretty much around the clock since . . . well, you know."

His smile faded a bit. "I'm sorry you got caught up in that crazy woman's mess like that, Abby."

"Me too."

It was hard to put on a brave face, but she was determined to put the whole episode behind her as quickly as possible. Hoping her smile looked more genuine than it felt, she said, "Gage wanted me to check in with him this week. Since I have an appointment with the mayor in a little while, I thought maybe I could see him, too. Can you check to see if he's available?"

The sympathy in the sergeant's eyes was almost her undoing. She suspected he knew it, too, but at least he didn't comment on the sudden sheen in her eyes. Instead, he picked up a bag. "Come on, I'll carry this one for you. Even if he is busy, Chief Logan always makes time for a friend."

When they reached the bull pen area, she opened one of the bigger containers of cookies and set it near the coffeemaker. Smiling at the handful of people working at their desks, she called out, "Come and get it."

They were up and heading toward the unexpected bounty before she made it as far as Gage's office door, where Sergeant Jones handed her the other bag. Before he walked away, she stopped him. "Could you take one of the containers down to whoever is on guard duty today?"

"Glad to. Deputy Chapin will appreciate it."

Gage stood up as soon as she appeared in his doorway. "Hey, Abby. How are you doing?"

There was no reason to pretend with him. "Not great, but a little better every day."

She set the bags down against the wall. "Sorry, but I may have overdone it with the cookies this time, but maybe you can freeze some. I already put some out in the bull pen and gave Sergeant Jones and Deputy Chapin their own containers to make sure they don't miss out on the goodies."

He motioned her to take a seat. "You know you're always welcome here. You don't always have to bring cookies with you, not that I'm complaining."

She sat in her usual chair in front of his desk. And how worried should she be that she actually had a usual chair in the police chief's office? That was a concern for another day. She already had enough on her plate today.

"I know, but baking helps me relax."

That didn't surprise him. He knew her habits all too well. "I just wish you weren't in need of therapy baking again."

She met his sympathetic gaze head-on. "You know, I really tried to stay out of the mess this time." Honesty had her adding, "Mostly, anyway."

"And I appreciate it even if it wasn't enough to keep you out of the line of fire again." He sat down and leaned back in his chair. "Seriously, are you okay?"

"Mostly. Well, other than my mother keeps threatening to kidnap me and drag me up to Seattle where she can keep an eye on me. That would be disaster for both of us, and she knows it. Tripp goes back and forth between worrying about me and being really mad I got caught up in another life-and-death situation. Then there's Zeke. He follows me around the house and pitches a fit if I try to leave without him. I think being tied to that lamppost must have stirred up his abandonment issues."

She frowned. "Come to think of it, I'm not sure anyone said who found him. Or if they did, I don't remember."

Gage's worried expression softened just a little. "Tripp got to him first, but it was a close thing. I got there just a minute or two after him. Evidently he decided to catch up with you and Zeke on your walk. He might have even gotten there before Francine managed to force you into her car if he hadn't started down the trail into the forest first. When he decided you wouldn't have gone that way without him, he headed over to Main Street instead. The second he spotted Zeke, he sounded the alarm and then took off running. I happened to be heading home and was only a block away when the call came in."

"Was Zeke okay? It nearly killed me to leave him there like that."

"He wasn't there all that long, but he was definitely happy to see us. And if I haven't said so before, that was brilliant of you to leave the phone with Francine's license plate on it."

"How did you know to look for us at her father's house?"

"It seemed logical, but I also sent people to check her home address, too."

Abby toyed with a loose thread on her sleeve before looking up at Gage. "I can't believe I bought into her wishing she could reconcile with her father."

Gage shook his head. "Don't beat yourself up over that. We all believed her story to some extent, and some of it was even true. DiSalvo did reject her when she married Curtis Denman. He also never made much of an effort to get to know his own grandson. And when she asked him for help, he turned her down."

"But was her husband even sick?"

Gage nodded. "Yes, but it wasn't as serious as she led us to believe. We may never know what triggered her breakdown. When I spoke to her husband, he said he'd tried to convince her to see a therapist to deal with her anger, but Francine wouldn't listen. Somehow she blamed everything, including her husband's illness, on her father. Her fixation became so extreme that Curtis felt like he had no choice but to get their son away from her. He hated doing that and had hoped it would finally convince her to seek help. We all know how that turned out."

Abby's heart hurt for all of them, but especially for Francine's husband and son. "It's just so sad for all of them."

"It is, but no one can help someone who won't let them." Then Gage shifted the subject of their conversation to a happier one. "The good news is I talked to Gil this morning. All the charges against Gary have been dropped, and he'll be home later today. Gil also said to tell you he still owes you a ride on his motorcycle. Just name the day and time, and he'll be there."

He paused to give her a puzzled look. "What's that all about?"

She laughed for the first time all day. "Gil was horrified when he found out I've never ridden on a motorcycle. He says it's his duty as a friend and a biker to correct that situation. I can't wait to tell Mom. She *hates* motorcycles."

There was one more person she was worried about. "What will happen to Casey? I know he was involved in what happened, but apparently it was Francine who planned it all and actually killed her father. He also did his best to talk her out of hurting me."

"The prosecutor is still working on all of that. Like you said, he wasn't exactly innocent, but he wasn't the kingpin, either. Evidently, Casey did lure her father off the main trail by yelling someone was hurt and needed help. Afterward, he helped Francine toss the body down into the ravine. Regardless, I'll keep you posted as I learn more."

She'd already given a detailed statement the night of

Francine's arrest. "While I'm here, do you need me to do anything else?"

"Nope, we're good for now. I heard Francine's attorney is working on a plea deal for her. I'm guessing Casey's will, too, so I doubt either case will ever come to trial."

"That's a relief."

She checked the time. "Well, I'd better get going. Connie Pohler called to say the mayor wanted to talk to me today. Any idea what that's about?"

He shook his head. "Nope, I haven't talked to Rosalyn for the better part of a week. Are you worried?"

"Not particularly. She probably wants to know if Gil and I want to run the Salmon Scoot again next year. We've already decided we'd give it another go."

"That's great, Abby. Everyone I talked to was thrilled with how smoothly everything went." Then he grimaced. "Well, up until the very end."

"Yeah, I think that's why both of us want a do-over."

She stood. "Well, I'd better head over to the mayor's office. I dropped Zeke off with Tripp, but I don't want to be gone too long. They both have a tendency to fret, you know."

With good reason, but at least Gage didn't feel obligated to point that out.

She waved at the people in the bull pen on her way out, but Sergeant Jones wasn't at his desk. That was okay. She could always say good-bye to him after she was done talking to the mayor.

Connie, the mayor's assistant, looked up and offered Abby a bright smile as soon as she spotted her. "Hi, Abby. You're right on time. The mayor said to send you straight in."

"Thanks, Connie."

Although there was something mildly worrisome about the woman's smile. Abby hated to be unnecessarily suspicious, but had there been something slightly predatory about it? No, she was just imagining things. It was natural to be a bit suspicious of people in general when you've been recently kidnapped. This meeting had to be about next year's race and nothing else.

She held on to that comforting idea right up until she was seated in front of the mayor's desk. Rosalyn's smile was a twin to Connie's, just a shade too cheery for comfort. At least the woman didn't keep her waiting. She came around her desk to perch on the front edge right in front of Abby's chair.

"Thanks for coming in today. I've been needing to talk to you."

Tamping down the odd surge of panic, Abby said, "If it's about the race, Gil and I have already decided we'd be glad to do it again next year."

If her voice cracked just a little, Rosalyn either didn't notice or didn't care. "That's really great, but this is about something else entirely."

Abby swallowed hard. "And what is that?"

"I hope you know what an amazing asset you are to the people of Snowberry Creek."

Feeling the sharks circling ever closer, Abby glanced at the door and calculated the time it would take her to reach it. "It's nice of you to say that."

"Here's the thing. James DiSalvo's death left a vacancy on the city council, and there's a year left on his term of office. Luckily, the city charter has a special provision that says the mayor can appoint someone to the position on an interim basis as long as the majority of the council approves the selection."

Rosalyn's predatory smile was firmly back in place. "I'm happy to tell you that of everyone who was considered for the position, you're the only one who received unanimous approval from the board. Please let me be the first to offer my congratulations."

When Rosalyn held out her hand, Abby watched in horror as her own slowly reached out to shake it, even as a panicky voice in her head pleaded with it to stop. But it was too late, the bargain was made, the deal was done.

After releasing her hold on Abby, Rosalyn picked up a thick notebook and held it out. "Welcome to the Snowberry Creek city council, Abby. Here's everything you need to know about how we operate and what your duties will be. We meet next week, and I'll see you there."

Abby clutched the notebook to her chest as she stumbled back out of the building, all the while still trying to figure out what had just happened. As she got into her car and started the engine, there was only one thought rattling around in her head—that maybe being kidnapped and held prisoner by her mother wouldn't be such a bad thing after all.